BUNDLE OF LOVE

A LONG VALLEY ROMANCE NOVEL - BOOK 7

ERIN WRIGHT

WRIGHT'S READS

To Emily Pennington – *Thank you for your help with the cover and inspiration for the story. I hope I included enough horses.*

~ *~

To Geeta – *Thanks for everything, but especially your love and support. I don't know what I'd do without you.*

CHAPTER 1

KYLIE

MAY, 2018

KYLIE VANLUEVEN SUCKED in her bottom lip. She could do this. She could totally, absolutely do this.

This was her *mom*, who loved her dearly. After all, it was her and her mom against the world – how many times had she heard her mom say exactly that?

So it wasn't admitting defeat to come crawling back to her mom's house, her tail tucked between her legs.

Well, maybe it was. A little. But her mom would still be happy to see her.

And right now, more than anything in the world, Kylie needed someone to be happy to see her. To want her.

She raised a trembling hand and knocked on the faded, wooden door of her childhood home. The one she'd busted through without a second thought a million times as a kid...*when* she'd lived here.

It seemed awkward as hell to knock on this door – the front door to a house that was the very embodiment of "home" to her, even though she hadn't lived here for four years. But just busting through and yelling, "SURPRISE!" didn't seem like a stand-up idea to her, either.

Her mom opened up the door, her hair up in curlers, peering out into the fading evening light. "Kylie?" she said, the shock almost palpable. "Kylie, what are you doing here?!" Even as she said it, she stepped back from the door to let Kylie in, her faded housedress flowing around her legs as she backed out of the doorway.

Kylie pulled her oversized suitcase in behind her, leaned it against the shoe bench, and then threw herself into her mom's arms, sobbing. She'd kept it together until now, but like a toddler whose scraped knee was fine until she lays eyes on her mother, all of the pain and frustration and anger and confusion and hurt that'd been boiling inside of Kylie came spilling out as soon as she saw the one person in her life who she knew loved her unconditionally.

Even as her mom pulled her against her generous chest, patting her back and whispering consoling words that Kylie didn't need to hear to understand, she was also pushing the door closed, the night sounds disappearing, leaving only Kylie's sobs and her mom's whispers and the ticking of the clock on the wall.

Finally, Kylie got herself under control enough to pull back and give her mom a watery smile. "Hi, Mom," she said weakly. "I'm home." She tried to say it in a sing-song voice, to play it off as a joke, but nothing was funny right now.

Nothing was going to be funny ever again.

Which was an exaggeration and Kylie knew it and she didn't care. It's how she felt, dammit.

Her mom draped her arm around Kylie's shoulders and pulled her against her soft, welcoming side. "Come on, let's go talk. Nothing can be as bad as all this, I promise."

They moved into the living room and sank down into the worn, soft couch, its embrace as inviting as her mom's had been. Kylie loved this couch. In fact, all she wanted to do in this very moment was hide in its flowery depths and never come out again.

She remembered back when she was 18 – just four short years ago – when all she had wanted was to get out of this town and never come back. Now...

Well, the world hadn't been quite as amazing as Kylie had thought it would be, that was for damn sure.

"Okay, tell me what's going on." Her mom's pale green eyes were caring and concerned...and laser focused on her.

Carol VanLueven could be horribly intimidating, even when she didn't mean to be, something her only daughter was all too aware of.

Kylie bit her trembling lower lip, fighting back

another wave of tears. Dammit all, she could cry in a minute, but right now, she needed to talk.

No matter how tempting it was to dissolve into a puddle of tears again.

She took a deep breath.

"I'm pregnant."

CHAPTER 2

ADAM

DR. ADAM WHITAKER pulled to a stop in front of the fire station and strode inside, trying to hide his yawn behind one hand while carrying his vet bag in the other. The story of his life right there, in a nutshell. It was gonna be another long day, but before he could get to the must-do's on his list, he had to look over a stray dog found up in the foothills just outside of town. It had been found in the aftermath of a wildfire – or during it, Adam wasn't too clear on the details just yet – with no tags or identifying information.

Moose Garrett, one of the local volunteer firefighters, was the one who'd called Adam this morning to ask for his help. He believed that the dog had been abused, and Adam was pretty sure he had to be right. Any dog left to wander in the hills in the middle of a wildfire probably wasn't being taken care of by its owner, whether or not it was also being kicked around.

There were levels of abuse, and from the sounds of it, this dog was definitely on one of the tiers. It remained to be seen which tier. Adam could only hope for the sake of the dog that Moose was overstating the case, although Moose'd never struck him as being someone to exaggerate.

Jaxson Anderson, the new Sawyer fire chief, was inside the station bay, along with Troy and a couple of the other volunteer firefighters. It didn't look like Moose had made it there yet. Adam shook hands with everyone, chatting as he went. He'd known most everyone here since they were knee-high to a grasshopper; all of them except for Jaxson, of course. The new chief had just moved in from Boise and although Adam hadn't had a chance to get to know him real well yet, he was impressed with the guy regardless. Anyone willing to go charging into a burning building to save people ranked pretty high in Adam's estimation.

"So, did we get the fire in the foothills under control?" Adam asked, once the greetings were over. He figured it must be if the guys were all here, but he was curious anyway. It must've been a small fire if it was killed off that quickly.

"Yeah, late last night. Thank God it's early enough in the season that there are still patches of snow around, keeping the fire from spreading too quickly," Jaxson said, rubbing his eyes wearily. "With this wind that keeps howling through, though, any spark can easily mean an inferno, especially because the more the wind blows, the more things dry out, which means the faster shit catches on fire. If we could only get the wind to stop—"

Just then, the man door to the fire station opened, and in came a very dirty Moose, ash and sand and dirt streaked everywhere. He looked like the lone survivor of a dirt hurricane. He was bent awkwardly at the waist, his hand securely wrapped around the collar of a beautiful white-and-black setter, which Adam assumed was the stray he'd been called in to look at. But setters, an expensive and sought-after hunting breed, didn't tend to be strays.

What the hell...?

Then came Georgia Rowland trailing in behind Moose and the dog. She was the local branch manager of the Goldfork Credit Union, and someone with a good head on her shoulders. Adam was a little surprised to see Moose and Georgia together – had they spent the night out in the wilderness? By themselves? All alone? *I wonder what Rocky Garrett will have to say about that...*

Eh. None of that mattered right now. Even as Adam hurried towards the trio, his eyes were trained on the setter, inspecting her for injuries, watching for limping or an unwillingness to bend in a certain direction.

"There's the woman of the hour," he said softly, once he'd reached her side. She was skittish as hell, but didn't appear to be limping, so that was a plus. He looked at Moose, his mind running through the possibilities of where to do his examination. "Let's take her back into the supply closet. It's got that table in there for organizing, and it's nice and enclosed. She won't be able to run too far if we corner her in there."

Moose nodded, his face a mask of concentration as they made their way to the closet. Poor guy – it wasn't easy to wrestle a dog of this size into submission. Life would've been a lot easier if Moose had slipped his belt underneath her collar to use it as a makeshift leash, but instead, the firefighter just had a death grip on the dog's collar. If Adam remembered right, the Garrett family had never had any pets, and to be honest, Moose's inexperience was showing.

Well, he'd gotten the dog to the fire station in one piece, and there was definitely something to be said for that. Adam was impressed with his grit. The dog probably put up one hell of a fight.

He put his vet bag down and then together with Moose, they maneuvered the gorgeous setter onto the table in the storage room, her trembling legs almost refusing to keep her upright. The sight tore at Adam's heart. She was completely terrified; probably a half an inch away from pissing herself.

Whoever had done this to this dog deserved to end up in a special level of hell, as far as Adam was concerned.

Moose turned to Georgia, who was hanging out in the doorway of the small closet. "She knows you better, plus I have to file some paperwork for last night's fun. You mind helping Adam out here?"

"No, not at all," Georgia said. Moose sidled past and out into the main area of the fire station as Georgia closed the door to the closet and turned to Adam with a smile. "What can I help with?" she asked.

"Just help keep her on the table so I can look her over. Actually, I have some small dog treats in my bag in the corner," he jerked his head towards his beat-up vet bag, "if you could grab those for me."

He continued to pet the beautiful dog, using his hands and voice to try to convey peace and calm, even as he used his pettings to do surreptitious inspections, searching out broken bones or lacerations or bruises. The poor thing was trembling so much, it was hard to tell if she was flinching from him touching a particular part of her body, or because she was just terrified in general.

Adam was glad in that moment that he didn't know who'd done this kind of psychological damage to this dog. He didn't fancy spending the rest of his life in jail for murder, although he was pretty damn sure it'd be worth it.

Georgia began feeding the small treats to the dog, her hand sliding into place over the collar so Adam could use both hands to get to work on a full-blown inspection. He was impressed that she didn't need to be told what to do; she just got into place without needing him to say a word.

As he inspected every inch of the dog, checking out the pads of her feet, trying to find a scar for a spaying procedure on her belly, feeling for any joints or bones out of place, he wondered idly why it was that he wasn't attracted to Georgia. Not at the moment, of course – she was covered from head to toe in ash and dirt and looked like she'd been dragged along behind a pickup truck for a couple of miles – but just in general. She was pretty in an understated way, athletic, intelligent, funny, good with animals…

And she did absolutely nothing for him.

This was probably why he was 38 and single. He'd loved his wife; he'd loved Chloe. That was it. Two women in almost 40 years. Did that mean he was going to find the next woman to love when he was 60?

That would just be his luck.

While Georgia kept the dog occupied and in place on the table, Adam asked her questions about how they'd found the dog – she'd apparently named her Sparky, an on-the-nose name for a dog found in the middle of a wildfire – and what had happened up in the foothills. As Georgia recounted her harrowing experience of trying to escape the fire, Adam pulled his handheld chip scanner out of his bag, waving it carefully over the dog.

Nothing.

Whoever abused her and left her to die in a wildfire had also failed to chip her.

Real winners, here.

With any luck at all, they'd catch the rat bastard

who did this and make him wish he'd never bought a dog. And if the justice system didn't, maybe Adam would. A few years in jail would totally be worth it.

He finished up his examination and together, they headed out into the main bay of the fire station to give a report to the gathered men. As they were chatting about what to do with the dog, Michelle Winthrop – the Sawyer city dog catcher – showed up. Large and in charge, animals were her first (and sometimes only) priority, something Adam sure could admire about a person.

Here was *another* single woman, as focused and interested in animals as he was, beautiful in an understated way, someone to be admired...

And someone who did absolutely nothing for him.

He sighed to himself.

"I don't recognize Sparky," Jaxson said to the group, pulling Adam back into the discussion. "That doesn't mean much, of course, since I only moved here five months ago. Does she look familiar to any of you?"

They all turned as one to search out Sparky in the corners of the station. Considering how much the setter hated people, Adam figured she'd be hiding under a fire truck or behind a pile of equipment, but was shocked to see that she was instead sprawled out on Troy's lap, her tongue lolling out happily, a mostly empty bowl of water off to the side, as Troy quietly ran his hands over her fur rhythmically.

Troy sensed the eyeballs on him, and he looked up

from his pettings of the beautiful dog to see them all staring at him. "She likes me," he said simply.

Wow. Adam could hardly keep his eyes in his head at the sight. Seeing how relaxed the dog was around Troy...

Stunning, to say the least.

As they discussed who would take the dog home — Troy, obviously — and how it was that Sparky was lost out in the wilderness to begin with, Adam noticed something.

A little...*spark* between Georgia and Moose, if he could be forgiven for using the pun in a fire station of all places.

Huh.

They were practically kids compared to him — at 12 years his junior, they'd been entering first grade when he'd been entering his senior year, a thought that made him feel ancient beyond his years — but even Adam knew that Moose's parents had decided who Moose would marry almost before he was born.

And that person *was not* Georgia Rowland. It was, in fact, her cousin, Tennessee Rowland.

Tennessee was the daughter of the older brother, the one who'd inherited everything — the one who owned the biggest farm in Long Valley County and didn't hesitate to use that fact whenever and wherever he could. Adam could only be grateful the man was a farmer, not a rancher; the few times a year he had to deal with him because of his horses was pushing the limit as it was. If he had to constantly be out at the Rowland place to work with a herd of cows and interacting with Robert Rowland every time... Well, Adam might've picked a new profession by now.

Georgia was the daughter of the younger brother, on the other hand; the one who'd inherited nothing and was now the high school biology teacher. Obviously, that wasn't good enough for Rocky Garrett and therefore, wouldn't be good enough for his oldest son, Moose.

But damn...if the sparks between Moose and Georgia were so obvious even he could see them – and Adam would be the first to admit that he tended to be blind to that sort of thing to an *ahem* extreme degree – well, things were about to get real interesting in the farming world. He could only wish the two of them luck, 'cause they were gonna need it.

Well, it was time to get a move on. He said his goodbyes to the group and then headed out to his late-model Ford truck, pulling his miniature calendar out of his shirt pocket and looking it over as he went. He let out a huge yawn even as he tried to focus his eyes on his scribbled notes. Shit, he was already tired, and the day had just begun.

Hmmm...He had a horse with a tender leg, a cow that refused to let her calf nurse, two rabies shots to give, and a neutering to perform back at the clinic, all before 3 pm. Then the *real* fun would begin – absolutely no sarcasm intended – when he would hurry over to the riding arena to work with the kids in therapy camp for a couple of hours. Those kids were truly the highlight of his day, no doubt about it.

But he also needed to submit invoices for vet work, figure out when he could squeeze in some time to do vaccinations, and then there was also the vet-as-a-career presentation that Miss Lambert over at the elementary school really wanted him to give to her fifth grade class.

He yawned again, his jawbone cracking, and he rubbed at his burning eyes with the palms of his hands. Maybe he'd stop by Mr. Petrol and get a coffee to go, and *then* tackle his day. He pulled out of the parking lot and headed for the gas station. As he drove mostly by instinct, he tried to think of how to be more efficient with his time. Type up an invoice as he was helping a cow give birth? Return phone calls as he did vaccinations?

Yeah, not gonna work. Each scenario was more ridiculous than the last.

He tried to force his non-caffeinated brain to do something more useful than just shrug in helplessness at him.

He could hire another vet to help him; they could share the practice, like a lot of dentists and lawyers did. But there just wasn't *quite* enough work to pull something like that off. Adam had too much work for one person to handle; too little work for two.

*Actually...*He tapped his chin, thinking. It wasn't so much the vaccinations and birthings that were kicking his ass − it was the paperwork. He felt like he was drowning in it. If he could just hand the office work off to someone else, hell, *that'd* make all the difference in the world.

He did have someone right now...kinda. Oliver Blank was a high school student who he had coming over after school to help with the animals staying at the clinic for one reason or another, but as much as Adam liked the kid, he wasn't exactly prime office help. Although he was an absolute gem around animals, he was equally as awful with people. Hell, just last week, he got into an argument with a client who'd had the temerity to ask for a business card. Oliver had told the woman hotly that if they handed out business cards to everyone, well, soon they'd run out of them!

Yeah, it'd taken precious minutes to smooth that one over. He'd tried to explain to Oliver after the slightly mollified woman left the clinic (business card in hand, thankyouverymuch) that the whole point of business cards *was* to give them away, but...

Well, it hadn't exactly gotten through to the kid. Adam half expected that next, he'd let loose on a client's head that if Adam took the time to talk to the client about vaccination schedules, Adam wouldn't have the time to actually vaccinate any animals!

Which, while being somewhat true, also greatly missed the point.

No, he needed to stop relying on Oliver to man the desk, no matter how desperate Adam was for an extra set of hands upfront. He needed to keep Ollie in the back, far, far away from any being that walked upright. Let him stick to the four-legged variety, where he could work his magic. Ollie understood and loved animals on a level that Adam wasn't even sure he was at. He'd make a damn fine vet one day…as long as he never had to talk to another soul while doing it.

As Adam walked out of Mr. Petrols, sucking at the brown, life-giving liquid, he sighed to himself. Whether he wanted to admit it or not, it was time to face the facts: He needed to hire an honest-to-God receptionist. An older woman who would be steadfast and unflinching in the face of growling dogs…and humans. Someone who could help him keep on track and get to his appointments on time. Someone who could do his billing for him.

You know, all the shit Adam hated to the depths of his soul.

A part of him cringed in pain at the idea of adding someone else to the payroll of Whitaker's Vet Clinic, but if they would actually bill clients on time and get both his accounts payable and accounts receivable under control, hell, they'd probably pay for themselves just through the avoidance of late fees. Oh, and by actually collecting money owed, something Adam wasn't exactly the best at.

So instead of heading out of town towards the Cowell spread to look at their mare's lame leg, he took a right and headed over to the local *Sawyer Times* office. It was time to bite the bullet and hire someone to help him shoulder the load. An even-keeled, placid, heavyset, 50-year-old woman with a touch of gray in her hair and a steely-eyed gaze that could bring even the most riled-up dog to heel with a glance.

Hells to the yes.

Now, he just needed to find this paragon of perfection and hire 'em on the spot.

CHAPTER 3

KYLIE

THERE WAS SOME PART OF HER — very small and very distant and oh-so-very quiet — that recognized that she was spiraling into some sort of depression. She'd never been one to be depressed before. There was just too much to do and see and experience and learn. She loved life.

She just didn't happen to love life right now. Or, more specifically, love the idea of giving birth to life.

At least, not at the moment. It just wasn't part of the plan. She'd always believed she'd become a mother…someday. She would marry a handsome guy and they'd have 2.5 kids and a house with a white picket fence and she'd be happy and fulfilled in her Unnamed Career doing Unnamed Things.

Just because she was 22 and hadn't figured out what that Unnamed Career was, let alone what those Unnamed Things would be, didn't mean she was a failure.

But the fact that she was pregnant, single, and homeless probably did.

She snuggled back down underneath the covers. She was so tired. So very, very tired. She'd get up in a minute. Maybe eat breakfast. Hell, maybe even brush her teeth. That'd be true progress.

But...not for another minute. She needed her rest. She was carrying another human inside of her, after all. That sort of thing was exhausting. She couldn't be expected to be Superwoman, right?

She was drifting in and out, the world a hazy blob around her, when she heard a knock on her bedroom door. She sat up slowly, blinking owlishly at the door. "Co–come in," she croaked out. She cleared her throat. Why was it so hard to talk? She tried to remember what she'd last said to her mom, but the days had slipped by like water down a mountain stream, and she couldn't remember what she'd said, or when she'd said it.

The world had turned into this murky, indistinct disaster zone, and Kylie couldn't keep straight what she'd actually done versus what had happened in her dreams. Which *should* freak her out but she was too tired to freak out. She'd worry about it later. Maybe after another nap.

Her mom popped her head around the door, surprising Kylie. She'd already forgotten about the knock on the door. Her mom sent an overly bright smile at Kylie even as her eyes said, "Danger ahead!" Even through her sleepy eyes, Kylie caught the look that spelled trouble. It was the same one her mom had given her in high school, right before sitting her down and lecturing her about getting B's in her classes, when she could be getting A's.

Ah. Back when life was so much simpler.

Kylie tried to plaster a happy look on her face. "Hi, Mom!" she said, a touch bit too cheerfully. She cleared her throat again. It was strangely hard to talk. "What's...what's going on?" She ran her fingers through her hair, hoping to straighten it out, but she hit a few too many snarls and knots, and gave up on the task. *Ugh.* When had she last brushed her hair?

She couldn't remember that, either.

Her mom crossed over to the bed and sat down. "I just got home from my book club meeting," she started out. Kylie's eyes widened with surprise. Book club? That was an evening thing. A Monday-evening-from-7-to-9-pm thing, if she remembered correctly.

But, that couldn't be right. That'd mean that she'd been here a week, *and* that it was nine at night.

But...but...she'd only been here a day or two, and it was still morning.

Her head hurt.

She surreptitiously grabbed her phone off the nightstand and checked it.

Holy shit.

How was it May 14th? And how was it 9:34 at night?

That couldn't be right.

Her head hurt even more.

Her mom stopped talking and Kylie looked up blankly. "Sorry, Mom, I missed that. Come again?"

With a disgruntled look, her mom snatched her cell phone out of her hands and set it down on the other side of her. "I saaiidd, the women at Between the Covers mentioned that Doc Whitaker is hiring a receptionist for the clinic." Kylie gave her a blank look. "The *vet* clinic," her mom said, trying to clarify. Kylie blinked. Why was her mom talking to her about the vet? She didn't have a pet. Hell, she didn't even have a goldfish.

What she did have was a human being growing inside of her, which was unfortunately much more terrifying than a goldfish. For starters, she didn't have to push a goldfish out of her—

"You should go apply for the job," her mom said bluntly, finally giving up all pretense of dancing around the subject.

"Work at the clinic?" Kylie repeated, confused. She'd planned on getting a job someday, but right now, it just seemed overwhelming. She'd have to get out of bed and put on clothes and take a shower – hmmm...maybe, take a shower and *then* put on clothes – but this all sounded like a lot of movement, no matter what order the steps went in.

"Kylie, you're in a depressed funk." Apparently, her mom was sticking to the blunt plan. "You've been here a week almost to the hour, and I don't think you get out of bed except to go pee and occasionally shuffle to the kitchen to eat a bowl of Cap'n Crunch cereal. I love you, but enough is enough. I am not here to be your source of sugary breakfast cereal for the rest of your life. I am not here to be your babysitter when you give birth to this baby. I am not here to be your refuge where you get to hide from the world. I kept thinking you just needed some time to pull your head out of your ass and get it together, but apparently, that time isn't going to happen on its own. So, I'm going to force it. You need to get up, take a shower, brush your teeth, brush your hair for hell's sakes, and then come into the living room. It won't kill you to go somewhere else other than this bed. We can talk when you're done."

And with that edict, her mom walked out of the room and shut the door with a *click* behind her.

Kylie stared at the door in shock. She couldn't believe it. Dammit all, she was pregnant and she didn't know what she was going to do with her life! Her mom could cut her a little slack.

Hot tears of indignation trailed down her cheeks as she headed to the adjoining bathroom, stripping as she went. Her mom could *try* being nice. Kylie was her only child, after all, and—

The smell hit her nose, stopping her thoughts in their tracks. *What the hell is that smell?* It was putrid. Had her mother let a dead body rot in the bathtub?

She pulled the shower curtain back cautiously, peering in. Huh. Clean and shining, like always.

Hold on...right before that smell hit, Kylie had just taken off her sweatshirt and tank top that she vaguely remembered wearing on the Greyhound bus to Sawyer.

Which meant that she hadn't taken them off in eight days.

Could that be right? It couldn't be right.

She took a tentative sniff of her armpit and yanked her face away in disgust.

Okay, so maybe that was right. Shit, she had no idea body odor could be so offensive.

Kylie peeled the rest of her clothes off and stepped into the shower, holding her breath as much as possible as she quickly adjusted the water to the hottest temperature her skin could bear. As the hot water pounded down on her, the fog that'd wrapped her up in its comforting embrace over the past eight days began to dissipate. She began to feel energy and thoughts and clarity return, ever-so-slowly at first. She scrubbed her scalp with shampoo twice, trying to get the layer of oil and grease out of it that she'd allowed to settle in, and then started in on shaving. The more she scrubbed and shaved and rinsed, the better she felt.

By the time the hot water was gone, her legs were shaky and she felt lightheaded, but she also felt... herself. More alive and present than she had been in weeks. Maybe months.

She brushed her teeth and then tugged on yoga pants and a tank top – a clean one – and headed to the kitchen. She needed to find something to eat, and *then* she could talk to her mom. She needed fortifications for this convo, she was pretty damn sure. Her mom met up with her in the kitchen as she was rummaging through the fridge. "Feeling better?" she asked, leaning against the counter.

Kylie pulled out a stack of items and piled them on the counter. Mustard, horseradish, sprouts, pepper-jack cheese, sweet pickles, and strawberry jam. Her mouth watered at the sight. This was going to be a *glorious* sandwich.

"I do. I…" She paused in her slathering of the jam on the rye bread and smiled meekly at her mom. "I'm sorry. I don't know what happened. I'm still in shock, I guess." She went back to spreading a thick layer of sprouts, smooshing it into the jam with the back of a spoon. She ignored the strangled groan of disgust from her mom. "I didn't realize how long I'd been here, honestly. I thought it'd only been a day or two. I can't believe it's been a week."

She piled some baked ham slices on, and then squished the two sides together with a pleasing *smoosh* sound. She took a huge bite and let out a groan of happiness. Her mom watched her, a smile playing around the edges of her mouth. "I don't even need to see the pee stick," she said dryly. "No one can fake those kinds of pregnancy cravings."

Kylie shrugged, chewing and swallowing just enough to make room to shove some more in. She hadn't realized how hungry she'd gotten, either. She had vague memories of pouring herself some Peanut Butter Crunch but she couldn't remember when or how often. Based on her stomach rumblings, she was going to guess not often enough.

The food began to hit her bloodstream and she felt the trembling in her legs start to go away. She started to feel...human again. It was a wonderful feeling.

"Okay, so tell me about the vet job again," Kylie said, and then took another huge bite of her sandwich.

It was time to start making some changes, and that began with getting back on her feet. She wasn't here to be a mooch.

It was about time to act like it.

CHAPTER 4

KYLIE

KYLIE WENT WALKING up to the front door of the clinic the next afternoon, wiping her palms on the thighs of her jeans before reaching for the door handle. Today had been exhausting – all she'd managed to do was eat more sandwiches and take more naps between last night and now – but she *felt* like she'd been running a marathon. After a week of almost no movement whatsoever, walking between the bed and the kitchen was a bigger struggle than she really liked to admit.

And now, she'd managed to walk her happy ass all the way down to the clinic, three blocks of walking in the bright sunshine and everything. She was damn happy to be out and about, even if there was no way Dr. Whitaker would hire her as a receptionist, considering she had neither receptionist nor animal experience. This was a fool's errand, there was no doubt about it.

But on the other hand, he was actually hiring — not a small consideration for a town the size of Sawyer — *and* the clinic was within walking distance of her mom's house, also not a small consideration for someone who didn't own a car.

So, it was worth a try. After this, she would walk over to the Shop 'N Go and see if they were wanting cashiers or grocery cart chasers or something. No matter what, she wanted to be able to go home that evening with at least a job prospect to share with her mom.

She plastered a smile on her face as she walked into the air conditioned building, the bell overhead jingling, alerting Dr. Whitaker to her presence.

Except...

This can't *be Dr. Whitaker.*

Because instead of an old man coming out of the back, a pimply teenage boy not even old enough to shave came walking out. He tugged on the brim of his baseball cap nervously when he spotted her. "Yeah?" he grunted, picking up a pen from the desk and clicking the end rapidly.

"Umm...I'm here about the job opening. Is Dr. Whitaker available?" She tried to keep her voice calm and in control, as if this was normal to go apply for a job. As if she wasn't at all nervous.

The kid turned towards the back and hollered, "Adam, some chick is here for you!"

Kylie did her best to cover her startled snort of laughter with the fakest cough *ever*, so when the kid looked at her suspiciously, she just shot him a bright smile.

One guess as to why Dr. Whitaker wants a proper receptionist, and the first three guesses don't count.

If this was the bar the vet would measure her performance by, she could stop being nervous now. Anything short of accidentally murdering a patient would probably be seen as an improvement.

Dr. Whitaker came walking up from the back, and Kylie had the strongest sense of *déjà vu* wash over her at the sight of him.

This can't *be Dr. Whitaker.*

She remembered the vet – she'd met him when he came to her fifth grade class and did a presentation on the animal sciences and what it was like to be a vet. He'd been *old*. She remembered that much. Well, that and how pretty his horse was.

But the man standing in front of her with an easy smile on his face, putting his hand out to shake hers… he wasn't old. He was older than her, sure, but not *old*. Shouldn't he have a potbelly and whiskers and ruddy cheeks and white hair? A veterinarian version of Santa Claus?

She felt a little off-balance as she put her hand out and grasped his. "I'm Kylie VanLueven," she said, trying to keep her voice even, even as electrical sparks went shooting up her arm from his warm, calloused hand. "You're hiring?"

Nervous. So damn nervous. Her heart was racing and her breath was short and she was just staring up at this monstrously tall guy and shaking his hand and...

She finally realized that they'd been shaking for longer than was probably normal and yanked her hand away. A smile played around the edges of Dr. Whitaker's lips as he drawled, "Nice to meet you. Carol VanLueven's daughter?"

She nodded, smiling confidently. *Fake it 'til you make it, sister.* "You know my mom?"

"Everyone knows your mom," Dr. Whitaker said with an easy chuckle. "She sure does a lot for this community. We're lucky to have her. So, you're interested in the receptionist job, eh?"

"Yeah." She wiped the palms of her hands on her thighs again. She didn't expect to be this nervous.

She didn't expect...him. Dr. Adam Whitaker, country vet for Sawyer, Idaho, was quite possibly the cutest guy she'd ever laid eyes on.

No, she didn't expect that at all.

CHAPTER 5

ADAM

*A*DAM'S EYES SKIMMED over Kylie, taking in her appearance. She'd come dressed in jeans, a sweatshirt, her hair pulled back in a ponytail, and tennis shoes.

In other words, she came ready to work in a vet office.

He appreciated that. If she'd come in high heels and nylons, he would've sent her packing on the spot. He didn't have time for that kind of bullshit. He dealt with enough shit – *real* shit – on a daily basis. A girl who spent more time primping than working wasn't gonna cut it.

But speaking of not cutting it, she also wasn't anywhere near 50 years old. Hell, she probably wasn't even 25. He tried to remember when the VanLueven girl had graduated from high school, but after a while, that sort of thing just blended together. Too many teenagers and kids and infants to keep track of.

Well, she was here. He might as well see how she did around the animals in the back. "C'mon back here," he said with a jerk of his head, heading down the hallway to the back. "You should meet our current crop of patients."

She followed him, her tennis shoes squeaking on the worn gray tile floor. "I heard about the job opening," she said as they walked, "from my mom, who heard about it from the book club, Between the Covers, so honestly, I'm not sure if I even have the qualifications you're looking for."

They got to the back, where the dogs were barking, the cats were meowing, and there was just a general sense of chaos.

So, a typical day at Whitaker's Vet Clinic.

"Do you love animals, and do you want to work with them?" he asked bluntly, watching her as she began to wander around the crowded room. She stuck her fingers through the wire of Pickles' cage, and Adam bit back his warning not to stick her hands into cages with random animals. Pickles was an older dog, though, that'd just had a growth removed and was docile as a sloth. The worst he could do was slobber someone to death.

She nodded as she laughed lightly, Pickles' pink tongue lavishing her fingers with kisses. "Yes, very much. My mom wouldn't let me have a pet growing up; she said one human child was quite enough for her, without my dad around to help, you know? But I've always loved animals and they seem to like me."

She moved down a couple of cages to Sir Grouch, who got his name for a reason. Before Adam could yell out a warning, though, Kylie had unlocked the door and was pulling out the crotchety old cat, snuggling him against her chest. "Oh, aren't you a sweetie," she cooed as the cat's rusty, loud purr filled the air.

Adam was pretty sure his mouth was dragging on the ground. In all of the time he'd been taking care of Sir Grouch — and keep in mind, his owner had adopted the damn cat when he was being weaned from his mom — he'd never missed an opportunity to let loose with his claws at least once per visit, if not multiple times per visit. Adam tended to wear long-sleeve shirts even in the heat of summer exactly because of cats like Sir Grouch.

And yet...

"So you're at college, right?" Adam asked, tearing his eyes away from the insanity in front of him. "In Oregon? Or Washington? I can't remember."

"I was in Bend, Oregon, attending a small community college there." Adam could hardly hear her over the din of the dogs barking and Sir Grouch purring, but what he didn't miss was her 100-watt smile. "I'm home for a bit; I got my generals done but I didn't want to keep going until I figured out what I wanted to do with my life."

He moved a little closer. So he could hear her better, of course. Nothing else. "So you're not going to school to become a vet tech or something?"

She shook her head, her straight blonde hair swishing with the movement. Sir Grouch was now bathing her chin in kisses.

Adam felt faint. Kisses. The damn cat was *kissing* Kylie. Was he dreaming? He might be dreaming.

"It never occurred to me, honestly," Kylie said, answering his question. "I love animals well enough, so I could, but I won't lie and say that it's been a lifetime goal of mine."

Adam stared down at her, thinking. She wasn't 50 years old. She didn't come equipped with a steely-eyed gaze, at least that he could tell. She didn't have a single gray hair on her head. She wasn't a vet tech in training.

"Any receptionist or billing experience?" he asked hopefully, grasping at straws. Despite her complete lack of any characteristics that he'd been looking for in a receptionist, he still wasn't willing to turn her away.

Not yet.

She shook her head again, nuzzling her face against Sir Grouch's mangy coat. "I worked at a gas station in Oregon for four years while going to school. Pumping gas for customers." A shadow passed over her face and then it was gone again, replaced by a... 60-watt smile. Flickering from being plugged into a shitty outlet. "It's taken me four years to do two years' worth of generals because of working full-time, but I've been trying hard to stay out of debt. Now, though, I need to make a decision about what my career is going to be, so here I am. I'm staying with my mom for the moment, while I contemplate my choices."

Sir Grouch had snuggled down and appeared to be drifting off to sleep in Kylie's arms. A nap. In the arms of someone else other than his owner.

It was stupid and impulsive and would probably go down in history as one of the dumbest reasons on the planet to hire a person, but Adam couldn't help it. Sir Grouch had voted, and had overridden every one of his reasonable concerns.

"When can you start?"

CHAPTER 6

KYLIE

*K*YLIE CAME WALKING UP to the vet clinic, the morning rays just beginning to peek over the horizon. She was grinning to herself. *I have a job, I have a job...*When she'd been talking to Dr. Whitaker the afternoon before, she'd been so sure she wasn't going to get hired. She didn't have bookkeeping or receptionist experience. She wasn't on the fast track to become a vet tech. Hell, she'd never even owned a pet.

And yet, he'd hired her.

She wasn't about to question why, but instead, just thanked her lucky stars that finally, something in her life was going her way.

She felt a little twinge of guilt over not telling Dr. Whitaker about her pregnancy, but she quickly shoved the thought away. No one wanted to hire a young girl who was almost four months pregnant, unmarried, with no place to live, and no prospects. She'd just have to work hard, hope her morning sickness continued to stay under control, and wear loose-fitting clothing for as long as possible. Hopefully, by the time the vet realized the truth, he'd also know what a great employee she was, and wouldn't want to fire her.

Could he even fire her for being pregnant? She had no clue. They didn't exactly hand out legal advice along with defective condoms, although she was pretty damn sure that should be changed in the future.

Either way, this was Idaho, not exactly home of workers' rights. Getting fired for being pregnant totally seemed plausible to Kylie, not to mention that even if it wasn't legal, how would she fight it? It wasn't like she had deep pockets, let alone a lawyer on speed-dial.

No, her best bet was to just work as hard as her body would allow her, and make him realize she was indispensable. Let the bad news hit when it would, and hope for the best.

She wandered down the hallway to the back where she found Dr. Whitaker working on cleaning cages and filling water bottles. "Good morning, Dr. Whitaker," she called out. He looked up and shot her a huge grin.

"Hey! Is it that time already?" His eyes flicked up to the clock on the wall. "Time flies when you're having fun." He strode over and shook her hand. "Ready to have some fun of your own?"

The butterflies that were busily dancing up her

arm at his touch told her that she was already having fun, but she tried to ignore that thought. This was her *boss*. Nothing more than that. She'd already been dumb enough to fall for one completely ineligible male. She didn't need to bat twice at that pitch.

"Sure, sure!" She looked around at the cages, suddenly realizing that if he wanted her to clean up cat shit, she was up shit creek. She couldn't fake an allergy to cat poop, could she? That seemed like a strange substance to be allergic to, to say the least.

Dr. Whitaker caught her glance and said, "Most of the stuff back here is taken care of by Ollie – he's the teen you met yesterday. He's better back here than up front, so best to leave these tasks to him or me. Where I need your help is with paperwork. And coffee. I have a coffee pot and supplies for it over there," he jerked his head towards what appeared to be an employee kitchen, which mostly seemed to just be a dorm fridge, microwave, and coffee pot, "but I never take the time to make a pot. It'd be great if you could do that."

She laughed a little. "I'm pretty sure I can make coffee every morning," she said with just a hint of wryness in her voice. She didn't want to appear to be laughing at her new boss...even if she was.

He grinned back. "I knew there was a reason I hired you. Okay, let's go over the phone system and files and stuff." They walked back upfront, Kylie trailing along behind him, studying the sway of his ass in his tight Wranglers as he walked. She gulped. She'd heard that sometimes, hormones could get out of control when a girl was pregnant, and considering the bolt of desire that just shot through her, she was going to guess she was one of those girls.

This was gonna be one tough job, if only because she had to keep her hands to herself while doing it.

He ran through the phone with her, how to check messages, what he wanted her to say when she answered, how to turn on the computer – she noticed he had no password or login for it; she didn't even know computers could be set up that way anymore – and then, the grand finale.

"I have a calendar," he said, pulling a small book out of the front pocket of his shirt. She looked at it, trying to hide the surprise on her face. When he said he had a calendar, he meant an honest-to-God *calendar*, not something online or on his phone.

She mentally revised his age in her head. She'd thought that maybe he wasn't so old after all, but this…this was starting to make her think her original guess was correct. Maybe he just had good genes, and appeared to be 35 when he was actually 85.

Really good genes.

"One of my biggest struggles is keeping all of my appointments straight," he said, holding the calendar out for her to take. She began flipping through it, reading the bold if sloppy handwriting as she went. "I realized that this was only going to get worse if I hired you. I can't have my calendar in my pocket *and* here at the clinic at the same time, but we're both going to need access to it if having you here is going to do me any good. So! I realized: You could take my calendar and put it into the computer. Then I can see it on my phone and you can see it on the computer *at the same time!*"

He sounded like he'd just discovered the joys of the internet last week, and was now excitedly spreading the knowledge to others. Next, he was going to start telling her all about those handy-dandy apps that can be downloaded to a phone, or how he finally set up a profile on Facebook last week.

She bit down so hard on the inside of her cheek, trying her damnedest to keep from busting out with laughter, that she tasted the iron tang of blood filling her mouth. Her best wasn't good enough, and he read her like a book. "I probably sound like the world's biggest idiot when it comes to computers, don't I?"

"Uhh…"

"They never did much for me," he continued on, thankfully not requiring her to reply. "I've always been happiest around animals, not electronics. I only got a smartphone when my flip phone died a violent death under the hoof of a cow and the Verizon Wireless store didn't have another one in stock to replace it." He was holding out the newest iPhone as if it was a snake that was going to bite him, and she struggled to hold back another laugh.

To go from a flip phone to the latest and greatest iPhone was a bit like upgrading from a Geo Metro to a Lamborghini. The fact that the sheer power and capabilities that he was holding in his hand seemed to be completely lost on him was…endearing. She'd even go so far as to say adorable.

Completely insane, but adorable.

She took the iPhone from him after he thumbed it to unlock it, and began flipping through. He only had the basics installed, so she quickly downloaded the Google Calendar app and showed him where she'd put the icon. "I'll put all of your appointments into Google Calendar here on your computer," she gestured towards the hulking monstrosity on the desk that was probably old enough to be her mother, "and it'll show up on your phone. Easy peasy—"

"—Pumpkin squeezy," he finished for her with a grin. She grinned back. Yeah, impressing Dr. Whitaker wasn't going to be hard after all.

CHAPTER 7

ADAM

*A*DAM WAS STARING DOWN at Kylie, panic blossoming inside. He'd made a mistake. Absolutely, positively made a mistake. She was way too beautiful, way too smart, way too…young. He should *not* have hired her. Forget a 50-year-old woman; he needed a 60-year-old woman in here. Hell, make her 70 and then she'd be the same age as his mom and his heart would absolutely not be going a hundred miles an hour just being around her.

This was a bad idea. A very, very bad idea.

He should just fire her now. Except, he had no reason to fire her right now, and jerking her around was an awful thing to do. Not to mention that bringing the wrath of Carol VanLueven down upon his head wasn't exactly something he was looking forward to. Now, *there* was a woman who couldn't be trifled with.

No, firing Kylie would be a real jackass move to

make. He just had to stick it out. Maybe not spend so much time in the office. Or any time at all in the office. Not if she was going to wear perfume that smelled like wildflowers, anyway. He could pretend an allergy to her perfume; ask her to stop wearing it. Anything to keep his sanity.

She was waving her hands in front of his face. His eyes jerked up to hers. "You okay?" she asked. "You were gone there for a minute."

"Good, good, going to go check up on some patients," he said, heading for the door before he realized he had no idea which patients those would be. He turned around with an embarrassed grin on his face, plucked his calendar out of her hands, scanned through today's entries, and then handed it back. "Leaving now. I'll be back at 5," he promised her, and then he walked out the door, breathing in the fresh, non-wildflower-perfumed air once he got outside.

Well, she knew how to run a computer, and at least in that arena, she was a huge step up from him. Hiring her was a great idea, even if she made his heart twist in his chest.

Maybe.

CHAPTER 8

KYLIE

OLIVER BURST THROUGH the front door and stuttered to a stop, his eyes taking in her sitting behind the desk. "Oh," he grunted, sounding like he'd accidentally swallowed his tongue. She stood up and walked around the desk to him.

"I'm Kylie VanLueven. And you are?" she said, holding her hand out to shake his. She was pretty sure he wouldn't follow formalities otherwise. His gaze darted this way and that as he put his hand out to shake.

"Oliver Blank," he mumbled, "but you can call me Ollie." And then he took off for the back like his ass was on fire.

She laughed a little to herself as she sat back down at the desk. Had she been that uncomfortable around boys when she was in school? Probably. Hell, she felt like doing just that this morning around Dr. Whitaker.

She got back to work on the calendar project. She'd finished putting everything in until the end of the year, and, for a lack of something else to do, had started back on January 1st and began working her way forward. At least this way, Dr. Whitaker would have all of his appointments in his calendar to refer back to whenever he needed.

And anyway, there was no way she was going to sit around and just wait for the minutes to tick by until five o'clock hit. There was no faster way to make her completely insane than to be stuck doing absolutely nothing.

Well, that week-long stint of hiding in bed aside, of course, but that wasn't exactly a normal thing for her.

She'd almost caught up to May when the front doorbell jingled and in came Dr. Whitaker, shit and hay and animal hair all over his clothes...and never looking better than he did right then. How did he manage to make cow shit look good?

She shoved the thought aside and grabbed the stack of messages from the desk. "Hi, Dr. Whitaker," she said, smiling as she walked around the front desk and over to him. "Here's your phone calls for the day. I marked the ones that seemed urgent in the corner with a star." She pointed those out. "I also have almost all of the calendar entries done. Did you play around with Google Calendar at all during lunch?"

He shook his head, not even looking at her as he thumbed his way through the messages. "Kylie," he breathed, "this is...amazing!" He looked up and grinned. "Wow! You're wonderful!"

"It's just some phone messages," she pointed out, but her cheeks were glowing red anyway. Her previous guess that as long as she didn't kill a patient she'd be a step up in Dr. Whitaker's eyes was turning out to be true. Which was embarrassing as hell, honestly.

"But I can read them all! And they make sense. And I bet you didn't tell a single person today that they weren't allowed to have one of my business cards."

"What?" she said, dumbfounded, just staring up at him. Praise was nice, sure, but praise that made sense would be even better.

"Don't worry about it," he said, waving her off. "Listen, do you want to go down to the Muffin Man Bakery and grab a donut to eat? My treat, as a way to say thank you for—*dammit!*"

"What?" she said again. She rolled her eyes at herself. Her vocabulary really needed some variety. Maybe she could start adding in the word "Huh?" for shits and giggles.

"We can't go to the Muffin Man," he said, clearly disappointed. "There was a big fire a couple of months ago, and Gage just got the insurance check recently from what I've heard. It hasn't reopened yet."

"Oh. Damn." Kylie was genuinely depressed right along with her boss. A donut sounded amazing to her at the moment, even though sugar was awful for a person...but hell, she was pregnant. It wasn't like watching her figure was going to do her much good at this point. "Well, I'll take a raincheck on the idea. We can do it later, when they reopen."

She started to gather up her things so she could walk home when Adam asked, "Hey, do you know of anyone who'd be willing to rent a farm?"

"A farm? Like, a whole farm?" She turned to stare up at him, mouth agape. "Ummm...who'd need to rent a farm who didn't already have one?"

"Well, it's just a hobby farm, really. There's acreage, but I have cows running on that. I mostly need to find someone to stay in the house and take care of the few animals I have in the barn. I keep hoping I can move back to it, but I haven't been able to yet, and the current tenant is moving out as we speak. She got engaged to her boyfriend and is moving in with him." He gave her a tight smile that didn't reach his eyes, and Kylie smiled back, the wheels in her mind spinning. Whoever this tenant was, Dr. Whitaker wasn't happy about her moving out, that much was obvious.

She wished she were more plugged into the gossip center of Sawyer. She was pretty sure there was a story here that Dr. Whitaker wasn't sharing.

But she couldn't say that out loud. Not to her boss, anyway. She shrugged. "I'll keep my ears open and tell you if I hear of anything. I wish I could, but I'm staying at my mom's for free, at least for now. I'm saving every penny I can for college and...and stuff," she stumbled, "so I can't splurge on something like rent. But if I hear of anyone looking for a place to stay, I'll be sure to tell you."

He had a funny look on his face. She paused, waiting for him to say something, anything at all, but he was just standing there, opening and closing his mouth so she finally just gave a mental shrug. "Well, I'm heading out. I'll see you in the morning." She grabbed her purse, slinging it over her shoulder and heading out the door.

Tonight, she needed a long, hot bath. Nothing but relaxation. Somewhere far, far away from her weird but sexy-as-hell boss.

CHAPTER 9

ADAM

*A*DAM JUST STARED AFTER HER, long after the door closed behind her, thinking, thinking, thinking. Dammit all, he *had* to stop trying to save every damsel in distress that came knocking on his door. Kylie hadn't said it, but he'd be willing to bet the farm on the fact that she was running from someone or something. Nothing else made sense.

Hell, all she'd need to be was pregnant, and then she could just be a younger version of Chloe. He could stand around and wait in the wings for nine years until baby daddy came swooping back in, and then she could run off with him, leaving Adam behind.

Again.

Well, Kylie wasn't pregnant, thank God, so at least that part of it wasn't going to happen.

And anyway, he needed to stop renting his farm out to beautiful, if poor-as-church-mice women for virtually nothing. His bank account was telling him loud and clear that another revenue stream would be greatly appreciated. So he couldn't offer the place to Kylie.

Case closed.

After a stop to check on a newborn colt on the way, and then another stop to check on a rabbit with pink eye, he finally made his way to his mom's house.

The thought drew him up short. He'd moved back in with her nine years ago so he could help her out, what with her debilitating arthritis and all, but even after all this time, it was still *her* house. Not his.

It was starting to get old, that. At 38 years old, he was still living with his mother, in her house. Granted, he owned his own home and business, so it wasn't like he was living with his mom because he was incapable of making it on his own, but whatever the reason for the situation, it still wasn't easy.

Ruby Whitaker may be slowly having her vitality and ability to move taken away from her by an insidious, severe case of arthritis, but it had done nothing to affect her mind. It was *her* house and *her* rules and although he respected that, it sure as hell wasn't ideal.

He pulled into his spot in the gravel driveway with a sigh, looking up at the grandmotherly house that'd been his home since he was born. The late evening rays were lighting up the baby blue planks, casting a golden light on them. He was late getting home, again. He'd moved in with his mom to help her out, but honestly, the only reason they hadn't killed each other yet was because he was gone so often. Which didn't exactly mean that this plan was working out the way he'd thought it would.

Good intentions, bad execution.

He pulled himself out of the truck and headed inside, noticing distractedly that the lawn needed a haircut in a pretty bad way. Maybe he'd have Ollie come out here and mow his mom's lawn tomorrow after feeding and cleaning out the animal cages at the clinic. God only knew that if it was up to Adam to do it, the grass would be long enough to cut with a scythe and bundle as hay before he got around to it.

"Hey, Mom," he said tiredly as he came through the baby pink front door. He pressed a kiss to her cheek, hiding a yawn behind his hand as he headed to the kitchen to scrounge up something to eat. Sassy was rubbing up against his ankles, begging for loving, when he spotted a pot of stew bubbling on the stove. He silently thanked the heavens that his mom had felt well enough to cook today. He would've been eating a peanut butter and jelly sandwich for dinner – again – otherwise.

"Hi, baby!" his mom called back cheerfully from the dining room table. Sassy gave up on getting his attention and wandered back over to Ruby instead. "You spotted the stew, I see," she said as he began scooping the food into a bowl. "So, you hired a new girl today?" she continued on.

Adam had to wonder for a moment how his

mother knew that, but then mentally just shrugged. Even though she was housebound, she still managed to stay firmly planted in the flow of the Sawyer gossip chain. It was a skill, really.

"Yeah, Kylie VanLueven, Carol's daughter," he said, sliding into a creaky wooden chair next to her and blowing on the soup. It smelled amazing – not surprising, considering his mom was an excellent cook – and there was a part of his brain that was all for discarding the temperature level of the soup and instead begin just shoveling it in.

Had he eaten that day? He couldn't remember. His stomach was saying, "Hells to the no" loud and clear, but it quite often lied. Like a fat, lazy horse, Adam's stomach was a bottomless pit that was never full.

"Well, I heard she's doing an excellent job. Much better than that *boy*."

Adam bit back his smile. His mom was no fan of Ollie, not after he told her that a cat didn't care if its collar had jewels on it, when she'd cooed that her baby "looked like a princess" with its pink crystal-studded collar on.

Ollie was right, of course, but sometimes, there were thoughts best left unspoken. The teen hadn't exactly discovered the joys of tact yet.

"Ollie's specialty definitely isn't…humans," Adam finally said.

His mom sniffed. "Understatement of the year," she muttered under her breath. Adam ignored that.

Convenient deafness was a game both of them could play, and she was surely the queen of that trick.

"Well, it was only Kylie's first day," he said, moving back to safer topics, "but she seemed to do real well, even without me needing to show her every little thing. The animals love her, I can actually read her handwriting, and she knows more about computers and smartphones in her little pinky than I do in my whole body. She's going to drag me, kicking and screaming, into the 21st century yet."

His mom let out a belly laugh. "It sucks to get old," she said ruefully, "but the good news is, no one expects me to learn how to run those things – they've all given up on me getting that through my thick skull. I'm afraid you got your computering skills from me."

"At least I know who to blame," he said with a wink as he stood up and began collecting the dishes from the table. He'd clean up and then head to bed.

Another day, another dollar. He wouldn't say that his life was boring – there were too many kicking cows and ornery horses for that to be true – but it was stagnant. As he lay in bed that night, staring up at the patterns cast by the full moon on the ceiling, he began to wonder what he was living for. He was working hard – getting up early, going all day, only to collapse into bed at night – and the animals he helped take care of appreciated him. The kids at the therapy camp appreciated him even more. But still...

What did it all mean, in the end? Would he lie on his deathbed and say, "I'm sure glad I got that calf castrated for the Cowells"? He would look back on his life, and…what? Be proud of what he'd accomplished? Wish he'd found his purpose? Wish he'd done something else?

He turned in bed, punching the pillow into submission before trying to settle in. It seemed like 38 was a little young to be hitting a midlife crisis, but that's all this whining and complaining seemed to be. He had a good life, for the most part. He was doing what he loved. He owned his own business. He was his own boss.

So why did it all seem so pointless?

CHAPTER 10

KYLIE

*S*TARING DOWN AT THE PAPER, Kylie chewed on the end of her pencil, trying to figure out how to squeeze just a little bit more out of her budget. Belt tightening was going to become a skill she would become black-belt master in, considering what she needed in her savings account in another five months.

How do people do this? She groaned. Well, for starters, most people could go after the father and have them help with expenses, but…well, that wasn't exactly an option in Kylie's case. He didn't even know she was still pregnant, and if he found out…

She shivered.

Six months ago, she would've sworn up, down, and sideways that Norman would never get violent with her, but she'd be the first to admit that six months ago, she was about as naïve as they came.

Now, she just didn't know what he'd do – something even worse than what he'd already done? The thought terrified her.

A knock on her bedroom door pulled Kylie out of her ruminations. "Come in," she called out, shoving her hair out of her face as she looked up to see her mom enter. "Hey, Mom! What's up?"

Kylie was staying in her childhood bedroom, which she'd always thought spacious and beautiful as a kid. Once she'd moved out, though, her mom had converted the space into her sewing room, and it was now stuffed to the gills with sewing machines – yes, *two* of them – along with fabric and thread and batting and ribbons and...

Her mom made her way through the maze to the bed where Kylie was sitting cross-legged, a notepad splayed open on the bed beside her. The corners of her mouth were a little tight, and instinctually, Kylie knew she wanted to discuss something difficult. Or bad. And/or not even in the slightest bit fun.

Kylie's stomach sank.

"I'm so glad you got that job down at the clinic," her mom said brightly, trying to act as if this was going to be a pleasant conversation. Kylie wasn't even vaguely fooled. "It's been two weeks now – have you received your first paycheck yet?"

"Yeah, just today. It's only a partial, because of how the pay schedule runs, but I at least have some idea of what the taxes and whatever will be now. I was just trying to put together a budget." She looked down ruefully at the budget in the notebook, with big X's and arrows and stars all over it as she'd tried to rearrange expenses, to make an extra dollar or ten somehow appear in the bottomline.

"Oh good!" her mother exclaimed, the tension on her face disappearing in a flash. "How much did you put in for rent? I can keep my ear to the ground and tell you if a rental comes up in your price range. You know how it is around here – it's easier to find a pile of gold hidden under a four-leaf clover than it is a decent rental in a good price range." She laughed a little at her own joke; laughter that quickly disappeared when she caught the look on Kylie's face.

Rent…

Kylie hadn't even added that in. She'd just assumed that her mom would at least let her stay here until the baby was—

Her mom was shaking her head. "Kylie, I love you," she started.

The "but" on the end of that sentence was so large, Kylie was pretty sure she was going to get smothered to death by it. She felt tears prick in the edges of her eyes, hot and embarrassing, before her mom even continued.

"But I *can't* have you staying here. You've been gone for four years. Four years! And even though I love you, I love my space, too. I'm not used to having someone else here after all this time. I'm not used to worrying about cooking for two. And I can't sew a damn thing when you're living in my sewing room."

"I…I just thought…" Kylie's voice was warbling and she hated herself for it and she couldn't stop it and she hated her mom, too, in that moment. "I didn't…"

"Ky, I've got the project I'm starting up with Nicky's mom, where we're making care packages for soldiers overseas, and then I have the soup kitchen that I'm running with Mrs. Frank once a week over at the Methodist church. I have this whole life that I'm living, and you're a part of that because you're my daughter and I love you, but I can't have you right here in the middle of it. I told you before – I can't be your babysitter, either. A grandma loves their grandchild, of course, but I'm my own person, too, with my own interests and passions and hobbies."

Kylie nodded, trying hard to snuffle back the sobs threatening to take over. She understood…sort of. It was selfish of her to expect her mom to rearrange her entire life just because her daughter was too stupid to run a condom properly, but it was also damn hard not to hear "I don't want you" as the message being conveyed loud and clear.

"I'll…I'll look, Mom. I'll tell you if I find anything. And…and you look, too." She gave her mom an overly bright smile, trying to hide the pain stabbing through her. Her mom leaned over and hugged her hard.

"I do love you, you know," she whispered into

Kylie's hair. "So very much. Never forget that." And then she stood up and made her way back out of the room and Kylie lay back on the bed and cried a river of tears that she wished could somehow wash her away to the sea.

CHAPTER 11

ADAM

*A*DAM PULLED UP to the clinic, surprised and pleased to see that the neon open sign had already been flipped on. Kylie had beat him there. Granted, he'd accidentally slept in that morning and then after feeding his horses and running over to his old farm and feeding and milking the animals there, he was more than a little bit behind, but still…

Having someone who he could rely on to show up and work hard was a giant relief, a relief he hadn't even known he needed, but now? It was only two weeks into it, but he already couldn't imagine living without Kylie there to rely on.

He went walking into the clinic, breathing in the pleasant scent of animal mixed with coffee. Of course – she'd already brewed up a pot. He was pretty sure she was Mary Poppins in disguise.

Kylie looked up from the front desk with a smile. "Hi, Dr. Whitaker!" she said cheerfully.

"Call me Adam," he told her, for what was probably the 17th time.

She nodded. "Adam," she said awkwardly. She seemed to much prefer his official title, although he couldn't begin to guess why.

He headed into the back to grab a cup of coffee and check on the animals, and was surprised to have her trail along behind him, her ever-present scent of wildflowers trailing along too. He'd kept telling himself to inform her of his non-existent allergies to her perfume, but apparently, sheer willpower only went so far, and then…stopped.

His willpower apparently stopped right at the doorstep of doing what was smart and logical, and then disappeared without a trace.

Not the most convenient place for his willpower to conk out on him.

He waited for Kylie to say something as he poured himself a cup, but she just stood there, gnawing on her bottom lip.

"Everything going okay?" he prompted her as he began wandering around, checking in on his patients. Sniffles seemed like she wasn't favoring her leg quite as much, which was a marked improvement. He should check her—

"Well," she burst out, "I…I'm wondering if you have another project for me to do."

He stopped rummaging around in the supply drawer and looked up at her, surprised. *Another* project?" he echoed. She sure seemed like she was getting a lot done to him. How could she possibly have time to do anything else? She got more office work done in a day than he did in three weeks.

"Yeah. All of the appointments from your calendar are in the computer, all of the paperwork is filed, all of your bills are paid, and the phone doesn't exactly ring every moment of every day. I can't stand being bored. I need something else to do. Do you have cleaning supplies?"

His head spun a little from the abrupt change in topic. "Like Windex and a broom, you mean?"

She nodded enthusiastically.

"Yeah, uhhh, probably," he mumbled, closing the supply drawer and heading over to the corner where he stashed the random shit he didn't use very often.

Honestly, the office was fine – a little dirty in places but hell, it was a veterinarian office. What really mattered was the cleanliness of the animal cages, and *those* were kept in tip-top shape.

But if Kylie wanted something to do, far be it from him to keep her from entertaining herself. After all, what kind of boss complained about an employee wanting to do more work?

She was simply staring down at the broom and Windex bottle he was trying to hand her, though, refusing to take them from him, and he looked at them too, confused. Why was she staring at them like they were venomous snakes, just ready to strike?

"Ummm...would it be okay if I bought new ones from the store?" she asked tactfully.

Huh. He held the broom up to inspect it. Now that he looked at it a little closer, he did have to admit that it'd seen better days. Maybe, like, 50 years ago when this vet clinic was started and this broom was first purchased.

"Yeah, sure," he said slowly, his stomach twisting a little at the idea of spending yet more money; his gut reaction to spending money of any kind on anything was instinctual and automatic. But, he began to reason through it, since she'd started actually billing customers on a regular basis, his bank account wasn't *quite* as empty as it had been before. In fact, it could stand the onslaught of a shopping spree for cleaning supplies – not something he'd always been able to say.

Kind of a nice feeling, really. Unusual, but nice.

"Sure, just tell David down at the hardware store to put it on my account and send me a bill," he said a little more firmly.

"Great!" she said, the brilliant smile back on her face. She headed up front and Adam got back to work on the morning check of his patients. When he'd finished, he headed up front and found that she was gone. She must've headed for the store already.

He shook his head, smiling to himself as he got in his truck to start making his rounds. The office was fine as it was, but if it made her happy to clean it… well shit, then it made him happy, too.

～

IT HAD BEEN A LONG DAY – but honestly, what day *wasn't* a long day – and he stifled a yawn as he pulled to a stop in front of the clinic. Time to go inside, pick up his messages, do another check of the animals, and then stop out at his old place to milk the cow and goat and feed the chickens before he could, blessedly, go back to his mom's and collapse into bed.

Was everyone this exhausted all the time? He felt like he was walking in a thick cloud, trying his damnedest to keep up with everything but slowly failing.

He forced himself out of the truck and towards the front door. One foot in front of the other. He could do this. He could totally—

He stopped.

This *was* his office, right?

He stepped back and looked over to the right, where WHITAKER'S VETERINARIAN CLINIC was emblazoned in big gold letters on the plate-glass windows. Yup, his office all right.

It just didn't look like it.

Had the front glass door always been encased in aluminum? He didn't remember it shining like that before. He had a vague recollection of it being gray before. Or black. Or some version of "grungy" anyway.

He gingerly pulled the door open, the doorbell overhead tinkling to announce his entrance, and Kylie looked up, huffing stray hairs out of her face. "Dammit!" she said, scrambling to her feet. "I was hoping to have it done before you got back. Is it really five already?"

But Adam couldn't answer her. His eyes were too busy scanning the room. The cement-block walls, previously painted a dingy yellowish color, were now white. Shining, clean, brilliant white. "Did you paint in here?" he burst out, his nose wiggling as he tried to detect the odor of fresh paint in the air. Nothing. Just lemons and wildflowers.

She laughed. "I just scrubbed them," she said with a huge grin and a shrug. "If I had to make a guess, I would say that was something that hadn't been done in a while."

The office was a disaster, to be honest. The left half of the room had been emptied, with everything shoved to the right side so she could do a thorough cleaning without anything getting in the way. It was the most orderly aftermath of a cleaning tornado he'd ever witnessed.

But the walls…and front windows…all of the nose prints from the countless dogs that'd passed through the clinic were gone. The black footprints, the hair everywhere…

It had all disappeared, like magic, under the hands of the most amazing employee he'd ever had the good luck to hire.

"Will you rent my farm from me?" he said, the words bursting from his lips impulsively. "Rent free. Just take care of the animals and the yard so I don't have to."

It was something he'd been telling himself that he absolutely, positively could not offer to her ever since the thought had first popped into his head, but looking around his clinic, he knew that it couldn't be in better hands than hers. Hell, she'd probably have his hobby farm turning a profit within six months, if his clinic was anything to judge her by.

Her eyes grew wide. "Really?" she breathed, and then she threw herself at him. "Thank you, thank you, thank you!" she cried, quite literally, as tears streamed down her face.

He patted her awkwardly on the back. Gratitude he could handle, even if it was a little embarrassing. Tears, on the other hand…not his favorite.

She pulled back, snuffling and wiping at her cheeks with the backs of her hands. "I can't even tell you how much this means to me," she said through her tears, grinning at him. "I just…my mom last night…I…thank you!" she finally sputtered out.

He laughed a little, his cheeks red with embarrassment. "I don't think I could find someone who'd take better care of it than you, honestly. Want to go tour it?" In for a penny, in for a pound. If he was going to offer her free rent, he might as well go show her around, right?

"Absolutely!" she said, spinning back to the desk and grabbing her purse and lunch bag from underneath it. "Is it okay if I leave the clinic like this until Monday?" she asked, coming to a stop and looking around the torn-apart office.

Adam shrugged. "If I get calls on the weekend, I normally just go out to a client's place. I don't have many customers come here on the weekend. It'll be fine."

She grinned. "Then I'm ready whenever you are."

He started to head towards the truck so they could drive out to his farm, but he stopped short, remembering in the nick of time. "Wait, I need to go look at the patients in the back real quick and then we can go. Did Ollie come in today?"

"Yeah, he was here until just before you arrived," Kylie said, trailing along behind him as he made an about-face to head down the hallway. "He said he needed to leave a little early tonight."

Adam nodded, getting to work checking on the animals. It was Friday night, and Ollie was a teenager. For all Adam knew, the kid had a hot date. Hell, stranger things had happened. Maybe.

And as he worked his way around the room, he could see that Ollie had done his job perfectly, as always. Between Kylie taking care of the front and Ollie taking care of the back, life was just a little more manageable. And if Kylie could move out to the homestead and start taking care of his animals, that'd be one more huge load off his plate.

He could almost feel his shoulders relax from the relief of having so many stressors removed from them. He could breathe a little deeper, and the constant knot in his stomach loosened up just a smidge.

Damn, this was a glorious feeling. A man could get used to this.

They headed out the front door, flipping off the lights and the open sign as they went, and Kylie climbed into the passenger side of his truck, tactfully moving all of the random paraphernalia off her seat before sliding into place. "Sorry," he said, a little embarrassed as he put his truck into reverse and backed out into the street. "I don't have passengers very often. It's an easy place to store things."

She smiled over at him. "No worries," she said. "You don't normally act like a taxi service. It's all good."

The businessman inside of him was screaming and yelling at him that he was being an idiot for giving away his rental property for free – *again* – but even as he thought the words, he couldn't make himself regret the offer. The 100-watt smile on Kylie's face was all the payment he needed.

Bank account be damned.

CHAPTER 12

KYLIE

*T*HEY PULLED UP in front of an older farmhouse, long on charm, short on paint. And window screens. But there were fun wooden scallops that ran the length of the porch and a gorgeous front door that Kylie was positive was original to the house, making it easy to overlook its few shortcomings.

"It needs some love and attention," Adam began apologetically as Kylie hopped out of the truck and hurried up to the house. "I've had a lot on my plate lately and it's been easy to—"

"No worries, I promise!" she broke in. A little peeling paint? Hell, she could live with that.

In fact, she could probably scrape and paint the place this summer. If she did the legwork, maybe Adam would provide the supplies. Her life was at critical levels of boredom – other than work at the clinic, she didn't have much else going on. Fixing up the house would give her something to do in the evenings and weekends. Her only other hobby of late seemed to be reworking her budget, but she could only do that so many times before there was nothing left to tweak.

Money did not appear from thin air, no matter how many times she tried to make it happen.

He unlocked the front door, which swung open to reveal a small entryway that opened up into a living room with what appeared to be original hardwood floors. A beat-up couch paired with a beat-up wing chair graced the room, both of them looking like they'd seen better years. "The furniture comes along with," Adam said as she looked around, oohing and aahing over the original wooden baseboards. "The former tenant is moving in with her boyfriend, so she didn't need to take it with her. She said to leave it behind for…well, for you, I suppose."

Kylie stopped trailing her hands over the nicked and scuffed woodwork to look back at him. He had that tight smile on his face that wasn't even vaguely convincing, and this time, Kylie was absolutely sure that the previous tenant was more than just a tenant. Were they in love? Did she dump him for this boyfriend dude? Kylie felt a little anger and indignation well up inside of her on his behalf. Who would choose someone else over Adam? He was kind and thoughtful and giving and sweet and handsome as sin and…

She stopped herself right there. Granted, it was

about ten thoughts too late, but at least she was trying to stop. She couldn't let herself look at her boss that way. Especially not if he was going to be her boss *and* her landlord.

If she fell in love with him…oh Lordy, wouldn't that just wreak some havoc. What would happen if it didn't work out? He could fire her and evict her in one fell swoop.

Falling for Adam Whitaker would be one of the worst ideas of her short life, and truly, that was saying something.

She smiled at him, scolded herself when her heart went into overdrive as he sent her a heart-stopping smile in return, and then turned towards the kitchen. She walked past the scarred dining room table and into a country kitchen – not horrifically small, but definitely on the efficient side. She looked around, an honest grin spreading across her face; not forced, not required, not trying to hide anything, but rather a joyful grin as she took it all in.

"Oh, Adam!" she exclaimed as she began opening and closing cupboards and drawers, even peering into the fridge.

When she'd left Oregon, she'd been forced to leave most of her kitchen equipment behind, too. That night of frantic packing, trying to escape, there'd been a brief moment of levity when her roommate had held up a meat baster that Kylie was leaving behind in a kitchen drawer. "Kylie, what the hell am I supposed to do with this? It looks like a tranquilizer needle for a horse!"

Yeah, all of that specialized equipment was definitely lost on her former roommate, and no doubt, she'd already sold all of it on Craigslist and bought pizzas from Domino's with the cash. But here was Kylie's chance to rebuild all of that. For the first time in her life, she'd have her own home.

She spun in a circle and grinned up at Adam. He had a funny look on his face when he said slowly, "You called me Adam. That's the first time you've ever called me that without me prompting you to."

She shrugged, her eyes dropping to the ground. She probably shouldn't have called him that, honestly, but she'd been caught up in the joy of the moment. It was much better to keep him at arm's length. Formality was going to be the only way to get through with her heart still in one piece.

She knew all of that. And yet...

"Thank you for this...Adam," she said softly, looking back up into his warm, brown eyes. "I cannot tell you how much it means to me. Truly. I will be in debt to you for the rest of my life."

A flustered grin spread across his face. "You're gonna be a big help to me, honestly," he rushed to assure her. "After the former tenant moved out, it's fallen on me to take care of this place and these animals again, and it's slowly killing me. Either I find someone to take this over, or I sell it. I can't keep spreading myself this thin. But...I'm not ready to sell it yet," a shadow crossed his eyes at the admission, "so I'm thrilled to have you helping me out."

She wondered again about the secrets this man in front of her held close to his chest. He was friendly and kind and thoughtful to everyone, but she wondered if that was a front somehow; a way of hiding the painful spots in his past.

If there was one thing Kylie understood, it was pain emanating out from the past to haunt a person. It was the kind of pain that a soul didn't get over easily.

She rubbed her belly absentmindedly. It wasn't a big house, but honestly, she didn't need a big house. She just needed enough room for her and the baby, and this would do that and more.

"Can we check out the upstairs?" she asked. "I'm assuming the bedrooms are up there."

His smile came back full force, happy and believable again. "Absolutely! There's this antique brass bed up there that you'll enjoy; from what I understand, the people who originally built this place ordered the bed out of a Sears catalog and had it delivered here on the train. You really can't get much more historical than that."

She followed him up the creaking wooden stairs, her eyes trained on the easy movement of his hips as they went.

She gulped.

She should definitely not be calling him Adam. Not if she wanted to keep her sanity.

CHAPTER 13

ADAM

$\mathcal{H}$E OPENED UP the gate to the small pasture that was connected to the barn and let Kylie pass by him before closing it behind them. The chickens went crazy, running over, wings outstretched as they competed for space next to him. They knew what the arrival of a human meant: Food.

"Oh, they're friendly!" Kylie said, leaning over to pet one that had gotten up close to her to investigate her shoes.

"Don't—!" Adam exclaimed, just as the chicken reached out and pecked Kylie's hand. Hard. Kylie pulled back with a yelp, and scared, the chicken took off running, her ass waddling as she hurried as fast as her two short legs would take her across the green grass. Kylie looked down with a rueful smile at her hand, a small stream of blood running down it.

"So, not that friendly?" she said wryly.

He laughed.

"Not pets, that's for sure. They tend to think that anything you're putting within reach of their beaks must be food. She wasn't trying to hurt you; she was just trying to eat you."

It was Kylie's turn to laugh. "You're really good at reassuring people, you know that? So, you've got killer chickens who want to eat me. What else do you have here for me to take care of?" She'd pulled a used Kleenex out of her sweatshirt pocket and had wrapped it around her small wound; Adam was happy to see that she didn't break down into histrionics over it. Once again, he patted himself on the back for his amazing hiring skills. Forget 50-year-old women; he didn't figure they could get any better than Kylie.

"Over there," he said, pointing to Skunk who was placidly grazing and ignoring the whole ruckus, "is the milk cow. Her name is Skunk. She was named by a little boy who thought that everything that was black and white must be a skunk." She laughed, and encouraged, he pointed to the goat. "And that is Dumbass."

At the sound of her name, the goat looked up and then came trotting over, apparently believing that if they were going to talk about her, pettings were obviously part of the deal. Meanwhile, Kylie was just staring at him, caught between laughing at what he said and gasping in horror. "Dumbass? Really? You named a goat Dumbass?!"

The old girl had put her head underneath Kylie's

arm and was quite forcefully pushing it up in the air, begging, goat style, for a nice head rub. Kylie must've found just the right spot at the base of her horns because Dumbass began leaning into the pettings with all her might. Adam was a little afraid she'd knock Kylie on her ass at this rate.

He shrugged in response to Kylie's question. "The old tenant…she renamed her Ivy, but honestly, that's too nice of a name for this ol' girl. Just wait until—"

Dumbass grabbed the bottom of Kylie's sweatshirt and began pulling it into her mouth, chewing happily as she went.

"—Until she tries to eat your clothes," Adam finished, too late. Kylie was laughing again as she began pushing on Dumbass, trying to wrestle her clothes back out of the goat's mouth, and her white, soft, rounded belly shone in the bright sunshine. Actually, Adam was a little surprised by how round her stomach was. That must be where she carried all of her weight, because there was hardly anything at all to the rest of her.

That definitely wasn't the body shape of her mom, who tended to be round all over, so Kylie must've gotten that from her father. No wonder she wore so many sweatshirts and oversized tops. She probably thought she was getting fat. *Women.* Adam thought her rounded stomach was adorable, but of course he couldn't tell his *employee* that.

Absolutely no mention of body parts, adorable or

otherwise, was going to come up in his conversations with Kylie, that was for damn sure.

Out in the sunshine, watching Kylie trying to pet Skunk, who let her for a moment before starting to wander away again, pooping with every step, Kylie laughing her ass off at the casualness of the whole affair...the past that had begun to haunt him inside of the house slipped away.

There for a minute, he'd been stuck in the past, hearing the voice of his dead wife as she exclaimed over every little feature of the house, making plans about how to turn it into a home for the Whitaker family that was sure to come. She'd loved to bake and had waved away his concerns about the size of the kitchen, telling him that it was efficient and smart in its design, so she'd make it work.

Listening to Kylie today say almost the same things had been...painful. An ache in his chest that had loosened over the years came stabbing back, punishing him once again. She hadn't known...it wasn't Kylie's fault.

And yet, back in the house, a small part of him had hated her for it. Had hated her for making him remember all over again.

But watching Kylie in the beautiful sunshine, light bouncing off her thick golden hair, swinging with every step...it was slowly helping him move on from the past.

Everyone had said that time healed all wounds. Everyone had said that after a while, you wouldn't spend all of your time remembering and wishing for your old life back.

No one had said that you'd hate yourself for it – that the guilt of moving on was almost as bad as the pain from not moving on.

But watching Kylie, right here and right now, *was* helping him move on – just a little – both from his wife and from Chloe, and he *wasn't* hating himself for it.

And that scared him more than anything else.

CHAPTER 14

KYLIE

$\mathcal{S}$HE GRINNED AT HER MOM HAPPILY, who, thank God, was grinning back. "He said I can move in this weekend. Can you believe it – a whole farm for me to take care of! I mean, not the beef cows out in the field, thank heavens, but Skunk and Dumbass and the chickens – it'll be my job to take care of all of them."

"Skunk? Dumbass?" her mom repeated, one eyebrow raised.

Kylie shrugged, laughing. "Skunk is the black-and-white milk cow, and Dumbass is the milk goat. She's definitely got...personality."

"Well, I'm just glad to hear that you have a place of your own." Like a light switch that had been flicked, she went into Mother Mode. "Do you need help with the utility bills? You'll need to put a deposit down with the power and the gas company. Maybe even the trash company. I'm assuming you'll be with

Custom Waste Systems since Adam's place is a rural address, not a city one."

"Hold on, what's the difference?" Kylie asked, confused. She felt a little stupid asking, but she'd always lived inside the city limits. Even as small as Sawyer was, there was still a basic level of services that came with living there, and of course, in Bend, Oregon, she'd lived inside city limits, too. She might be from Idaho, but ironically enough, she was still a city slicker in a lot of ways.

"Well, you won't have a city bill, for starters," her mom said, settling easily into the role of educator. As an employee of the local county partnership program, she spent a lot of time working with, and educating, people on choices, and how to climb out of the vicious cycle of poverty.

Kylie realized with a sinking feeling in her stomach that this was something she'd need a lot of help on herself. Unfortunately.

"You'll have a septic system for your waste water, like the water from your kitchen sink drain, tub, toilet, that sort of thing. As the landlord, Adam will take care of cleaning out the septic tank periodically, so you won't have that worry, which is nice. Your garbage will be picked up by a private company called Custom Waste Systems. People out in the country used to simply burn all of their garbage in burning barrels, and there are still some older people who do that, but most people have moved towards using a private garbage company."

Kylie nodded, appreciating the information, but then she felt her eyes cross and a full-body yawn steal over her. She was *exhausted*, what with her day of cleaning the office and then touring the farm. This much excitement in one day was a little overwhelming.

"I'ma-gonna-goto-sleep," she slurred, "so I can get started," another yawn, "wanna move first-shing in da morning."

"It's a good thing I'm fluent in Exhausted Kylie," her mom said, laughing, and then stood up to help her off the couch. "I'm proud of you, dear – I hope you really do know how much I love you." She got serious for a moment and said softly, "Just because I like having elbow room in my house doesn't mean I don't love you with all my heart and soul. I just know that if I didn't say anything, it'd fester inside of me and eventually, I'd start to get angry with you over it and you wouldn't even know why. That sort of passive-aggressive behavior isn't right."

Kylie leaned into her mom's side with a laugh and another rub of her eyes. "You're right," she agreed, her words coming out a little more legibly this time, "and I appreciate you telling me the truth. I won't lie and say that it was the easiest thing in the world for me to hear, but it does make sense."

They were heading back to Kylie's room, arms around each other's waists, when Kylie said with a laugh, "Do you remember when I was a kid – I don't recall where we were at, but I'd taken off my jacket and I'd handed it to you to hold. You took it from me, looked down at it, then back up at me, and said, '*I* don't want to hold your jacket for you.' I remember I was in shock; it just blew my mind. I was only six at the time and it had never occurred to me that you didn't want to follow me around and act like my personal coat rack. What do you mean, you don't want my coat?! Of course you do! You're my mom. Your highest goal in life is to be a human coat rack and food dispenser, don't you know?!"

They laughed together for a moment, and then it was Kylie's turn to get serious. "I didn't mean to fall back into that. I was so stressed out when I finally faced the fact that I was pregnant that I don't think my brain was operating at full capacity, you know? I just wanted to hide from the world. I wanted to run back to my mom and have her take care of all of my problems and make my life okay again. Sounds childish, doesn't it?"

Her mom shrugged, her pale green eyes kind. "I know Grandma died too young for you to remember her, but almost until the day she died, I felt the same way with her. I think it's encoded deep into our DNA – no matter how bad the rest of the world gets, when things really get awful, you want your mom. Hell, when I'm sick with a cold, I still miss my mom. I want her to bring me chicken noodle soup and tuck me into bed. Your grandma's chicken noodle soup was the best. She never did teach me how to make it, so I can't replicate it, dammit. But it warmed you to the depths of your soul.

"So tonight, let me tuck you into bed," she pulled the covers back on the bed, "and wish you a good night," she bent over and kissed Kylie on the forehead, "and tell you once again that I love you, and I'm proud of you. This isn't an easy situation you've been handed, and you've been doing nothing but trying to make lemonade from it…after your eight-day pity fest, of course."

Kylie laughed at that, her eyelids drifting shut even as she mumbled, "Well, I can't be totally perfect. No one wants to deal with someone who is *too* perfect. That would just be obnoxious."

"Yeah, that's it," her mom agreed dryly, laughing. "Truly, I appreciate your thoughtfulness. Well, goodnight." And the door closed with a *click* behind her and Kylie drifted into a world of dreamless slumber almost instantly.

SHE AWOKE to someone knocking on her bedroom door. "Yeah?" she croaked, trying to get her eyelids to open and her voice to work correctly. Either it was really early or she was still recuperating from her hard scrubbing of the vet office yesterday.

"Dr. Whitaker is here," her mom said through the closed door.

Kylie jackknifed up in bed. "What?!" she hollered.

Well, her voice was working just fine now.

"He says he's here to help you move out to the farm."

Kylie scrubbed at her eyeballs with the palms of her hands. "Umm...yeah...okay. Give me a minute here." She rolled over and peered at the alarm clock blearily. 7:22. The man was here at 7:22 in the morning.

What

the

hell

Granted, she had to be to work at the clinic at 7:30 in the morning, but that was Monday through Friday. She didn't tend to get up *quite* so early on the weekends.

Le sigh...

She hurried to get ready, pulling on yoga pants and a tank top, with a sweatshirt over that. Yoga pants were her saving grace; they were the only reason she hadn't needed to go buy pregnancy pants yet. This particular trick wouldn't last forever, but it would be damn hard to explain away a wide stretchy band of material around her waist if, say, Dumbass grabbed the bottom of her shirt and lifted it up into the air again – *thanks, Dumbass* – so she'd stick with the yoga pants for as long as possible. That and the biggest shirts she could find meant she probably had another month before her pregnancy bump became impossible to hide from even the least discerning Sawyer residents.

It was really too bad she carried her baby like her mom had carried her – loud and proud, upfront and noticeable to all. Her mom had already warned her that by the end, she'd look like she'd swallowed a basketball, maybe even a beach ball, for breakfast.

No, there was no hiding that from anyone.

Hair pulled through the opening in the back of her hat, teeth brushed, and tennis shoes on, Kylie was ready to face the day. She hurried out to the living room where she found Adam standing there, shifting from foot to foot, a baseball cap in hand.

"Hi, Dr…Adam," Kylie stumbled out.

He raised one eyebrow, a quirk crossing his lips. "Dr. Adam…that's a new one for me."

Kylie laughed, embarrassed. "Thanks for coming over. I didn't know you were going to help me."

He shrugged, his turn to look embarrassed. "You've done so much for me, I thought it'd be a good way to help you in return. I didn't remember Carol driving a pickup around town, so I figured my truck would come in handy."

"It's true, I only have a little Toyota Prius," her mom put in with a laugh. "We could've gotten it done, but it would've meant more trips back and forth."

"Are you all packed up?" Adam asked, his whiskey brown eyes trained on Kylie. She gulped. He wasn't trying to be sexy – in fact, the words, "Are you all packed up" couldn't be less sexy unless he started discussing the digestive tract of the snail in there somewhere too – and yet, just him looking at her was making her heart go into overdrive.

Which, considering the fact that he was her boss and her landlord, was quite an unfortunate thing. She really needed to stick with "Dr. Whitaker."

And start wearing a pair of blinders around him.

Because *that* wouldn't be obvious at all…

She smiled at him, trying to act confident. It was a stretch, for sure. "Pretty much. I haven't had much of a chance to unpack since I got here, and I didn't have much stuff to begin with, so this should go fast. Mom, while I'm packing up my clothes and toiletries, would you mind showing him where my boxes are at?" She turned back to Adam. "I have some memorabilia from high school that I left behind when I moved to Oregon, so I might as well take that with me now. Give my mom *all* of her house back."

Her mom shot her a huge smile. "Great idea!" she exclaimed happily. Adam and Mom headed out to the garage where her mom had stashed the keepsake boxes while Kylie got to work packing up her clothes and toiletries. After she was done, she looked down at the oversized, overstuffed suitcase with a sigh.

When she'd left Oregon in a rush, she'd had to leave so many things behind, but what she missed most of all were her kitchen gadgets. She'd pumped gas and gone to school and scrimped and saved for four long years to buy all of that stuff, and to know that it'd all been sold to support her former roommate's pizza habit…it was not a happy thought.

Well, now that she had a house to live in, she could start all over again. If nothing else, this whole thing was teaching her that life did not start and stop with the collection of items.

She wheeled her suitcase out into the living room, and Adam took it from her, hauling it outside and pushing it into the bed of the truck, next to the half-dozen plastic totes. "Is…is that it?" he asked, looking at the load.

Kylie shrugged. "I travel light," she said, trying to play it off. His answering smile, confused and concerned, told her that he didn't believe her, not one bit, but he didn't say anything and for that, she was grateful. She didn't want to talk about why it was that she'd had to leave Oregon in the middle of the night, without most of her stuff, a refugee from her own life.

No, she didn't want to talk about that at all.

Her mom gave her a huge hug goodbye and slipped something into Kylie's sweatshirt pocket as she did so. "Utility deposits and a little extra something to help you get by," she whispered into Kylie's ear, and then pulled back with a big smile on her face. "I'm proud of you," she told Kylie. Turning towards Adam, she added sternly, "I'll be out to do an inspection on your place in a couple of days. If it isn't in good operating shape, you'll be hearing about it."

Kylie laughed at the worried look on Adam's face; that was her mom all right – protective mother hen even when she didn't need to be. "It's not a palace," she warned her mom, "but all of the toilets flush and the fridge runs."

"Well, I *suppose* that's good enough for my little girl," she said like a queen bestowing a favor upon her subjects. But she winked at Adam as she said it, and they laughed, the relief evident on Adam's face when he realized she'd been kidding around with him.

Kylie bit back her grin. Poor Adam; Carol VanLueven could be intimidating as hell when she wanted to be. Something her only daughter was all too aware of.

Climbing into his truck, Kylie felt like she was practically vibrating off her seat with energy and nerves. She'd lived for four years away from home, of course, but she'd always lived with a roommate, and she'd always lived in an apartment. This was the first time she'd be living in a real house, *and* living all by herself, and it was surprisingly intimidating to her.

If the floorboards were creaking during the night, she couldn't send her roommate in to see if a burglar had broken into the house.

She'd be the cause of − and the person who had to clean up − all of the dirty dishes.

All utility bills were her responsibility.

She had a lawn to mow and flower beds to weed.

She had the sexiest man this side of the Continental Divide as a landlord.

No, this wasn't like living in Bend, Oregon at all.

And hell, that wasn't even touching on the fact that she'd be in charge of feeding and taking care of animals, something she had absolutely no experience in at all. She had a sudden urge to go adopt a goldfish, or three. The smart thing to do would be to start out small, and move up from there.

But she forced herself to face the fact that the reason that her boss was giving her a place to live – for free! – was because she'd agreed to take care of animals slightly larger than goldfish.

She tried not to groan out loud with worry.

The drive out to the new place passed by in a blur and before she knew it, they'd pulled up in front of the farmhouse. Kylie bounded out of the truck like a dog finally let off a leash. She hurried to help Adam carry everything into the living room to stack it in the corner out of the way, where she could work on unpacking the items over the next week or two, and then stood back with a satisfied grin. At least this part was under control.

The whole entire house was all hers – she couldn't believe it.

All the way out in the country, far, far away from…

"Oh no!" Kylie groaned just as Adam said, "Oh shit!"

They looked at each other.

"I have no way to get back to town," she groaned, gnawing on her bottom lip.

"No, you don't," Adam agreed, his eyebrows creasing with worry. "I can't believe I didn't think of that before."

"I can't believe *I* didn't think of it! In Bend, there was a great public transportation system in place so I just used that, and then here, since my mom's house is in town, I could just walk everywhere I wanted to go. *Shit.* I'm trapped here."

The excitement she'd been feeling quickly turned to panic. Being stuck out in the country, with no way to get to town, was just about the loneliest prospect *ever*. What if something happened? And how was she supposed to get to work? And—

"I don't know how you feel about grandma cars," Adam broke into her rising internal hysteria, "but my mom's had this car for probably 20 years, and since she doesn't get around real well anymore, she keeps telling me I should sell it. It's just sitting in the garage, dry rotting away. You could pay for it out of each paycheck – $50 a check or something."

Kylie quickly did the math. That would be $100 a month plus insurance and gas, which damn, that was a gut punch to her budget, but on the other hand, she *needed* a car. She couldn't exactly give birth to a baby and then cart it home on her back. Plus, if she had no car, she had no job and because her boss was now also her landlord, that meant she had no place to live, either.

Yeah, that wasn't going to work out so well.

$100 a month plus insurance and gas it was.

"That sounds amazing," she said, a little tremor in her voice. She cleared her throat. She was *not* going to start crying again. Damn pregnancy hormones. "I feel like such a mooch – first you give me a job and then a place to live and now a car to drive. I promise I'm not normally this needy!"

He laughed off her concerns. "First off, I'm not *giving* you anything. You've done an amazing job with the clinic, moving out here to take care of the animals is a huge weight off my shoulders, and actually getting my mom's car sold without having to list it in the newspaper or on Craigslist is a wonderful gift. My mom will be thrilled to know it's finally going to be used by someone instead of just dry rotting away."

"You said 'dry rotting' before; what does that mean?"

"Oh," Adam said, a little surprised by the question. He probably wasn't used to dealing with people who barely knew what an engine was and had no idea what an alternator was. Kylie was embarrassed by her ignorance, but she also knew that if she never asked any questions, she'd never learn anything.

"Well," he started out hesitantly, "vehicles are meant to be run. Whenever you drive or start a car, the oil is moved around, re-lubricating everything, so the longer a vehicle just sits there, unused, the worse condition it ends up in. If a car sits out in a car lot for a long time, not being sold, it'll eventually end up with 'lot rot,' which – you can guess just from the name – isn't good for it."

"Wow. I had no idea." Her cheeks flushed red and she stared down at the hardwood floors in embarrassment. How was it that she was technically an adult and yet, there was so much she still didn't know? If she was old enough to get knocked up, it seemed like she ought to be old enough to know the most basic of information.

Lot rot? Septic systems? Burning barrels? Was adulthood this confusing for everyone or had she missed a class somewhere on how to become a *real* adult?

Adam reached out and gave her a friendly hug. "Don't feel bad!" he reassured her. "You've never owned a car; you can't be expected to know every... every little thing about them." Except the last part came out in a mere whisper as he stared down at her, tucked up against his side, and she was drowning in his whiskey brown eyes, her breath caught in her throat.

I can't, can't, can't do this. I can't fall in love with my boss/landlord/car salesman.

Absolutely, positively cannot.

CHAPTER 15

ADAM

*H*E WAS FROZEN, his arm around Kylie as he looked down at her. She felt it too, he could see it plain as day. She'd make the world's worst poker player because every thought and feeling was right there on her face.

And her face was telling him that she felt the arcs of electricity between them with every strangled breath.

"Well-I-better-get-going-and-look-at-the-car-and-see-what-needs-to-be-fixed-before-you-can-buy-it-see-you-later," and he was out the door, running as if someone had set his ass on fire and he jumped into his truck, gunning the engine and tearing down the dirt driveway like a convict making a break from prison.

He couldn't fall in love with Kylie VanLueven. No way, no how. She was his *employee*, for God's sake. And a good fifteen years younger than him. And...and...

well, he was sure there were other reasons too, that he'd think of in just a moment.

Oh, like the fact that he was in a position of power over her – that was a damn good reason that he couldn't fall in love with her. He couldn't take advantage of her.

Yeah, she felt the sparks right now – he was plenty sure the fine folks of Franklin, 30 minutes away, felt the sparks between them – but what if that changed in the future? She could feel pressured to continue to date him even if she didn't want to, and how despicable was that? He couldn't stand the thought of being *that* guy. He wasn't built for it.

He couldn't shake the feeling that he *was* built for Kylie, though, and the idea of giving her up, no matter how "right" it was, felt like someone had landed a nice right hook to his solar plexus. It was hard to remember what life had been like a few short weeks ago – behind on bills, behind on billing, the office a mess (okay, so it was still a mess but at least it was now a clean mess), incoherent phone messages scrawled out by the world's worst secretary, no scent of wildflowers to drive him absolutely crazy, no bright smile and cheerful attitude to cheer him up no matter what was happening…

He didn't want to face a world without Kylie VanLueven in it.

But he also couldn't take advantage of her youth and naïveté by dating her.

But he also, *also* couldn't imagine continuing to

keep his hands to himself – his self-control was rapidly disappearing every day that he spent around her.

In short, he was screwed six ways to Sunday, and he had no idea how to even begin figuring out how to save himself, or what "saving" really meant.

CHAPTER 16

KYLIE

*K*YLIE WAS NIBBLING on the end of her pencil, looking down her needs list, trying to think if there was anything else she needed to scour Second Time Around for, when she heard the low but insistent *moo* of a cow.

A cow that seemed quite unhappy with her status in the world.

Kylie shoved some Crocs on and hurried outside. Maybe the cow had gotten her head stuck in something. Maybe she needed more food and water. Actually, come to think of it, she and Adam hadn't exactly gotten around to talking about the finer points of taking care of the animals. She'd figured they'd go over that after he helped her move in, but then he'd touched her and taken off like a rabbit with a sparkler tied to its ass, and…well, feeding instructions hadn't exactly happened.

She let herself into the small pasture that was

connected to the barn and this time, all of the animals came running at her. The hens, the rooster, Skunk, and Dumbass were all high-tailing it in her direction. She saw the heavy udders of Skunk sway with every hurried step and a lightbulb went off in her head.

Duh.

She was supposed to be milking the milk cow. And the milk goat. Herself. She hardly knew how to set up utilities in her name; barely knew what a septic tank was; only had the vaguest clue about lot rot after Adam's quick description of it; and was now the sole person in charge of the care and upkeep of real live animals.

She was pretty sure God was laughing his ass off on some cloud up there, watching the light bulbs going off over her head. *Yeah, Kylie, you are responsible for real animals who need real food and real care. Get with the program, yo.*

Apparently God had a ghetto accent. Who knew!

Dumbass was busy pushing her head up against Kylie's side with all her goat might, reminding her that Skunk wasn't the only one that needed milking, while Skunk stood directly in front of Kylie, lowing so loudly, Kylie's teeth were rattling from the strength of it.

Good fun.

The evening light was fading fast but Kylie figured out how to get the latch undone and open up the door to the barn. There was a general stampede of fur, feathers, and madness as all of the animals tried to thunder inside as one. Kylie jumped to the side and watched as the stream went by, finally breathing in deeply when everyone had disappeared into the shadowy depths.

"I can totally do this," she said to the world at large, and then went inside, closing the door behind her. She patted around on the walls, searching for a light switch and finally found one, a solitary light bulb flipping on above to reveal a dusty barn with creaking rafters and walls that were nothing more than gray, weathered slats. They were covered with a generous helping of spider webs and a smattering of farm implements that Kylie could only guess had been used at the turn of the century.

The 19th century.

The chickens were busy going in and out and in and out of their coop, obviously wanting to settle in for the night but not quite sure they were ready to make that large of a commitment yet, while Dumbass was preoccupied with chewing on some wooden slats. Skunk was in a stall, her head stuck in the feeding trough, happily eating away for the moment and blessedly not mooing her discontent to the world.

Now Kylie just had to figure out how to milk the poor girl.

She spotted a three-legged stool in the corner, cleaned by regular usage from the dirt and dust that was so thick elsewhere, and pulled it over to Skunk's side.

Grand, she could now sit down next to the cow.

This didn't mean much since she didn't know how to do the next step – actually milking the cow – but hey, it was a small victory nonetheless.

Her eyes were darting around, searching for a bucket or pail or some sort of catching-milk-from-a-cow's-teat device, when she heard the crunch of gravel under tires and then a diesel engine shutting off. She hurried out through the main barn doors to find Adam swinging down from his truck.

"I realized I forgot a couple of important pieces of information," he called out as he loped over to her with that easy gait of his. Her eyes followed his body with an eagerness that she wasn't willing to put a name to just yet.

"Ummm...like how to milk a cow?" she said, laughing easily, as if just being in the same vicinity as Adam Whitaker wasn't the most torturously amazing thing she'd ever lived through.

"Yeah, like that." He grinned down at her when he reached her side. "I see you at least got the animals inside."

"That part wasn't too hard," Kylie said with a shrug. "I just opened up the door over there and they practically ran me over to get into the barn."

"They've been doing this for a while, so they're pretty used to the routine by now. The chickens are the easiest – they like to roost at night, so as soon as the sun sets, they want to go inside where they can get up onto their perches. So, did you find the milk buckets yet?"

She shook her head. "All I found so far was the milking stool."

"C'mon, I'll show you where the milk fridge is at." He led her into a side room with a fridge and some metal buckets stacked on the counter. He rinsed them out quickly in the shop sink, explaining that he did a thorough cleaning job after milking but always rinsed them before milking again just in case dirt or dust got into them, and then they headed back out into the main part of the barn.

As Adam set up the stool and the buckets, showing how to lean against the cow while milking, how to pull down on the teats, how to direct the milk into the bucket, Kylie couldn't help but stare at him. She shouldn't, of course, absolutely positively shouldn't, and yet, it was hard not to. The way his shirt stretched over his broad shoulders, the way his strong hands flew over everything like magic…it was like watching a milking maestro at work.

"You ready to give it a shot?" he asked, looking up at her. She swallowed hard but nodded. Adam knelt next to her, wrapping his arms around her and moving her fingers into place around the warm, soft teats. "Okay, start at the top and pull down," he said, his deep voice in her ear, sending shivers down her spine. She tried to pay attention to what she was supposed to be doing, she really did, but the world's sexiest teacher was in her ear, his arms wrapped around her while he gave milking lessons…

She couldn't really be faulted for not being able to pay attention, right?

They finally stumbled their way through poor Skunk, who looked back occasionally to see who was yanking on her teats with such enthusiasm, but she didn't otherwise seem too perturbed. Kylie was grateful for the old girl's patience, because 30 minutes of milking a cow did not an expert make.

They'd moved over to Dumbass and had gotten to work on her when Kylie's hands began cramping from the strain. "I can't believe how hard this is," she said with a small laugh, massaging her hands. "How come you don't have a milking machine?"

Adam moved into place, letting Kylie sit off to the side for a minute to give her hands a rest. He began rhythmically pulling on the teats, never missing a beat, never causing Dumbass to bleat out in pain or surprise, each stream of milk aimed perfectly into the bucket.

Kylie was pretty sure she'd never be this good, even if she milked for the next 20 years.

"It isn't worth it for two animals," he said with a shrug, his hands continuing to move rhythmically even as he chatted with her. "That kind of setup can be thousands of dollars. It just isn't worth the money for one cow and one goat. You need a whole herd to make the numbers work, and I'm not interested in being a dairyman."

"So why do you have these guys?" Kylie asked, stroking Dumbass' side as they talked. The ol' girl definitely had what could only be described as "goat aroma," but Kylie found she didn't mind. It was earthy and real and so authentic compared to games on her cell phone or chatting with friends via texts.

There was a visceral pleasure to being around animals that she hadn't realized she'd been missing all her life. Her friends back in Bend would think she'd gone around the bend, but Kylie didn't care. There was something tactile and pleasurable and so *real* about this.

"That's a good question," Adam answered with a rueful grin. "Both of them were surprises. I had patients who couldn't afford my vet bill, and somehow, I got these guys as payments instead of cold, hard cash. I'd originally thought I'd sell them or butcher them or something, but they started to grow on me, even Dumbass here, and pretty soon, I didn't want to think about getting rid of them. But the next time someone offers to trade an animal or two for services rendered, I need to remember what a massive pain in the ass it is to take care of those animals." He shot her a grin. "I am a veterinarian through and through. It's hard for me to turn down any animal, no matter the circumstances."

She chuckled even as her heart twisted a little inside. She wondered for a moment if Adam saw her as another stray animal; someone to feed and house and take care of, even though it shouldn't be his job. Did he ever do something just because he wanted to, not because he felt obligated to do it? Here he was, taking care of his crippled mother, and animals he hadn't even intended to get, and running a therapy camp for kids with special needs, and practically adopting a girl on the cusp of adulthood who was stumbling around, lost and clueless, no real idea of how to move forward.

Except she didn't look at him as a guardian and a father figure. No, she definitely wouldn't classify her feelings like that. But maybe this was all one-sided and he felt nothing towards her. Maybe—

His hand cupped underneath her chin, pulling it up to meet his gaze. "What are you thinking about?" he asked softly, his fingers running over her chin. She trembled a little – whether from the cold of sitting on the concrete floor or from the nearness of Adam, she couldn't begin to guess.

"You…why are you helping me out so much?" she whispered. Her face flushed hot under his gaze. She hated bringing this topic up again, but dammit all, he'd asked. She couldn't lie to Adam and tell him she'd been thinking about daisies and sunsets and how beautiful the Goldfork Mountains were.

Because as much as she loved daisies and sunsets and the Goldfork Mountains, she also felt like a loser. She was struggling not to be a mooch off her mother, but she'd somehow turned into a mooch off her boss instead.

It was embarrassing enough to be a mooch off her mother, but she was at least, well, her mother. Being a mooch off a total stranger was much, much worse.

Especially a total stranger who she was falling head over heels in love with, and yet he probably didn't see her that way at all.

She'd never been one to pine over an unattainable guy but there was always a first time for everything…

He shook his head slowly. "You really don't realize how much of a help you are to me, do you?" he murmured. "Remind me to tell you a story about business cards sometime. And pretty pink jeweled collars." She stared at him in confusion. He gave her a sexy-as-hell grin that threatened to set her panties on fire. "Never mind that," he said with a small laugh. "The point is, I think I need you just as much as you need me. I was just thinking this morning that it'd only been a few weeks since I brought you onboard, and already, I don't know how I'd live without you. Trying to balance the whole world on my shoulders is exhausting, and you've helped me just a little with that balancing act. That means more to me than anything."

She nodded. She believed him…mostly.

But more than that, her stomach was just a ball of nerves and butterflies and shooting sparks as his eyes dropped down to her lips and then back up, locking in on her with an invisible bond that felt unbreakable in that moment. She couldn't breathe or blink or look away and then he was coming closer, ever so slowly closer, giving her every chance to back off, to scramble to her feet and announce that she needed to go inside *right then* but she didn't move an eyelash because she didn't want to go inside.

She wanted to kiss Adam Whitaker and as her heart almost beat out of her chest, she realized that for once, she was going to do exactly what she wanted to do, consequences be damned.

Finally, his lips closed over hers, soft and demanding and needy and she leaned forward, pouring her soul into the kiss. Her blood was thundering in her ears as his lips molded to hers and then his tongue swept out, seeking the boundaries of her lips, prodding to find its way inside and she opened up with a moan, her whole body wanting to meld together with his.

Breathing and eating and thinking all seemed so complicated and unnecessary in that moment. All she wanted to do was to melt into Adam and to never let go.

Dumbass let out a bleat, turning her head and knocking Kylie over and into Adam's side with a powerful jerk of her head. Adam caught her and they laughed for a moment, a quiet breathless moment filled with promise, and then it was broken, disappearing into the ether as if it had never existed.

"I better get on my way," Adam said, scrambling to his feet and offering his hand to Kylie to help her up. "Tomorrow, I need to look over your car and... and lots of other important stuff, so I should get to bed early."

And then he was gone, jumping into his truck and

pulling away with the deep growl of the diesel engine, leaving a breathless and flushed and scattered Kylie in his wake. She stared after him, her fingertips resting lightly on her lips where Adam had kissed her, wondering if he regretted kissing her.

Knowing that she should regret it.

Knowing that she never would.

Even if she never got to kiss Dr. Adam Whitaker again, tonight's kiss would warm her at night. She could lie in bed and remember it, reliving every moment of it.

And never, ever regret it.

CHAPTER 17

ADAM

*A*DAM HURRIED TO THE DINING ROOM, running behind as always. First he had to feed the horses and then get started on looking over his mom's car. The sooner he could sell it to Kylie, the better. She needed it; leaving a person stranded like that with the closest neighbor being over a mile away and no way to get into town if she needed to...well, it just wasn't right.

He couldn't believe he hadn't thought of that particular problem before, when he'd been offering the farm to Kylie. He could only blame her perfume on that particular slip-up. It was intoxicating, like the finest whiskey a man could buy, and impossible to overlook.

Or forget.

"Hi dear!" his mom said, already sitting at the dining room table, the *Franklin Gazette* spread out in front of her. "How'd you sleep?"

"Good, good," he said absentmindedly, pressing a kiss to her cheek and then hurrying into the kitchen to get a cup of coffee. "Hey, I should let you know — I think I found a buyer for your car. Kylie is all settled in at my place," he poured himself a cup of the steaming brown liquid and then came back into the dining room, sipping as he went, "but she doesn't own a car. She's just been walking from her mom's place to the clinic every day. I didn't even think about it until I had her all moved in and set up. My place is way too far out in the country for her to hike into town every day."

His mom studied him for a minute, her faded blue eyes taking in every detail. He squirmed a bit under her gaze. The moments ticked by, and then she asked bluntly, "Is she another Chloe?"

He let out a flustered laugh even as his mind skipped back to the kiss he'd shared with Kylie the night before. "No, I'm not falling in love with her, I promise," he said, a trying-too-hard smile on his face. He toned it down a bit. "She's a great employee who needs a helping hand right now, is all."

His mom nodded, an inscrutable look on her face as she continued to study him. He couldn't tell if she believed him or not. He'd never been the best at hiding stuff from her; that's why she'd realized that he was in love with Chloe even as Chloe had been oblivious to it all. She'd never said a word about it to anyone, something that he was eternally grateful for.

His mom knew how to keep secrets, thank God.

As tough as the Chloe situation had been, and as hard as he'd taken it when she'd fallen in love with Dawson without a backward glance, Kylie was different. After all, she wasn't pregnant. God had a funny sense of humor sometimes, and he seemed to believe that Adam could handle a lot more than Adam thought he could, but even God wasn't *that* cruel.

Kylie and Chloe were totally different people in different situations. He wasn't getting himself into trouble this time. And as for love, well, it was too early to tell. *If* he did fall in love with Kylie, he'd tell his mother the truth then. No need to talk about something that hadn't happened yet, right?

His mom finally nodded. "Well, I'm glad to hear it, anyway," she said blandly, which Adam took to mean, "I think you're lying to yourself but I'll pretend to go along with it regardless."

He sure loved his mother sometimes.

"Listen, I need to talk to you," she continued, and this time, it was her turn to look uncomfortable. Her normally paper-thin white cheeks flushed a rosy red color and she was studying the elaborately embroidered tablecloth in front of her intently.

He set down his coffee cup. "What's wrong?" he asked softly.

"Well, I'm not complaining because I do appreciate all of your help, but...well, I need a...a woman's help, you see." His mother stumbled to a stop.

Adam nodded, hoping that he did see and wouldn't have to question his mom any further. She was of the generation who didn't speak to men about *women's problems* with anything except generalities and euphemisms, to the point that it was sometimes difficult to know if they were talking about a vagina or a new TV show on Netflix.

The more nonspecific the platitudes, the better, in his mom's opinion.

"You want me to hire a CNA – a *female* CNA – to come help you out?" he asked, hoping he was on the right track.

She nodded gratefully. "Yes, please. I'd really appreciate it."

"Sure, no problem," he said with a smile, happy that he'd decoded her request correctly. "I'll look into it tomorrow. I imagine most places are closed on Sundays."

"Wonderful." She beamed a huge smile at him, her face back to its normal paper-thin white color, and he grinned back at her in return.

"Well, I better get a move on. Lots to do today." He kissed his mom goodbye on the cheek, and then headed out to the barn to check on the therapy horses. Sonny knickered happily when he saw him, pushing his nose over the stall door and snuffling Adam's shirt as soon as he got into range. "Checking for a carrot or two?" he asked Sonny with a laugh. "You're a big beggar, you know that? No wonder you and Genny with a G get along so

well. She loves to feed you and you love to eat."
Sonny knickered his agreement and Adam laughed
again.

Genny (or Genny with a G as she liked to
introduce herself) was one of the students who'd been
coming for a while to Adam's therapy camp. She had
Down Syndrome but was on the high functioning end
of the spectrum, and loved nothing more in the world
than horses, and more specifically, Sonny. Adam was
pretty damn sure Genny would sleep in Sonny's stall
if he let her.

Which he didn't, much to Genny's dismay.

After a quick check of the horses and their water,
Adam opened each stall's door and the barn door to
the adjoining pasture, letting the horses out to graze.
They all trotted out happily, their tails whisking in
tandem to swat the flies away.

He looked around, double checking that
everything was where it should be, and then decided
he ought to drive out to his old place and check on
Kylie. He'd shown her how to milk last night, sure,
but people didn't tend to learn a skill like that literally
overnight.

And she was just stubborn and independent
enough that even if things weren't going well, she
wouldn't want to bother him by asking him for help.
He remembered back to last night, when she'd
managed to find the milking stool but hadn't found
the buckets yet. If she'd found the buckets before he'd
gotten there, he had no doubt that she would've done

her best to milk Skunk and Dumbass without any lessons at all.

Yeah, he should definitely go check on her, just to make sure that she and the animals were doing okay.

No other reason at all.

Definitely no wildflower perfume or mind-blowing kisses reasons.

He pulled up in front of his old home, and as soon as he shut off the diesel engine, he could hear the cacophony − Skunk wasn't happy. Which, to be honest, she was a pretty easy going old gal, so if she was unhappy, things had really gone off the rails.

Adam jumped out of his truck and sprinted inside to find a frustrated Kylie and an even more frustrated Skunk, having a human-cow showdown worthy of a Wild West shoot-out. "I can't milk you if you−oh thank God!" she hollered, jumping to her feet when she saw Adam. "I tried what you showed me last night, I promise I did, but it's not working. I must not be remembering it right." The color was high in her cheeks and she looked flustered and frustrated and embarrassed.

Shit. He shouldn't have let her try to milk this morning without him; it wasn't fair to her or to Skunk. It really was a lot to take in all at once.

"No worries at all," he reassured her, pulling her to his side for a quick hug. It was like hugging an electric fence, though − the voltage shot right through him, and straight to his dick.

Why was it that tight Wranglers were so popular

among cowboys and veterinarians? In that moment, he couldn't think of a single good reason for them. He'd been alone for a long time. A really, really long time, and his body was doing its best to tell him that some female attention wouldn't go unwanted, that was for damn sure.

He did his best to ignore the lower half of his body by sheer dint of will. He could totally do that; he'd done it lots of times before. A man couldn't get friend zoned for nine years by a beautiful woman without becoming real practiced at the art of ignoring basic human needs.

"All right," he said, forcing himself to focus on the topic on hand, which was unfortunately *not* his dick or anything even vaguely close to it, "sit on the stool. Let's go over the basics again." He knelt behind her and wrapped his arms around her as he guided her hands to the milk teats, gulping hard as he did so. His vision went double and then a little dark around the edges as he focused as hard as he could on the task at hand.

"Remember what I said," he murmured into her ear, and suddenly, the words didn't have much meaning. He was holding her against his chest, his mouth buried in her hair, breathing her scent in, and he was pretty damn sure he was roughly 0.231 seconds away from complete insanity. "From the top to the bottom," he whispered, and he felt her trembling in his arms. Was she trembling from being near him? From being scared or nervous or turned on or simply because she was cold?

It couldn't just be that. She *had* to feel this between them. She wasn't another Chloe. She wasn't.

Finally, he realized that her rhythm was getting better and she was even getting most of the milk into the pail, which he thought was a pretty good sign, so he reluctantly pulled away and mumbled something about milking Dumbass while she milked Skunk. She nodded, her face turned away from his as she worked, and Adam moved over to the ornery goat.

She bleated loudly at him, clearly unhappy about waiting so long to be milked and he told her tartly, "I don't know why I like you." She jerked his hat off his head and began trying to eat the brim of it. He jerked it back out of her mouth and pulled it back down onto his head. "Well, now I *really* don't know why I like you." Dumbass bleated again and Adam huffed out a breath. Arguing with a goat wasn't going to get him anywhere – something all goat owners everywhere were already well aware of – so he was better off just getting to work.

He finished Dumbass up quickly and carried the milk pail to the fridge, setting it inside before returning to see how Kylie was faring with Skunk. "I think I'm about there," she said with a groan, scooting out of the way so he could give it a try, "but my hands…" She massaged them as Adam finished up. She hadn't done a half-bad job of it, actually. In another couple of weeks, she'd be a stand-up milker.

He patted Skunk on the back and then let her and Dumbass out into the pasture before carrying the cow's milk pail to the fridge. Kylie trailed along behind him and peered inside the fridge. "What am I supposed to do with all of this?" she asked, wonder in her voice.

He looked at the fridge and then back at Kylie. "Oh. Ummm…well, I take some over to my mom's house for us to drink, but I don't know what the previous tenant did with the rest of the milk. She had a son, so maybe they just drank it all? I never asked, honestly."

Kylie nodded, worrying her lower lip as she stared thoughtfully at the milk pails in the fridge. He knew her well enough to know that she was concocting some sort of plan even as they stood there. He couldn't help but watch with fascination to see what she ended up doing.

The thought that she'd turn his little hobby farm into a profitable one within six months popped back into his head. Kylie may be young and a little naïve about things, but she was also scary smart. He pitied the fool who tried to get in her way.

She was definitely her mother's daughter.

"So I was going to bring my mom's car over here for you to look at it," he said, interrupting her world-domination planning, "but I don't want to drive it that far before I do a full tune-up on it. What would you think about me driving you back to my mom's place and you can take a look at it over there?"

"Oh sure, that'd be great!" she said enthusiastically, grinning up at him. "I'm ready whenever you are." They double checked that the chickens, Skunk, and Dumbass were all in the pasture like they should be, the chicken wire that covered the bottom four feet of the fencing keeping even the smallest of the hens in place, and then they took off for his mom's house.

Adam's nerves jangled as they went. Having Kylie in the same vehicle as him, within inches of him...it was hard to think, honestly. He tried to cover by rambling on about what he needed to do to the car before he could turn it over to Kylie, but he wasn't sure if he was fooling her or just boring her to tears.

She listened without interruptions until he finally – blessedly? – couldn't think of another damn thing to say, and then said slowly, "I...well, it sounds like the car will be in great shape when you're done, which I really appreciate. A lot," she added, obviously worried that he didn't believe her.

"Buuuttt..." he said, prompting her when she didn't say anything else.

"But I didn't bring any food with me when I moved out to your house," she said in a rush. "I ate eggs and drank milk for dinner and for breakfast this morning, but I need a little variety in my diet. At some point, I'm going to need more than just eggs and milk, you know?"

"Oh, of course," he said, ruminating over his choices. He really shouldn't have "wasted" the morning showing Kylie how to take care of the animals; it was Sunday, which meant a day of catch up for him. He had stalls to clean out, he needed to go over to Frank's Feed & Fuel and arrange for a fill-up of his propane tanks, he needed to be working on soon-to-be-Kylie's car, he should…

"Why don't we drive to Boise together?" he asked impulsively, even as his brain was yelling at him for it.

So he ignored his brain. Some days, it was okay to listen to his heart.

And his heart was telling him not to let Kylie out of his sight. Which was stalkerish and creepy and he couldn't make himself regret it, not one bit.

"I'm sure my mom would love it if I did a grocery run," he continued as he flipped around and headed back towards her house so she could grab her wallet, "and honestly, I don't pay you well enough for you to afford Shop 'N Go prices. Hell, *no one* gets paid well enough to afford those prices. Speaking of, I should keep an eye out, and if I hear of a used chest freezer coming up for sale around town, you should buy it. It'd be a great investment to make. Anything to help lessen the number of times you're forced to shop here in Sawyer, and lessen the number of trips to Boise."

"Wow. Really? Wow! I just…are you this nice to all of your employees?" Kylie burst out.

Adam laughed it off, even as he felt heat creep up into his cheeks. "Well, like I said, I need to go shopping myself. Might as well take you along with. I'm pretty sure you don't weigh enough that I'd need to worry about my gas mileage dropping." He pulled to a stop in front of his old house. He'd just driven in a big circle, with absolutely nothing to show for it, but instead of getting frustrated with his lack of progress, he found he was smiling instead.

Being around Kylie was magical, that was for sure.

She threw her head back and laughed. "I think there was a compliment in there. Somewhere. Buried deep, but there. I'll take it!" She hurried into the house, grabbed her purse and reappeared, ready to go. No primping, no wasted time doing her hair or changing out of her oversized sweatshirt or yoga pants covered with straw and dirt.

As he helped her up into the cab of his truck and hurried around to his side, he realized that he wanted to compliment her on that too – he just loved how practical she was – but knowing him, he'd probably mess it up again. Every time he tried to tell her how wonderful he thought she was, he ended up saying things like she wasn't so fat that she'd affect his gas mileage on his truck.

Yeah, no one was going to mix him up with Casanova any time soon.

He drove over to his mom's house, laughing and chatting with Kylie as he went. He felt...free. His must-do's, his worries, the tension usually stretching across his shoulders, had all disappeared. Being around Kylie was like being inoculated against the stresses of the world.

And if there was one thing he needed to be inoculated against, it was that.

They pulled up in front of his mom's house, the baby blue siding and baby pink front door making it look as grandmotherly as ever.

"Oh, it's a cute house!" Kylie exclaimed, jumping out of his truck. "I love the gable over the front door."

Adam looked up at the gable in question, really seeing it for the first time in a very long time. Maybe ever.

"Yeah, the house has character, if you can look past the decorating choices," he said wryly.

Kylie just shrugged. "It's your mom's house. If she didn't decorate using blues and pinks and doilies, it wouldn't feel like her house."

Adam looked at her, surprised. "How did you know she decorated with doilies?"

Kylie just scrunched up her nose and laughed at the question. "I looked at the outside and made an educated guess."

Right. That was much more likely than her being a mind reader, anyway.

They went walking in, doilies and porcelain cats everywhere and Adam heard Kylie mutter, "Didn't guess the porcelain cats, dammit!" to herself, which made Adam choke with laughter.

"Hey, Mom, Kylie's here with me," he called out as they made their way down the hallway and into the living room, where his mom tended to spend the day reading. She used to crochet, too, until her hands got too gnarled. Now she couldn't make them work properly, something that she fussed over pretty much every day. Her slow slide downhill was slowly driving her insane, and Adam wished for the thousandth time that he knew what else he could do for her.

His mom's eyes lit up when she spotted Kylie. "You must be Carol VanLueven's daughter," she said, holding her hand out to grasp Kylie's in hers. Kylie hurried over to Ruby's chair, kneeling by it and taking her delicate hand in hers.

"I am," she said. "How do you know my mom?"

"Oh, dear, I know just about everyone in town," Ruby said, patting Kylie's hand affectionately. "I heard your momma's starting up a group with Mrs. Zimmerman to support the military troops from the Long Valley area. How is that going so far?"

"Pretty good," Kylie said. "They just started but there's quite a bit of interest already, so I'm thinking it's gonna takeoff."

"Of course it is. Anything your mom puts her mind to, she gets it done. Now, I heard that you want to buy my car from me?"

"Yes, ma'am," Kylie said, her hand still in Ruby's. She didn't seem to be uncomfortable at all with the close proximity to Adam's mom, and for that, he was grateful. Kylie just seemed to *get* people. It was an underrated talent in Adam's book.

"Well, I'm glad to hear it. Adam will look it over and make sure it's in good shape before you start driving it around. I don't want you stuck on the side of the road from a flat tire or something. It's a good car – it's lasted me a long time but I don't drive anymore, so there's no use in it just sitting in the garage, rotting away."

"I appreciate it, ma'am," Kylie said earnestly, squeezing her hand.

His mom laughed. "You can call me Ruby; everyone does."

Adam broke in before his mom could start in on the story about where her name came from; if she started reminiscing, they'd be there all night. "Hey Mom, Kylie needs to go grocery shopping in Boise to get her settled into my old place, and I thought since she doesn't have a working car yet, I'd take her over. I'm sure you've got a list of things you'd love for me to pick up?"

His mom's face lit up like a light bulb. "Oh, yes please!" she said with a delighted grin. "I haven't wanted to bother you, what with you being so busy lately and all, but I'm running dangerously low on coffee and a few other things. The list is on the side of the fridge, if you want to go grab it."

He headed into the large country kitchen and pulled the top sheet off the notepad that was stuck to the side of the fridge. His eyes skimmed down the list, easily reading her shaky handwriting. His stomach sank as he looked at how long it was. She didn't just need coffee; she needed just about everything that could be found in a grocery store. She hadn't said a word to him about needing him to buy food, and he felt guilty that he hadn't noticed on his own.

What was the point of moving in with his mother if he wasn't even going to do the simplest of things for her, like keep the fridge stocked?

He was a godawful son, there was no two ways about it.

He came back just as his mother was finishing up one of her favorite stories about him: The time he ate an entire raspberry pie out of the kitchen window and then had tried to blame it on a passing squirrel, not realizing that he had pie filling all down the front of his shirt while he was telling the tall tale.

Kylie looked up from her kneeling position on the floor and laughed. "You were an awful child!" she teased him.

Adam tried to laugh in return, but honestly, at that moment, he kinda felt like he was one even now. "I'm sorry I waited so long to go grocery shopping," he told his mom.

She shrugged her thin shoulders. "You've been plenty busy lately. We haven't starved to death. Now you two go on and have some fun. I've got a wonderful cozy mystery to read. It's set in a quilting shop, and I'm just sure I know who the murderer is!"

Adam kissed her on the cheek, Kylie squeezed her hand, and then they headed out the front door. "You want to check out the car now or later?" Adam asked, closing the front door behind them.

"Now would be great," Kylie said with a big grin.

"I just love your mom," she continued. "She sure is lucky to have you here to take care of her."

Adam nodded, trying to hide his worries that out of all of the things he was accomplishing right now, taking care of his mom wasn't even in the top ten on that list.

His mom deserved more but Adam was damned if he could figure out how to get more hours out of a day.

CHAPTER 18

KYLIE

KYLIE TRIED TO KEEP her eyes from crossing as Adam began explaining the repairs and checks he was going to do on the car. There were alternators and mufflers and hot plugs involved, or maybe they were spark plugs, and black thingies everywhere.

He finally stopped.

"You don't understand a word I'm saying to you, do you?" he said dryly.

She grimaced. "Am I that transparent?" she asked with a small laugh.

He raised an eyebrow.

She decided to keep talking before he could actually answer her rhetorical question.

"Honestly, what I know about cars is that when I put the key in the ignition and turn, it starts up. I'm many things, but mechanically inclined is *not* one of them. I can out-clean, out-organize, and out-cook almost anyone, but please don't ask me to find my timing belt."

He opened up his mouth, and she was just sure he was going to tell her where the washer fluid was and she was already mentally groaning at how literal men were about *everything*, and then his mouth snapped closed. "You know what? You're right. You don't need to know this. As long as you keep sending my invoices for the clinic out on time, something I don't think I've managed to do even once, I'll be happy to change your oil and check your washer fluid for you. It's more than a fair trade!"

She let out a happy sigh of relief. "Good!" she said. "Now let's go buy some groceries."

They headed back out of the old-fashioned garage, pulling the dangling cord to close the overhead door behind them, and then over to Adam's truck. He helped her up into the passenger seat, and just his hand on hers sent tingles through her.

Which was ridiculous, of course. Being helped into the truck wasn't in the least bit sexy – she was sure he did exactly the same thing for his mom whenever she actually left the house – but she was starting to realize that Adam had this amazeballs ability to make *anything* sexy.

Which really shouldn't be legal but somehow, it was.

"So, you like to cook?" Adam asked as they took some back roads to head out of town.

"Yes, very much," Kylie said happily, already

excited about the upcoming shopping trip. It'd be a little weird to cook food only for herself; she was used to cooking for her roommate or Norman when he was in town—

She stopped the line of thought right there. Any thought that included Norman wasn't a good idea.

"Anyway," she said after an awkward pause where she attempted to gather her derailed thoughts, "I just like how cooking makes me feel. I can take all of these ingredients that are nothing special on their own, and can mix them up to make magic on the tongue. With just my hands and a few ingredients, I can feed people – their bellies *and* their souls. I love experimenting and watching people's faces light up with pleasure when I've hit it out of the ballpark. Browsing through cookbooks is fun for inspiration, but I don't tend to follow the recipes very closely. In my world, recipes are more along the lines of a suggestion rather than a step-by-step guide."

Adam let out a belly chuckle at that, and she asked him, "What? What's so funny?"

"I'm just thinking how nice it is that not everyone is good at the same thing," he said with a shrug and a flash of gorgeous white teeth. "If everyone was like me, all of our vehicles would be in tiptop shape and every animal out there would be vaccinated, but there'd be nothing but peanut butter, jelly, and bread at the grocery store, because I don't know how to cook anything more than that."

"Are you trying to tell me that the pinnacle of

your cooking repertoire is PB&J?" she said with a disbelieving laugh. "Not even scrambled eggs or bacon make the list?"

He shrugged. "I can make scrambled eggs and bacon, sure, but that requires time, and honestly, that's not something I have a whole lot of."

She nodded thoughtfully. "I figured a small-town vet would be busy, but I don't know if I've ever met someone as overbooked as you are, and I'm including my mother in that list. She's busier than a centipede in a toe-counting contest, and somehow, your calendar is even more packed!"

"Centipede in a toe…" Adam repeated, and then bust out laughing. "I need to remember that one."

She grinned impertinently at him. "And when you were hiring me, you didn't even ask about all of the fun sayings I know! You lucky soul, you, getting that extra feature without even needing to ask." He let out another belly laugh at that. She grew more serious, and asked quietly, "Have you always been this busy, or is this just a lately sort of thing?"

He tapped his chin as he drove, thinking. "It just sort of snuck up on me, I guess," he said finally. "Years ago, I was married, and Wendy…God, she was so much help. We spent all day every day together at the clinic and we only came close to murdering each other a couple of times. Which I figure is pretty damn good, really." He flashed Kylie another panty-melting grin. "But, after she died, I stupidly tried making it on my own at the clinic. Eventually, I realized that it wasn't possible to be everywhere at once, and I hired on Ollie. Which, he does wonderful things with the animals in the back, but when it comes to people... well, I'm sure you've noticed that they're not exactly his specialty."

Kylie laughed lightly at that, not wanting to admit that she'd absolutely noticed that – it just didn't seem right to pile on Ollie that way. And anyway, her mind couldn't get past his dead wife. How had she died? When did she die? How long had he been alone? Her heart hurt at the idea of someone as thoughtful and kind as Adam losing a spouse.

Fate sure wasn't kind some days.

"My dad died just weeks before I was born; a farming accident," he continued. "My mother never really moved on. Told me that she'd loved enough for one lifetime and she was happy with just me. She really liked Wendy and Chl–another girl I...well, another girl," he stumbled out. Kylie's mind was going a million miles an hour. This was the mysterious renter before her, she was just sure of it.

"So after Wendy died and Mom's health started going downhill, she asked me to move back in with her. She didn't want to leave her house that she'd lived in her whole life – it's literally the house she was born in – but she needed some help around the house. I agreed, but honestly, I'm not sure how much help I've ended up being. I get up early, I come home late, I'm always dragging ass...now she's asking me for a CNA to come over and I feel guilty because I haven't been there enough myself.

"And because I have amazing timing," he sent her a sarcastic grin, "I started the horse therapy camp in the last year, which is a shit ton of work, and then my tenant moved out and I had to take over those animals too, and…it just sorta stacked up. There are days where my eyes are crossing from trying to keep track of it all."

Kylie nodded. That made sense to her. It explained why he'd been able to stay in business for as long as he had, despite having very little office expertise or desire to keep up on the paperwork himself. It explained why he drank a pot of coffee a day. It explained why he was living with his mother to help her out and yet, seemed to be very rarely at home.

She could see where his thoughtful and kind nature was in serious conflict with reality. He instinctively wanted to help the whole world, and hadn't yet mastered the concept that he was just one person.

He couldn't do it all, no matter how many pots of coffee he drank.

And here she was, just another burden on him. Sure, she was taking care of the animals at his old place (kinda) and she was taking care of the office work at the clinic (that, she was a lot more successful at, thank heavens), but she still needed things like rides to Boise to go grocery shopping, and for him to spend time fixing up a car for her.

She vowed to herself to work her ever-lovin' ass off for him over the coming months. No matter how hard it would get as her belly grew in size and maneuvering became an Olympic sport, she wouldn't be yet another burden for him.

Maybe she should start where she was always good at starting – in the kitchen. She could make easy-to-eat snacks and bring them with her to work. She doubted he was eating like he should be, so maybe some hearty muffins and some washed and sliced fruits and veggies would keep him going.

She straightened up, feeling better already. Mom didn't raise her to become a mooch, and Kylie wasn't about to start now.

THAT EVENING, after Adam dropped her off with a promise to pick her up in the morning to take her to work, Kylie set about putting her groceries away. She'd only bought the absolute basics this trip; running off a partial paycheck like she was, she couldn't afford to buy everything she'd wanted to, but she'd paid close attention to what had caught Adam's eye as they'd wandered down the aisles of Winco together, so she could be sure to buy those items later. Just as soon as another paycheck or two came in.

But once all of her groceries were put away, she

began wandering around her house aimlessly. She was tired, and couldn't seem to grasp and hold onto a thought for more than a few seconds.

She came to a stop in front of the small pile of boxes in the corner of the living room, and stared down at them. She really should be putting this all away, but focusing seemed like a gargantuan task at the moment. It would require her to make decisions, and that...well, that just seemed impossible.

Just as she was debating between a nap and a long, hot bath, she remembered.

Oh, duh! I need to take care of the animals. This twice-daily routine was a damn lot to get used to.

But after a mostly successful milking and egg collecting and animal gathering expedition to the barn, she found herself at loose ends again. Had she always had this much free time on her hands? She tried to remember what she'd spent most of her time doing back in Oregon, but could only come up with cooking and cleaning up after her roommate, and pining after Norman.

Neither of which she was doing any longer, thank God.

Norman...

Without thinking about it; without making a conscious decision of whether to do it or not, she somehow found her phone in her hand and she was pulling up her Facebook app. She paused for a second, trying to convince herself to put the phone away, but even as she was telling herself that, her thumb tapped into the search bar.

Well, okay, she'd just take a quick peek, nothing more. Just to see…

When they'd first started dating, she'd asked him if he was on Facebook, thinking that she'd friend him and start tagging him in the selfies that they took together. He'd haughtily told her that he didn't see any point in joining a social media site like that; after all, it was such a *childish* activity. She'd felt stupid for asking him; for being such a baby compared to him, but now…

She had to know.

She typed his name into the search bar at the top and began scrolling through the results. Just a half-dozen or so down the list and there was his smiling, confident face. He was snuggled up against his wife, taking a selfie as they laughed together.

Kylie's eyes burned with unshed tears even as her finger tapped on his profile. It was all there – his beautiful wife, his two adorable kids, even his damn dog. He was living the American dream…without her. Thankfully, of course – she didn't want anything to do with him now – but still, the ache of what she *thought* she had with him versus the reality of the situation washed over her.

She'd been his mistress, the other woman, and had been inadvertently breaking up this happy family.

Well, not so happy, as it turned out. She wondered wildly if the wife knew; if she knew what Norman did on his sales trips through Bend, Oregon. Hell, he covered all of the Pacific Northwest as a salesman; he probably had a half-dozen Kylies scattered between here and the Redwood Forest.

How many of them had he gotten pregnant? How many of them had he thrown money at and told them to "take care of the problem"? How many of them had he made feel like a child because he sneered at them for wanting to friend him on Facebook?

How many other Kylies were there?

Kylie sank down the living room wall, the cool hardwood floor under her ass offering no cushion, no comfort. She was alone in the world, just her and this unplanned baby, and a mom who didn't want Kylie living with her, and a boss who saw her as someone to keep animals fed and invoices filed...and nothing more.

She had no friends and no prospects. The person who she'd believed was her forever love was actually a cheater, a liar, and an asshole.

Kylie curled up on the hardwood floor and cried like a baby.

Maybe Norman was right about one thing – nothing good came from Facebook.

CHAPTER 19

ADAM

*a*DAM CAME STROLLING UP to the front door of his rental early Monday morning, a happy grin on his face. After spending most of the day with Kylie yesterday, he'd gone back home and had been able to get the barn cleaned out, and had even started in on her car.

It wasn't nearly enough, of course, but with a to-do list a mile long, it was *never* enough. Even though he hadn't completed 1/100th of the must-do's on his list, after his mom's huge smile and hug when he'd unloaded all of the groceries, he'd still felt ten feet tall.

And now, he had a whole week to look forward to, where he got to see and work with Kylie every day of it. He couldn't squash the feeling that he'd been handed a gift; a rare and precious gift.

He knocked politely on the front door; although he owned the house, he couldn't just go barging in. She was his tenant, not his roommate. But when she opened the front door, she wasn't smiling and happy like normal. Her eyes were red, her thick blonde hair was in the sloppiest ponytail he'd ever clapped eyes on, and she just looked…exhausted.

His cheerful greeting died on his lips. "Are you okay?" he blurted out.

She nodded and shrugged, shifting her purse higher on her shoulder, her lunch bag gripped tightly in her other hand. "I'm ready to go whenever you are," she said mechanically.

Adam was stunned. She must've used that phrase in conversations with him a half dozen times before, but this was the first time where she'd said it while looking like she was facing an executioner.

"Is it the animals? Did they give you fits again this morning?" He was already cursing himself for not coming out first thing this morning. The happy, accomplished feeling he'd had while bounding up the driveway leaked out of him like a deflating balloon.

Once again, he'd let someone down whom he cared about. She'd told him last night when he'd dropped her off that she thought she had it and she didn't need the help anymore, but obviously, he shouldn't have believed her. Maybe Dumbass had—

"They're fine," she said curtly. "I'd really like to go to work now." She brushed past him and towards the truck, climbing inside, not waiting for his help up into the cab.

He walked slowly around to the driver's side and climbed in, starting the rumble of the diesel engine, thankful for the noise. Anything to help hide the silence that had descended like a brick wall between them. Where the hell was the Kylie from yesterday? And the last two weeks? This morose person sitting next to him bore no resemblance to the Kylie whom he'd come to know.

In conclusion to the longest drive in the history of mankind, they finally pulled up in front of the clinic and again, Kylie jumped out before he could help her out, hurrying to open the front door using her own key. By the time he got through the front door after her, she'd already put her lunch away, flipped on the open sign, turned on the computer, and was making coffee. She was a whirlwind of activity – a tornado of efficiency – but still, no sound was coming out of her.

Oh, and she wasn't meeting his gaze.

If he didn't know any better, he'd think she was royally pissed at him, but for what, he couldn't begin to imagine.

After doing a quick check of the few animals in the back and filling his coffee mug, he headed out the front door.

"I'll be back at five," he said as he headed out. She nodded in acknowledgment but still said nothing.

He slid into the driver's seat of his truck, pulling his phone out automatically to check his schedule for the day, even as he turned the situation over and over in his mind. He couldn't make heads or tails of it, and with a muttered curse he was glad his mother couldn't hear, he put his truck into reverse and headed out of the parking lot.

Whatever was going on with Kylie, he could only hope to God it didn't have a damn thing to do with him. Maybe a day by herself in the office to think it over would help.

God only knew it couldn't hurt at this point.

CHAPTER 20

KYLIE

*a*s soon as Adam headed out of the clinic parking lot, Kylie sank into her chair at the front desk and just stared off into the distance, the vaguest pretense of being fine disappearing without a trace.

What a hellacious night.

She hadn't slept well, she'd cried her body weight in tears and then some, and then this morning, all she could think was that Adam deserved so much better than her.

In fact, as soon as he knew she was pregnant with a married man's baby, he'd never want to talk to her again. No one would. Dammit all, this was a small town. People didn't forgive *or* forget easily.

And, by convincing Adam to hire her without telling him the truth, she'd dragged him into her disaster of a life, and knowing some of the judgmental asses out there, she might actually cost him some business with this little stunt of hers. Some rancher could totally choose to use a vet out of Franklin or Copperton rather than associate with a business who hired people like *her*.

Her being unmarried was bad enough, but the unforgivable part was the fact that the father of the baby *wasn't* unmarried. That was the part that would earn her the most scorn and judgmental looks.

The hardest part of all was that Kylie had been so damn naïve not to have seen it before the pee stick came back with a plus sign. If she hadn't gotten pregnant, would she have ever found out about Norman's other life? How long would she have continued on in ignorance, thinking that he was going to propose to her any day now?

And, oh God, if he had…she would've said yes in a heartbeat. She really thought she loved him.

Truthfully, she really ought to be locked up for her own good.

She dragged her ass out of her chair and forced herself to start working on putting the office back to rights. If someone came walking in and saw this mess, they'd think Adam was a terrible vet, or at least had terrible taste in employees. She couldn't let herself sink into a funk and do nothing but keep her chair from floating away all day. It wasn't fair to Adam.

She made a quick stop in the employee bathroom, scrubbing her face with cold water before redoing her ponytail. The first iteration had more closely resembled the hairdo of someone who'd just stuck a fork into an electrical socket, rather than the secretary of a veterinarian clinic. She couldn't embarrass Adam by looking like that in front of his clients.

And then, she got to work.

The more she worked, the better she felt. The raw, rough feeling of the lining of her eyelids disappeared, and they no longer felt like they were made of sandpaper. She got a rhythm going, her heart pumping and her breath quick as she scrubbed and swept and shoved the worn furniture where it needed to go.

When she'd finally finished, she sat back with a critical eye and then smiled to herself. The smile grew into a grin. The office looked amazing – a thousand times better, and she felt a thousand times better.

This was the second time she'd allowed herself to drown in self-pity because of Norman and this pregnancy, but screw it, it was gonna be the last.

She was a doer, through and through, and just sitting around and thinking and whining to herself about poor, poor pitiful Kylie VanLueven, taken advantage of by an older, wiser man…

Well, it just wasn't her, and she wasn't gonna let it be her in the future. She owed Adam an apology for her surly attitude that morning, for starters, and that evening when she got home from work, she promised herself that she'd get started on the Keep Adam Fed project. Bringing some muffins to work the next morning would help make up for the start of today.

She gnawed on her lower lip with worry. When

Adam came back at five and was met with a cheerful, upbeat Kylie, he was gonna think that she was bipolar, and she couldn't blame him one bit.

How could she explain pregnancy hormones to him without, you know, mentioning being pregnant?

Dammit, she needed to just tell him. Sure, it'd only been a little over two weeks since he'd hired her and she'd been hoping to make it longer than that before having to confess the truth, but after all that he'd done for her, he deserved to find out from her before he somehow found out from someone else.

God forbid.

It was just her and her mom who knew, but still, this sort of thing tended to spread through whispered rumors and sideways glances when waistlines began to change shape. Kylie had gone to school with a gal who'd gotten pregnant their junior year, and the rumors were flying fast and thick way before she officially told anyone. She ended up dropping out of school and marrying the baby's father, some guy from Franklin, in the middle of what should've been their senior year.

They got a divorce two years later, the stress of marrying too young and caring for a newborn baby destroying whatever love they'd once felt for each other. At the time, Kylie had been a little smug – how did you accidentally get pregnant in an age of condoms and birth control pills? Hadn't anyone explained the birds and the bees to her?

But now…

The phone rang, pulling Kylie out of her swirling thoughts, and she hurried across the office to the landline. "Whitaker's Veterinarian Clinic, this is Kylie speaking," she answered, trying to hide being out of breath.

"Hey, sugar!" her mom said cheerfully. "How are things going?"

For a moment, Kylie felt the burn of unshed tears well up in the corners of her eyes, but she quickly blinked them away. Damn pregnancy hormones. She didn't used to cry this much, truly she hadn't.

"Pretty good," she said, trying to hide the warble in her voice.

She failed, of course.

"What's going on?" Her mom pounced immediately. Trying to hide this sort of thing from Carol VanLueven was an impossible task, frankly. "Do you need some money?"

Kylie wanted to laugh a little to herself. It wasn't hard to notice what her mom *wasn't* offering: A place to stay.

"No, no, I'm good. Adam took me grocery shopping this weekend, and I have enough to get through to payday. Life is good, I promise."

Her mom paused for a moment, and Kylie could see, clear as day through the phone line, that she was debating whether or not to press the point. She held her breath, hoping that her mom would just let it go. She didn't want to tell her mom about last night.

She'd start crying all over again and she was done with crying.

Done.

"Welllll," her mom finally said, deciding to leave the topic alone, at least for the moment, "I was calling to find out if you wanted to attend the Knit Wits meeting with me tonight. I was thinking about it earlier today and started to worry that you're out there in that house all by yourself. Maybe it'd be fun to get out and socialize."

The Knit Wits? Kylie debated her choices.

If she started baking as soon as she got home from the clinic, she could probably get the muffins made and on the counter to cool before the start of the monthly meeting of her mom's knitting club. That way, she could get her Keep Adam Fed project going right away, and God only knew, after her performance that morning on the way to work, Adam deserved whatever kind thing Kylie could think of to do for him.

But on the other hand, her mom's idea of socialization…? It wasn't exactly thrilling. Unless things had drastically changed in the last four years since Kylie'd left for college, Mom was the youngest knitter in the group. Kylie would be young enough to be the granddaughter or even the great-granddaughter of every other knitter there.

Honestly, though, her mom *was* trying to be helpful, and really, an evening spent with a bunch of kindly old grandmas wasn't a half-bad way to pass a couple of hours. It sure beat curling up in a ball on a hardwood floor and crying a flood of tears.

Not that that was much of a benchmark, but Kylie was setting the bar low.

"That'd be great, Mom," she finally said. "Could you pick me up and drop me off? Adam hasn't finished working on Ruby's car yet, so I'd need a ride into town."

"Absolutely," her mom reassured her. "I'll be by a little before seven. We meet at the Muffin Man and everyone buys a dessert and a drink to thank him for being open later for us, but I'll pay for yours."

"Thanks, Mom," Kylie said gratefully. She really didn't want to spend her precious cash on something as frivolous as coffee and a donut from a bakery, and as always, her mom was thinking ahead.

She really had been blessed with a wonderful mother.

She hung up with a grin on her face, feeling roughly a million times more cheerful now than she had been that morning. As she looked around the clean office, smelling like lemons and glass cleaner, every surface polished to a high shine, she decided that she'd tell Adam the truth about being pregnant in the morning. She'd make him muffins tonight after work and have them ready for him to eat tomorrow morning when he came to pick her up; tell him the truth while he was still grateful that she'd cooked for him.

It was just as good of a plan as any, and a large

part of her was thrilled at the idea of having the truth out in the open. Lying, even through omission, wasn't right, and even if she'd done it for a good reason, it'd still been bothering her, like a sliver under a fingernail.

She celebrated her decision by getting to work on the cramped employee bathroom. She could put in some elbow grease there, too, and really surprise Adam. If she worked hard enough, he wouldn't even care about the rest of it.

CHAPTER 21

KYLIE

K YLIE WENT WALKING into the bakery with her mom, the yeast and sugar smell almost overwhelmingly powerful, but in the most pleasant way possible. If she could drown in delicious smells, she'd die a happy death here in the Muffin Man.

She looked around, spotting a few signs of the recent remodeling after the fire Adam had told her about. There were some ladders and paint cans scattered about, and a big plastic tarp that separated the back from the front. Kylie didn't personally know the owner, Gage – he'd moved back to Long Valley to take over his grandparents' bakery after she'd already left for college – but she'd heard all of the comments down at the vet clinic. He was rumored to be Long Valley's most eligible bachelor, and after the amount of drooling that the man inspired, Kylie was curious to see if he lived up to the hype.

Her mom called out a greeting to some of the other ladies in the Knit Wits group, and then made her way over to the grouped tables to chat with them. A little overwhelmed at the idea of meeting such a big group, Kylie wandered instead up to the front counter to inspect a handwritten sign, informing customers that until further notice, only coffee, tea, and muffins would be served at the Muffin Man, while the bakery was under renovation.

Kylie was impressed that they were even partially open, and wondered if Gage had been forced to do it to try to keep the bills paid while the remodeling work was being done. Based on what Adam had told her, the fire had been fairly significant.

Just then, a muscle-bound guy who looked like he could swing a fifty-pound bag of flour up over his shoulder without breaking a sweat, came pushing through the plastic curtain, carrying a tray with an array of muffins on it. He saw her standing there and smiled, revealing a row of white, straight teeth.

"Hi, you must be Carol's daughter," he said in way of greeting, shifting the tray to the other hand so he could push his glasses up his nose. With his square jaw and brilliant blue eyes, he looked like he could grace the cover of a romance novel.

Kylie laughed. "Is the family resemblance that strong?" she asked dryly. Gage shrugged.

"Carol mentioned that you'd come back to town, and honestly, there aren't many people who attend the Knit Wits who are under the age of 90," he winked, "so it wasn't a hard deduction to make." He held the tray out to her. "Want one?"

"Oh sure!" she said delightedly, dithering over her choices before finally picking out a lemon poppyseed concoction. She followed him over to the gathered tables, watching him as he passed the muffins out with ease to all of the older ladies, charming them with his smile and his laugh.

Well, it was plenty obvious to see why every woman in town under the age of 102 was in love with him.

Everyone, that is, except for her. She could tell why there was an attraction there for other people, but he just didn't do much for her. He needed to be taller, leaner, replace the flour dusted across his jeans with straw and shit instead, change his eye color from deep blue to whiskey brown, and...

Well, then you'd have Adam Whitaker, of course.

Kylie tried not to groan out loud. She really was a hopeless case.

As Gage disappeared into the back, carrying a now-empty tray, Carol began introducing Kylie to everyone in the group. She remembered some of the ladies from functions around town when she was back in high school, but honestly, they weren't exactly in her age range. Her guess that she'd be the youngest person in the group by a half-dozen decades or so, wasn't too far off.

"Oh, and today we have Tiffany and Ezzy with us again," her mom said, gesturing towards two gals who weren't as young as Kylie, but certainly weren't as old as even her mom.

"Good to meet you," the Tiffany chick said, putting her hand out to shake, but it was a limp-wristed shake with lifeless fingers, the kind of handshake that Kylie just hated. She always felt like she was gripping a dead fish.

Not exactly appealing.

Her mom pulled out a chair for Kylie next to Ezzy, who flashed a quick smile at Kylie but said nothing, and then began pulling out needles and yarn for them to work with. Kylie snagged two knitting needles and a ball of fluffy, purple yarn. It'd been ages since she'd tried to wrestle yarn into submission, but she was surprisingly excited about giving it another attempt. Maybe it was that nesting instinct that the internet had told her would start kicking in, but she wanted to make a warm, soft blanket – nothing complicated, just cozy and inviting.

The chatter about gardens and the weather – the wind had finally died down – and who was sleeping with who swirled around Kylie but she only half-listened as she struggled to get her needles to cooperate. She'd thought that knitting would be like riding a bike and it'd all just start coming back to her, but either her analogy was wrong or she was slow on the uptake, because she couldn't seem to cast on more than a few loops before she found herself stuck.

She leaned over to her mom to ask for help but before she could say anything, the conversation died down and Tiffany turned to Kylie. She cleared her throat loudly and asked, "So, you've moved back to Sawyer, huh?"

Kylie straightened up, putting her yarn and needles on her lap for the moment. She could ask her mom for help just as soon as this conversation was over. Since Tiffany had waited until there was a lull in the conversation *and* had cleared her throat before talking, every eye in the group was now trained on Kylie.

She gulped.

"Yeah," she said lightly, trying to pretend as if it wasn't a big deal. "I worked full-time while going to school part-time so I could stay away from student loan debt as much as possible, so it took me four years to get a two-year degree." She laughed a little. No big deal. None of this was a big deal. Not a big deal at all. "Now that my generals are out of the way, I'm trying to decide what I want to do with my life, so I came back home for a bit. Once I decide which degree I want, I'll be heading back out again."

Tiffany just stared at her for a moment, one eyebrow arched, and then looked pointedly down to Kylie's stomach, as subtle as a wrecking ball. Even before her mouth opened, Kylie felt a rush of dread wash over her, cold and clammy.

"Interesting," Tiffany said cattily, in that tone of voice that said that she didn't believe Kylie, not one bit. "You see, I'd been hearing around town that you're prego. Are you *sure* that isn't why you came running back to Mommy? And, I see no engagement ring, either."

The outburst of sound – gasps of horror and outrage – swirled around Kylie. She was dumbfounded. *What the hell? What is wrong with this... this bitch?*

Ezzy snickered behind her hand at the look on Kylie's face.

Make that two bitches.

"I really don't know what business it is of yours," Kylie retorted, her ears red and her cheeks red and the anger boiling like molten lava inside of her.

Tiffany shrugged, studying her fake fingernails nonchalantly. Kylie noticed that the ball of yarn in her lap hadn't been touched yet. Tiffany hadn't even tried to pretend that she was there to knit anything.

"I was just curious, is all," Tiffany said innocently. "I mean, if you got pregnant without a guy willing to make it right by marrying you, well now, that's between you and God, isn't it? It does make me wonder if he isn't married already, though..."

She trailed off significantly, arching one eyebrow, waiting for Kylie's defense.

Kylie felt like she'd been thrown into a pit of vipers. This was the Knit Wits group? It was supposed to be a group of sweet old ladies who gossiped about who did the best job dyeing and covering up grays, not...not *this*.

"I'm not feeling well," Kylie announced, standing up, struggling to hold back her tears. She was *not* going to cry in front of this woman. Never. "Mom, I'd like to go home now."

She marched towards the front door, her needles and yarn clasped in her hands, trying to act as if nothing was wrong. Nothing at all.

It really was too bad that she was such an awful actress.

Behind her, the sound of chatter and uncomfortable laughter swelled up again. She didn't know and didn't care who was laughing. She was never going to see any of these women again. She was going to move to Mississippi and dye her hair black and adopt a southern accent and pretend her name was Susan Blackeye. She hated this town and this state and especially people named Tiffany and Ezzy.

She threw herself into the passenger seat of her mom's Prius, finally giving into the desire to cry her eyes out. She was crying so hard, she was hiccuping when her mother made it to the car, starting it and driving until they pulled into the empty parking lot of the library behind a small row of bushes. She turned off the car, and then pulled Kylie up against her side, holding her as Kylie let out a jagged breath, then howled with anger and hurt again.

She didn't know and didn't care how much time passed before she finally calmed down enough to pull out of her mom's arms. "Why?" she whimpered. "Why would Tiffany do that? I hardly even know her."

That, more than anything, was the most hurtful

part of all. If she'd been in a Hatfield-McCoy feud with the woman all through school, well, it'd make sense, at least. But Tiffany had graduated years before Kylie. She'd probably been in elementary school when Tiffany had been a senior.

"It just doesn't make sense," she whispered.

Her mom hugged her hard. "I've never particularly liked Tiffany," she said regretfully. "I was a little worried when her and Ezzy started showing up to the Knit Wits meetings a couple of months ago, but she never did anything wrong, per se, so I just bit my tongue. She never seemed all that interested in knitting or crafts in general, though, but *real* damn interested in the gossiping part. She probably just had a hunch that you were pregnant and asked tonight, wanting to get a rise out of you, hoping to get a reaction. So I'm going to say that the secret is out, darlin', 'cause no one back in that bakery was fooled in the slightest. Have I mentioned lately that maybe you shouldn't consider a Broadway career among your many options?"

Kylie pulled back, a hysterical laugh spilling out of her. "Not Broadway, huh?" she said, scrubbing at her eyes. "And I so thought I had a chance…"

And then she grew serious. "I knew it'd come out at some point, of course – you can't hide a baby forever – but I guess I just didn't think that people would be rude enough to ask me about it to my face. I knew there'd be gossip behind my back, but there's a difference between that and right here in front of me. And how did she know that Norman was married?!"

That was the bad part. That was the part that was going to cause her the most trouble, for damn sure.

Her mom pulled her against her soft side, cradling Kylie against her body. "Small towns can be vicious," she said softly, running her fingers through Kylie's hair as she talked. "Last I heard, Tiffany had been chasing the new county extension agent but apparently he fell in love with the younger McLain daughter instead. Maybe Tiffany turned her sights on Adam, and thought that you were her competition. She's the kind of person who'd look at the world that way. Which, by the way, *is* there anything between you and your hunky boss?"

Kylie pulled back with a startled laugh. "Of course not," she protested automatically.

Her mom just stared at her.

Kylie stared back...and then blinked first.

Dammit.

"Maybe," she allowed.

"Maybe, as in...?"

"As in we've kissed. But just once. He hasn't kissed me since. Maybe I'm not a good kisser." She gave her mom a pained smile. Her mom rolled her eyes.

"Knowing Adam, it's probably more that he feels like he can't take advantage of an employee, and especially not one who's so much younger than him."

"Okay, yeah. Probably," Kylie allowed. That did make a *bit* more sense.

"How much older is he than you?" her mom asked, settling back into the driver's seat and turning on the car. Being a hybrid, the start-up process hardly made a noise.

"Like, fifteen years? Maybe? I'm just guessing. I haven't actually asked him."

"That's quite a difference when you're only in your 20s, but when you hit your 40s, it won't be much of a difference at all." Her mom paused for a moment and then added, "But, since you're in your 20s right now, I'm not sure how much of a comfort that is to you."

Kylie let out a hollow laugh. "Well, I'm not sure if it matters either way, honestly. He's not going to want a girl who's pregnant with a bastard child."

No one did.

CHAPTER 22

ADAM

*a*DAM HURRIED INTO the dining room, behind as always. He could snag a cup of coffee from the kitchen, swing by and pick up Kylie, and then get to work without being too late. Hopefully.

Well hell, who was going to fire him? It wasn't like he had a boss he had to explain himself to, right?

It still bothered him, though.

He pressed a kiss to his mom's cheek, as always, as he rushed past. "Good morning, Mom," he called out cheerfully from the kitchen, pouring himself a cup of coffee. "How'd you sleep?"

She didn't answer but instead folded up the newspaper and put it neatly off to the side. Her unexpected silence caught his attention and he went back into the dining room, coffee cup in hand. She looked…upset. Angry. Worried.

Something not good, anyway.

"Adam, dear, there's something you need to hear and I think you ought to hear it from me," she said slowly.

Adam slid into his chair, kitty corner from his mother's, and picked up her hand in his. "What's wrong?" he asked, worried. His mother wasn't one for the melodramatic, so this was unusual, to say the least.

"Kylie VanLueven is pregnant."

He jerked his head back and shook it instinctively. "No," he whispered. "That can't be right."

Then he remembered the flash of her rounded belly in the sunlight when Dumbass had been trying to eat her shirt, and how she always wore sweatshirts and yoga pants and…

He was such an idiot. *Such* an idiot.

"How do you know?" he demanded defensively. "Are you sure?"

His mom nodded slowly. "That Tiffany gal – you know her? A couple of years younger than you – confronted her last night at the Knit Wits meeting. I sure don't like that Tiffany woman, or her friend Ezzy. Nothing good ever seems to happen around them. Anyway, Tiffany seems to think that the father of Kylie's baby is married to someone else, although she didn't have any proof for it."

"Did Kylie actually *say* that she was pregnant?" Adam demanded. He felt his world spinning off its axis.

Not again…

"I don't know. I wasn't there. You know I can't anymore…" She held up her gnarled hands. "But a couple of my friends called afterward and told me what had happened since Kylie is your employee and all. They thought you deserved to know. I know that nowadays, in some places, it's okay to have six children by six different men and never marry any of them, but this is *Sawyer*. If it's true, she's not going to have an easy time of it. And you aren't either. There are some prudes in town who might not want to use you as their vet because of this."

Adam nodded mechanically, but honestly, he didn't care about that part. He had enough business to keep him running at full speed 24/7. If he lost a little business, he'd probably be better off for it.

But Kylie…

All this time, and she didn't tell him. Why didn't she tell him? Did she think he didn't deserve to know?

Not again…

He stood up from the dining room table. "I better get to work," he said woodenly. "See you tonight." He kissed his mom goodbye and climbed into the truck.

He didn't remember a thing about the drive over to his old place. When he pulled up in front of the older farmhouse, he looked around, blinking. How had he gotten there? He could only hope he hadn't run any stop signs while driving on autopilot.

And then it all washed over him again and the haze disappeared and the anger rushed back and he jumped out of the truck, hurrying to the front door, pounding on it. Kylie opened up, a big grin on her face, a platter of food in her hands but before she could say anything, he demanded, "Are you pregnant?!"

Her face crumpled and her shoulders slumped. She put the tray of food on the entryway table. She looked back up at him.

She nodded slowly.

"How far along?"

"Four months tomorrow," she whispered.

"Why didn't you tell me?" he demanded. The pain swirled through him at the betrayal.

Not again…

"Would you have hired me if you knew?" she retorted right back, planting her hands on her hips and glaring up at him.

"Of co—" He stopped his instinctive response and thought about it, *really* thought about it. She hadn't known anything about animals. She didn't have any billing experience. She wasn't 50 and she didn't have gray hair and she sure as shit didn't have a steely-eyed glance. He'd been so close to turning her away as it was. Would he have hired her if he'd known she was pregnant?

Probably not.

His hesitation gave him away.

"I needed a job," Kylie said flatly. "No employer hires someone who is months along in their pregnancy. Oh, they come up with fake reasons for it – shit that has nothing to do with the pregnancy – but honestly, employers just don't want to be inconvenienced by hiring someone who has to take medical leave just months after starting, no matter how good they are in the meantime. And, in case you haven't noticed, I'm not married, and this is Sawyer-freaking-Idaho.

"So yeah, I didn't tell you."

Adam sputtered, his mind spinning in circles. He didn't know what he wanted to say or do. He needed some time to think, some space from Kylie. Maybe a nice round of vaccinations with a herd of cows that were dumber than a pile of rocks would help him get his head on straight.

"Well, are you ready to go?" he growled. He wasn't normally one to snap at people, but he couldn't make himself care at the moment. He'd care later. Right now, he felt too mixed up and stirred up and chaotic and panicked to be kind and thoughtful.

"'Go'? Hold on, you still want me to come to work?"

"Of course. I sure as shit don't want to have to start sending out invoices again." He turned back and started stomping down the walkway, his boots not making any noise on the dirt path. *Dammit.* What he wouldn't give for a concrete sidewalk in that moment.

They climbed inside and for a second day in a row, the drive to work was uncomfortable and awful and awkward as hell. Adam pulled to a stop in front of the clinic, waited for Kylie to climb out, and then drove off. He could go buy a cup of coffee from Mr. Petrols. Right now, he needed some space from Ms. Kylie VanLueven, and the chance to figure out what in the hell he was going to do.

CHAPTER 23

KYLIE

*W*ELL, that went about as awful as she thought it would go.

Actually, scratch that. It went way worse than she'd thought it would. After Tiffany at the bakery last night and then Adam this morning, she'd had about all she could stand of judgmental Sawyerites. There was a reason she'd moved to Oregon to get her associate's degree, dammit. She had wanted to be far, far away from this town and its small-mindedness, but then, when the shit hit the fan, where did she go running back to?

Sawyer-freaking-Idaho.

Argh.

The phone rang, and Kylie cleared her throat hurriedly and then answered as cheerfully as she could. "Whitaker's Vet Clinic, this is Kylie speaking," she said, working extra hard to add a pleasant lilt to her voice. Just because she was having a shitty day…

no, week…no, month…well anyway, it didn't mean she should take it out on the rest of the world.

Her cheerful greeting did her absolutely no good, unfortunately. She hardly got the word "speaking" out before Mr. Stultz began in on a 25-minute diatribe, angry because he'd received such a large bill in the mail the day before.

Kylie tried to explain a couple of times that Adam had gotten behind on his billing and so when she'd taken over, there was quite a backlog in place, but there was no reasoning with Mr. Stultz. All he took from that information was the idea that this was all her fault.

"So I can thank *you* for this huge bill?" he demanded angrily.

"I think you can thank your animals – they're the ones who needed the care," Kylie retorted and then squeezed her eyes shut. *Whoops.* She probably shouldn't have said that. Wasn't there some awful saying in the customer service world about the customer always being right?

Adam was *really* going to regret hiring her after he heard about this phone call.

"Listen here, you little twit, it isn't *my* fault that Dr. Whitaker couldn't get his bills out on time for months on end, and I sure as hell ain't gonna pay this gigantic thing now that he's finally gotten around to doing his damn job! So, tell him that if he wants *any* of this money, he'll call me."

And with that, Mr. Stultz hung up the phone.

Kylie's hand was shaking as she put the phone back in the cradle. Did she just get into a shouting match with a customer?

What

a

day

She wandered into the back and opened up the cage for Pugsies, a miniature pug that they were running some tests on, and snuggled his small body against her. "Hi, Pugsies," she whispered into his fur. "Do you still like me?" He licked her chin. "You might be the only one," she told him seriously. "You're adorable, so of course this town likes you, but me? I'm just a stupid girl who doesn't know how to pick a boyfriend or run a condom." She smiled, just a bit, at the phrasing, and then her shoulders began to shake as the tears began to run down her face.

Again.

This time, instead of having to wipe them off with the backs of her hands, though, Pugsies just reached up and licked her face, his stumpy little tail wiggling hard as he tried to comfort her.

"Such an idiot," she whimpered, her voice breaking, and then there were strong arms wrapping around her, pulling her tight up against a muscular chest. Adam reached out and put Pugsies back into the cage and then turned her around in his arms, running his hands up and down her spine as she just gave in and cried, letting the roiling fear and worry that'd been boiling in her guts spill down her face instead.

"Whhyyyy…" she wailed.

"Why what?" Adam whispered.

"Why are you here and not out vaccinating cows?" she blubbered.

She felt his chest shaking against her cheek.

"First off, kudos for having my schedule memorized," he said, laughter in his voice even as his hands continued their long, rhythmic strokes down her back. She felt a little like a cow getting milked, but instead of milk coming out, all of the stress and worry that she'd been carrying around with her were flowing out instead.

"Second of all, I'm here to apologize. I…it's better if I show you. Will you forgive me long enough to go on a drive with me?"

She snuffled, pulling back and wiping at her cheeks with the backs of her hands. She missed Pugsies' kisses just then. Adam disappeared for a moment and then he was back, pushing some Kleenexes into her hands. She took them gratefully, blowing and wiping her nose.

"Will you come with me?" he repeated. "Just let me tell you what's going on. Then you can decide whether or not to forgive me."

She nodded as she looked up into his warm, whiskey brown eyes, wrinkles in the corner as he peered down at her, worry etched on his face. "Yes," she whispered.

He took her hand, plucked the goopy tissues out of them before she could protest – he didn't want to touch those things! – threw them away for her, and then started tugging her towards the front. He flipped off the lights and the open sign, and then locked the door before leading her over to the passenger side of his truck.

"It's only 10:42," she protested automatically, even as he helped her inside. "We can't close right now."

He shut the door and walked over to the driver's side before responding. "Kylie, before you started here, I had all of the office calls forwarded to my cell phone, and I was only in the clinic when I scheduled it with a patient." He pulled out of the parking lot and began heading towards the foothills outside of Sawyer. "It was inconvenient as hell and people sure love having you there anytime they want to stop by, but you've only been working the desk for what two? Three weeks? Anyway, if people want to talk to me, they can call me, just like they always have. One day of closing early won't kill this community."

She nodded. She still felt guilty for playing hooky from work, but on the other hand, it was her boss who was insisting that she did, so really, who was she to tell him no.

His comment about phone calls reminded her, though. She grimaced. She really, really didn't want to talk about Mr. Stultz right now, but on the other hand, he'd hear about it sooner or later. She didn't want him to think that she'd tried to hide that from him also.

"Ummm...speaking of people calling," she said hesitantly, "I have a note for you back in the office. Mr. Stultz called and he's *pissed*."

Adam grimaced. "His bill?" he asked, not taking his eyes off the road.

Kylie nodded. "Said that it wasn't fair for you to wait so long to bill him for all of that work you did."

The corner of Adam's mouth twitched up just a little bit, and then he said dryly, "Don't take that personally. Every single time I send him a bill, he finds something to bitch about. One time, I ran out of black ink and didn't want to drive all the way to Boise that day for more, so I printed the bills using colored ink, and he called to complain that the color was wrong." Adam shrugged. "People like him...it just comes with the territory of working with the public. I'll call him back and listen to him rant and rave, and then he'll pay his bill. Sometimes, I wonder if he doesn't just want an excuse to call someone. He's older, and I think he's lonely."

He turned off onto a dirt road and they bounced along for a while, flashes of blue through the pine trees making Kylie think that they were following the path of a river. She wasn't entirely sure where they were at, other than up in the foothills outside of Sawyer, but she kept her mouth shut and just waited for Adam to tell her why they were taking a nature hike in the middle of the day on a Tuesday, and what on God's green earth this had to do with her being pregnant.

They rolled to a stop in a little pull-out and Adam turned off the engine, took a deep breath, and turned to look at Kylie.

CHAPTER 24

ADAM

"*Y*OU WOULD'VE LIKED my wife if you'd met her," he said. He wasn't entirely sure why he was starting with that part, other than it was the words coming out of his mouth, so he ran with it. "We graduated together, though, so I doubt you ever met her."

Kylie shook her head mutely, just watching him as he talked.

He gulped. He felt naked. Vulnerable. What he was about to tell Kylie was something only he, his mom, and the coroner knew.

So yeah, not a whole lot of people.

"Wendy was right there for me through it all. She moved to Boise and we attended BSU together. After I got my undergrad, I transferred to vet school. She transferred with me.

"Partway through vet school, we got married. It was one of those things where we'd always told ourselves that we wouldn't get married until I was out of school, but…" He shrugged. "We were both sick of waiting. So we got married by Judge Schmidt down at the courthouse and told ourselves that we'd have a grand wedding later, when we had the money, but for now, we wanted the piece of paper.

"We never did have a grand wedding. Life kept getting in the way. We were going to do it 'later,' and…later never came."

He tried to act as if it wasn't a big deal that he hadn't given his Wendy what she needed, but the guilt of that still haunted him.

A quick sideways glance at Kylie told him that she wasn't fooled, not one little bit.

He looked back out through the front windshield. There were no pale green eyes to haunt him out there. He wondered for a moment if she knew how much she looked like her mother, right down to that unique shade of green.

"We didn't start trying for a baby until I'd graduated from vet school and had come back to Sawyer to take over the practice. The former vet had held in there until I had my degree so he could sell it to me, but I don't think anyone in the world has ever been as happy as he was, the day he got to walk away from it all. Last I heard, he's been hanging out in the Caribbean, as far away from cows and horses and sheep as he could get."

Kylie's laughter tinkled out and Adam smiled a bit. Laughter. That was…nice.

"When Wendy got pregnant, I was thrilled to pieces. I don't know if you've done the math, but my mom had me quite late – she was coming up on forty before she finally got pregnant for the first time. She always called me 'my miracle baby.' And then, she lost my dad just before she had me, almost like God was telling her that she only got to have one or the other – she didn't get to have us both."

His voice broke and he felt the heat of unshed tears build up behind his eyes but he wouldn't let himself shed them. He'd cried too many tears too many times before.

He cleared his throat and plowed on.

"Wendy was only a couple of months along when…she lost the baby. Woke up to bloody sheets and her screaming. The doctors said to give her body some time to recuperate and heal, but that we were absolutely fine to try again after that. Said that some women's bodies reject the first baby, or even two, but that it would work. Eventually."

He breathed in and then out, slowly and evenly, trying to get a grasp on his emotions. It'd been such a long time since he'd torn the bandages off these wounds, and it turned out, they were just as painful and gaping and awful as they'd always been.

"She lost two more after that. Same thing every time. The doctors couldn't seem to figure out why – there was no medical reason for it that they could see. Her body just kept rejecting the pregnancies. Wendy eventually got it in her head that she shouldn't tell anyone that she was pregnant; that she was somehow causing this to happen by blabbing the news to everyone too early. So with the last pregnancy, she didn't even tell me.

"One day, it occurred to me that I couldn't remember the last time she'd had her period – when you're trying for a baby, you start to watch that sort of thing real closely – and asked her when she was supposed to have her next visit from Aunt Flo."

Kylie giggled at that, and Adam tore his gaze away from the windshield to grin at her. "'Aunt Flo' is such a better term than 'period,' honestly. Anyway," he waved his hand in the air, brushing the aside away, "that's when she told me that she was pregnant, and this time, she was four months along.

"I couldn't believe it. She'd never made it past the two-month mark before, and this time she'd made it to four? It was a miracle. But…I know it sounds crazy, but I also felt betrayed."

"Betrayed?" Kylie echoed. "Because your wife was pregnant?"

"No," he whispered, "because she didn't tell *me*. Her superstition about not telling anyone that she was pregnant meant that she'd kept this information from even me, her partner and husband. This was something that we'd worked for, for so hard and so long, and then…she hid it from me. I don't think she realized how hard I'd take that. *I* didn't realize how hard I'd take it until it happened. I could understand not wanting to tell all of Sawyer, but not even me? It was this wonderful, magical secret that she'd kept to herself for four whole months."

He let out a deep sigh. This was where it got bad. Kylie wasn't going to look at him as a good guy much longer, and the idea of that hurt his soul.

He wasn't a good guy, but he liked to pretend that he was, and he liked to think that others saw him that way, even if it wasn't true.

"We went to bed angry with each other that night. I just needed some time to calm down and get over myself, as my mother would say, but…I had no idea that it was my last night to hold my wife in my arms. If I'd known, I think I would've made myself get over the hurt and shock a whole lot faster." He let out a bitter laugh.

"The next day, I went straight out to a client's place, hoping to work my way through my problems. I am a doer. If I have a project in my hands and can work, it lets my brain think through shit. If I just sit somewhere, problems go around and around in circles, and never get resolved."

Kylie let out a little laugh, and Adam looked up, pulled momentarily from his story. "What?" he asked, perplexed.

Her gorgeous green eyes were sparkling with laughter, but she attempted to wipe the smile from her face. "Nothing. I'll tell you later. Keep going."

He shrugged. "So Wendy came out to where I was that day, and asked me to have lunch with her. She'd packed a hamper and everything. She wanted to say sorry for keeping this news from me. I'd already started to feel better about the whole thing, but hell, when your wife goes through all of the trouble to make you lunch and follows you out into a field to ask you out on a date, you don't tell her no. So I wrapped up quick and headed out with her. She took me here." He gestured at the forest towering on either side of the dirt road.

"There's a little spot just over there – flat, with soft sand instead of hard dirt – a perfect place to have a picnic. After we ate, Wendy went down to the river and was splashing around. Teasing me. She was flicking water on me and telling me that I was too chicken to get in there with her. It's a glacier-fed stream, so it's certainly not a nice warm bathtub you want to soak in. But before I could join her or flick water back at her – I hadn't decided which to do yet – her feet…"

He paused and then whispered, "They slipped."

He gulped, trying to shove down the sudden nausea that'd boiled up in his throat, the acid burning, bitter and nasty.

"She fell. Her head hit the rocks in the shallow river, and…that was it." He shuddered out a breath. "She was gone. I just didn't know it yet."

He looked at Kylie but he couldn't see her through the hot tears swimming in his eyes, and anyway, he was seeing his wife instead, drifting in the stream, blood swirling away, hearing his own screams as he frantically splashed through the water, dragging her to the edge...

"I wrapped my shirt around her head. It was the only thing I could easily get my hands on. I carried her to my truck, laid her down in the backseat, and took off like a bat out of hell for the hospital. She never woke up. They tried everything, but...she was gone.

"It took me years to get past it. The what-if's still haunt me to this day, to be honest. What if I hadn't been angry with her for not telling me the news right away? She wouldn't have felt like she needed to pack a picnic and take me out here. What if I'd been faster when I saw her slip? I might've been able to catch her. What if I'd insisted that we not try for another baby? There would've been no fight, and thus no picnic. People say that it doesn't do you any good to say 'what if' because you can't change the past, but dammit all, it's instinctive. And if someone has learned how to control that instinct, well, good for them. I'm not there. Not yet."

He blew out a breath and looked up at Kylie to find her face swimming in front of him. He brushed angrily at his eyes. He'd cried enough tears to fill an ocean. He didn't need to cry anymore.

"So, when I heard that you'd hid your pregnancy from me, I took it a lot more personally than I should have. Please forgive me. I am not your husband or your boyfriend or the father of the baby. You weren't obligated to tell me about your pregnancy, and I shouldn't have been upset with you over it. There's just…a lot of personal pain mixed up in this. And I haven't even told you about the time I helped a gal give birth on the side of the road in the middle of a blizzard! Traumatized for life with that one." He tried to chuckle, to laugh off the pain, but he wasn't sure that he was fooling anyone.

"I was going to tell you I was pregnant this morning," Kylie said softly. "I know that probably sounds suspicious – yeah, sure, easy for you to say now – but I actually decided that I would tell you the truth yesterday afternoon. I was waiting until this morning to do it, though, because I wanted to make muffins for you and while I had you softened up with food, tell you about the baby. I'm totally not above bribery." She flashed an unrepentant grin at him.

"Oh, I forgot about the muffins!" he exclaimed, happy to focus on *anything* but how it was that he'd failed his wife and unborn child. "You were holding them this morning when I came to pick you up."

She nodded. "Yeah, I…uh…started a new project." She suddenly looked embarrassed. Adam dashed the last of his tears away and cocked his head to the side, studying her intently. There was red blossoming on her cheeks, and the tips of her ears were a bright cherry color.

When she didn't say anything, he prodded her. "And that project would be…?"

"Keep Adam Fed," she blurted out.

He stared at her for a moment, and then he

couldn't help it. He burst out laughing. "Oh my God, are you kidding me?" he finally huffed out through his laughter. "Am I that hopeless that you need to take me on as a *charity project*?"

"Well, I wouldn't say hopeless," Kylie said loyally. "Just not as focused on taking care of yourself as you should be."

"Keep Adam Fed," he repeated, and then laughed again. "It was the PB&J comment, wasn't it?"

"I'll admit that it got me started," she allowed, her cheeks burning brighter than ever, "but you're just so busy all the time. It can't be good to only eat once a day."

"How do you know I don't eat breakfast or lunch?" he protested. "You're not at my mom's house or out in the field with me."

She arched an eyebrow at him. "Do you?" she asked bluntly.

It was his turn to squirm in his seat. "Sometimes," he said, stubbornly. "When I have the time."

She just continued to stare at him, one eyebrow perfectly arched.

"Once every six months or so, I do," he finally admitted, sighing in defeat.

She shook her head. "That isn't healthy. You need three square meals a day and snacks in-between. *Healthy* snacks. And no, donuts from the Muffin Man do not count as healthy."

"You're a terror, you know that?"

She grinned angelically at him. "You should meet my mother. She's got me beat to pieces!"

He let out a loud laugh at that. "I have met your mother, and I have to say, I absolutely believe you!"

They grinned at each other for a moment and then Adam said seriously, his eyes trained on every curve of Kylie's face, "I…Listen, I don't want to creep you out and this is all sorts of awkward because I'm your boss and two decades older than you—"

"Hold on, how old are you?" Kylie broke in.

"I'm 38. How old are you?"

"Not 18," she said hotly. "I'm 22."

"All right, fine, not two decades, only 16 years. Does that make you feel better?"

"Yes," she said, mollified. "Now, you were busy saying that you're my boss and 16 years older than me…?"

"And for those reasons and probably a dozen others that I can't think of at the moment, I shouldn't say a damn thing, but honestly, I already screwed this up when I kissed you in the barn so I might as well say something now, so the truth is, I like you, a lot, and that's actually the biggest reason why I took it so hard to hear that you're pregnant."

She jerked her head back like she'd been slapped. "Because you can't like someone who's pregnant with another man's bastard, is that it?" she whispered, her eyes filling with tears.

"No!" he exclaimed, reaching for her, but she jerked her hands back, out of range.

"Then what?" she spat out. "And choose your next words carefully if you actually want a future with me."

He sighed and rubbed his forehead. "I just meant that it hurt to hear about the pregnancy after the fact, rather than the person I love being uppp ffffrront..." He stuttered to a stop. Her mouth was gaping open, her eyes as round as two teacup saucers.

"Have I mentioned yet that I love you?" he asked weakly.

"You...wha...I can't..." She was sputtering, mouth opening and closing spastically. And then, she started laughing, until she bent over in the seat, holding her sides and tears running down her cheeks. "If someone ever calls you Casanova," she gasped, "just laugh in their face. Please."

"Funny you should mention that," he said dryly. "I was thinking that I needed some help in the suave department after I told you that you weren't so fat that you'd affect my gas mileage."

She started laughing again. "I have to admit, that was a hell of a compliment. One of the best I've ever received." She looked at him, her lips twitching with the effort of holding her laughter in. "So, Casanova, you really love me, huh?"

He looked at her seriously. "I really do. I know it's crazy, but I've only loved four women in my life, and one of them is my mother. The other two were Wendy and...and Chloe Bartell. Soon-to-be Chloe Blackhorse."

"Was she the gal who used to rent from you?"

He nodded, surprised. "How did you know?"

"You always acted so cagey and weird about your previous renter. I knew there had to be something between you guys, or at least on your end."

He nodded slowly. "Within weeks of meeting Wendy, I knew I'd love her forever. Within weeks of meeting Chloe, I knew the same thing. But you...I knew from the moment I clapped eyes on you. That's why the betrayal was so deep to me."

"Is that why you hired me?" Kylie asked, biting her lower lip. "Because you were in love with me as soon as you saw me?"

He squirmed a bit in the driver's seat. "Well, if you'd asked then, I would've told you absolutely not. I'm really not an impulsive person. Only my heart is impulsive."

She let out a belly laugh at that and he grinned back at her. "Honestly, I knew the paragon of perfection that I wanted to hire, and you didn't have a single qualification on that list. Not one. But my heart was telling me to do it, and then watching you with Sir Grouch...did you know that cat hates everyone except his owner and you? Even Ollie can't get away with picking him up. But there you were, cuddling the orneriest cat I've ever had in my clinic, and he was *purring*. If he'd started reciting Shakespeare sonnets, I don't think I could've been more surprised."

She laughed lightly. "Animals have always seemed to like me," she said, and shrugged, as if it was no big deal. She chewed on her bottom lip for another moment and then said, "Before we can go any further down this road, I need to tell you about me and this baby. You should know the truth, and then decide if you still love me. I won't blame you if you don't. I mean, I won't pretend to be excited, but I won't be surprised either. Can we walk as we talk? It's getting hot and sticky in here without the air running."

"Of course," he said. "Just...don't go down to the river?"

"I promise." And just to show how serious she was, she crossed her heart...and then winked.

He threw back his head and laughed. He couldn't believe that he'd told her the most awful story he had to share, and was laughing just minutes later.

He'd never met another soul like her; not even Wendy or Chloe did what Kylie did to him.

It was terrifying and wonderful, all wrapped up in one. Terriful? Wonderfying?

Definitely...something.

CHAPTER 25

KYLIE

*a*DAM HELPED HER out of the truck and they began to wander up the dirt road, staying on the far side from the river. She could hear it rushing by, a relaxing nature symphony accompanying their walk, but she had to wonder how hearing it affected Adam. She snuck a covert glance, but he seemed fine. Maybe it had been long enough that the sound of water didn't bother him anymore.

"So," she said, and then stopped.

"So," Adam echoed, and then winked at her. He was certainly a lot more playful than he had been just a half hour before. She wondered if he was trying to be upbeat and lighthearted in order to help her relax as she recounted her sordid history.

Unfortunately, there weren't enough jokes in the world to counteract *this* story.

"Since today is Confess Everything From Your Past Day," she started out, trying to inject a little levity into the situation herself, "I should tell you about Norman."

"Hold on, you dated a guy named *Norman*?" Adam interjected.

She sent him a mock death glare. "Focus!"

"I am focusing," he mumbled, "on what a terrible name that is!"

"I thought it was charmingly quaint," she informed him pertly.

"At least somebody does."

She glared at him. She was never going to get her story told at this rate.

He pantomimed zipping his lips and throwing the key away. Satisfied, she drew in a deep breath and began.

"I didn't date much here in Sawyer growing up," she started, kicking a rock down the road as they walked, "because damn, is it hard to fall in love with a guy that you've known since you were both in diapers. I'd look at some guy asking me out and all I'd see was him back in the fourth grade, when he used to pull my braids or whatever. I think it's sweet that you and Wendy were high school sweethearts; that just wasn't ever going to happen with me."

She kicked the rock into the bushes and then bent over to scoop up a pinecone to fiddle with instead. It made talking to Adam so much easier. She flipped it over and over as they walked, staring at it but not seeing it at all.

"Mom and I went to Bend, Oregon a couple of

times on vacation, and I just loved the city. It's a funny choice for college because all they have there is this little dinky community college. Most people wouldn't think to move across state lines just to attend there, you know? But I wanted to live in Bend. I was never – no *never* – going to come back to Sawyer, no how, no way." She rolled her eyes at herself. "You can see how that's worked out thus far. Anyway, I got a job pumping gas at a gas station – in Oregon, they pump your gas for you. I know it sounds weird, but I actually enjoyed it. I would hurry over to someone's car, greet them, squeegee their windows while the gas was pumping, I always had a big smile for everyone, and I made quite a bit in tips. Way easier than waiting tables – I didn't have to remember anyone's drink order – *and* I got to be outside.

"Then, one day, this older guy pulls up in a convertible, but not a new one. No, this was a Karmann Ghia."

Adam whistled appreciatively, and she said, "I know, right?! So of course I hurry over because if nothing else, I want to admire this gorgeous car. Cherry red, polished to a shine, top down – just beautiful. I found out later that this was part of his schtick. Norman was a traveling salesman, and he used this antique as a foot in the door. Potential customers would come out and want to look it over, and while he was giving them the full tour of the car, he'd start hitting them up for a sale. Apparently, this same trick also works on potential girlfriends."

She grimaced. She needed to stop referring to herself as his girlfriend. She'd been his mistress, whether she'd known it at the time or not.

"He gave a hefty tip, which of course made my day, but he played it smooth. He didn't ask me out at that point. He flirted with me, told me I was the most beautiful person to ever pump his gas, blah blah blah, but then he left. I didn't think much about it until a week later, when he came back through again. He was on the return route, and had specifically chosen to go through Bend, just to see if he could catch me at the gas station again. That was flattering, so when he asked me out, I said yes. Older, handsome man; nice car; he thought I was cute; he was good at giving compliments…"

She threw the pinecone as hard as she could and watched it bounce down the hill towards the river below.

"I hadn't had a serious boyfriend before Norman, and so I was ripe for the picking, I guess. I *wanted* to fall in love and find my happily ever after." She scooped another pinecone up and began tossing it from hand to hand as they meandered. "He wasn't your typical boyfriend, though. Because he was a traveling salesman, he wasn't in town every day. He'd come through every couple of weeks, take me out to dinner, a movie, bring me flowers, tell me how much he'd missed me, then rent some dinky motel room and we'd make love all night." She blushed, chancing a glance at Adam. She felt awkward as hell talking about sex with him, but he didn't seem to really react much, so she decided to follow his lead and act as if it was no big deal.

"We texted," *sexted*, she corrected in her mind, but decided that she wasn't quite *that* comfortable with the topic of sex with Adam yet, "between visits, but not all the time, and he rarely called. He always told me how busy he was. How important he was, and by implication, what a great favor he was doing by coming to Bend to see me. A pompous windbag, in retrospect. I should've kneed him in the nuts and run the other direction, but…live and learn, I guess."

She drew in a deep breath. This was where it was going to get rough. Honestly, the only reason she had the guts to tell him this part was because he'd already told her the worst of his past. It was just a tiny bit less scary because he'd taken the plunge first, and thus, she was just a tiny bit more brave herself.

"Since we didn't see each other all the time, it's fairly easy for me to pinpoint when it was that he got me pregnant: The end of January. He stopped by on a Tuesday night, we had dinner, went to the cheap motel and screwed like rabbits, and then he left. I'd stupidly started thinking right about in here that he'd propose to me soon. After all, he'd told me plenty of times that he loved me, couldn't live without me, I'm the best part of his life, blah blah blah, so I really thought that this was it." She grimaced, and then hurled the pinecone into the forest where it landed with an unsatisfying *puff* in the dirt.

She spotted a pale pink wildflower with petals sticking out in every direction and plucked it, immediately getting to work denuding the bloom. There was something satisfying about pulling the flower apart, just like her life had been pulled apart without her permission.

"I was pretty stressed at this point – working hard on my classes, working hard at the gas station, my roommate was a slob who couldn't cook, so working hard back at the apartment keeping things clean...I didn't notice that my period was late for quite a while. I've never been the best about keeping track of when it was supposed to hit, so it was just one of those, 'You know, I haven't bled in a while' moments when it finally dawned on me.

"But, it was coming up on the end of the school year, and I didn't want to know. I didn't want to be sidetracked with all of that right as I was finishing up the worst math class on the face of the planet: Introduction to Probability and Statistics. Bookkeeping makes total sense to me; theoretical math kicks my ass. So I decided to basically stick my head in the sand and ignore it all. If I didn't pee on a stick, then it wouldn't be real. And hey, some girls stop bleeding because of stress, and I certainly had enough of that. Maybe that's all this was. When you don't want to know something, you can justify ignoring it ten ways to Sunday, all before breakfast." She laughed, but there wasn't much humor in the laugh.

She tossed the completely denuded stem to the

side and snagged another wildflower, starting in on destroying it. It was something she could control, concentrate on, work on and succeed, and in that moment, it was the only thing keeping her sane.

"Fast forward to the beginning of May. Norman texts me that he's going to be coming back through, and I realize that with finals done – I'd finished the last of them that morning – I needed to confront the big, scary monster in the corner, and pee on a damn stick. I go over to Walgreens, buy a pregnancy test, and sure enough, the big ol' plus sign pops up. At this point, I'm feeling slightly ill – this was never part of the plan. Norman and I had *always* used condoms. He'd insisted on it. Usually it's the girl pushing for protection, but Norman told me that he cared too much about me to get me pregnant on accident. I'm thinking there was a hole in one of the condoms or something…? I guess we'll never know.

"He came over that night; I'd talked my roommate into leaving so I could have the apartment to myself. I told Norman about the pregnancy. I was hoping…I was hoping he'd be happy?" She said it like a question because looking back on it, it just seemed ridiculous beyond words. "I know that sounds naïve," she rushed on, "but he'd told me how much he loved me, and I just thought…I thought he'd want to marry me."

She stopped in the middle of the road and Adam stopped too, looking at her quizzically. But she wanted to be looking him straight in the eye when she confessed her sins so that when he blinked or turned away or looked at her with scorn, she'd know, and she could move on with her life without him.

Because she wasn't about to be in another relationship where the guy looked down at her as being inferior. Not now, not ever.

"What I didn't know was that he was already married."

She said it baldly, and then waited for the reaction. He could call her a whore or a home wrecker. He could stare at her judgmentally. He could—

But he didn't. None of that, or anything else. He just blinked, and then waited for her to continue.

"Aren't you going to say something? Call me a name?" she demanded, a little hysterically.

He cocked his head to the side, obviously surprised. "I already knew that, though," he said, and she could tell he thought he was pointing out the obvious.

"Hold on, what? How did you know he was married?" He couldn't know Norman, right? She rubbed her forehead.

"Well, I guess I shouldn't say that I knew for sure, but I was pretty sure. One of Mom's friends was at the bakery last night, and she called after the whole mess happened, wanting my mom to tell me so I knew who I'd hired." He rolled his eyes. "Anyway, at the bakery, Tiffany accused you of getting pregnant with a married man, and you didn't deny it." He shrugged.

"So you knew all of that, and you still told me that you loved me, back in the truck?" she said, completely confused. She rubbed her forehead harder. "Don't you hate me now?"

"Hate you? Because a guy lied to you and used your trusting nature against you? Because you fell in love with a guy who pretended to be someone he was not, and you didn't find out the truth until too late? I might think that you're naïve, but I wouldn't hate you. And anyway, you're 22 years old. It's easy to be naïve at that point. This mess says a whole lot more about Norman than it does about you."

She felt tears well up in her eyes, but instead of burning their way down her cheeks, they were happy tears. Tears of joy. "I can't believe it," she whispered. "I never expected…"

He pulled her up against his chest and stroked her hair, slowly, steadily, rhythmically. "Kylie darlin', you need to stop beating yourself up for this. Shit happens. It isn't your fault."

"Well, *I* know that," she said, laughing as she pulled away, swiping at the tears of joy running down her cheeks, "but this is *Sawyer*. You said it yourself – someone called to tell your mom to tell you so you could know what kind of trashy woman you hired to work at the clinic. No one would think twice about you firing me right here, right now."

He smiled sadly down at her, using his thumbs to catch the last of the stray tears off her cheeks. "You gotta stop thinking of every person in Sawyer as being ridiculously old-fashioned. Yeah, there's a few people here and there who are like that, but hell, I don't want to work with assholes like that anyway."

"But you might lose business over this," Kylie protested automatically, even as she snuggled her cheek into the palm of his hand. She missed human contact. She wanted to do nothing but lie with him, chest to chest, and soak up his presence, his smell, his muscles.

He laughed. "You and my mom. You guys seem to think that this would be some sort of punishment or something. You've seen my schedule – you know that it could stand to be a little less full. If some crusty, jackass of a farmer doesn't want me to help his horse with a lame hoof because my secretary is naïve and trusting and loving, well hell…I hope he finds another vet, only because the horse needs to be taken care of no matter what the owner says or does. But *I* sure as shit don't need the business."

She pulled back and looked up into his whiskey brown eyes. "Secretary…or girlfriend?" she whispered, her voice catching a little as she asked. She couldn't believe she had the guts to ask, but then again, this entire conversation was in the realm of unbelievable.

His eyes darkened as he looked down at her. "Girlfriend, if she'll have me. I was an ass to her just a few hours ago, so she might not—"

She leaned up on her tippy toes and kissed him into silence.

Well, not *silence*. He groaned, burying his hands in her hair and tilting her head to the side, plundering her mouth, his fingers pushing into her skull as he begged with his body for her to love him back.

She felt like she was floating on a cloud of lust and desire as she threw her arms around his neck, pulling him closer. How was it that such a beautiful man, inside and out, wanted *her*? But even as she wondered, she told herself that she shouldn't question fate. Because there was nothing else to believe, but that fate had brought them together.

Finally, he gently put her back down on the ground and her eyes floated open.

"Girlfriend it is," she whispered, stroking the light stubble on his jaw.

"Well, girlfriend," he said teasingly, "do you want to go on a date with me? A real one? Not a grocery shopping trip to Boise pseudo-date?"

"Oh, yes please. Can we eat on our date?" she asked eagerly. "I've been in a perpetual state of hunger lately. They weren't kidding when they said that you start eating for two."

He threw his head back and laughed. "I think we can arrange to end up at a restaurant," he said, pulling her back in for another quick kiss.

Okay, so maybe *quick* wasn't the right word. Ten minutes later or so, Adam scooped Kylie up into his arms and began carrying her back towards his truck. "Adam!" she squealed. "What are you doing?!" Even as she protested, she was wrapping her arms around his neck and instinctively, she began running her fingers through the curls at the nape of his neck.

He bounced her for just a moment, and she squealed and wrapped her arms around him even tighter. He grinned down at her. "Now that's better," he said with a naughty smile. "You weigh hardly a thing. It's damn good we're going to go eat. I can't have my girlfriend starving to death!"

She pulled one of her arms free to pat her belly. "I promise you, I'm not starving. I carry babies the same way my momma does, so in about another week, there'll be exactly zero chance of me continuing to hide this baby bump of mine."

He nuzzled her ear. "You are going to be the cutest pregnant momma this side of the Mississippi," he growled in her ear, sending shivers down her spine. He stopped next to the passenger door of the truck, letting her pull on the door handle so it could swing open. He slid her inside onto the passenger seat, not letting her feet touch the ground. "In fact, while we're in Franklin, I think we ought to take you clothes shopping. I'm assuming you've been wearing the oversized sweatshirts and yoga pants to try to hide the pregnancy?"

"Yes…" she said hesitantly, "but I also don't have the money to buy a whole new wardrobe, at least not right now. I was going to wait for another couple of paychecks and then—"

"You say I'm no good at being Casanova," he said gently, breaking into her worried stream of consciousness, "but you're not much better at being spoiled."

"'Spoiled'?" she echoed.

"Yeah, spoiled. Because of the most amazing secretary on the face of the planet, I actually have money in my bank account to spend on my sexy, sexy girlfriend." Her mouth made an O as she stared at him. *Sexy?* Maybe Gage wasn't the only Sawyerite in need of glasses. Her waistline was getting thicker by the day, and she was already getting stretch marks that she was pretty sure she was stuck with for life.

Before she could inform him of his apparent need for glasses, though, he planted a kiss on her lips – a short one for realsies this time – and whispered, "Let me spoil you. Let me do everything I'd wanted to do with Wendy but couldn't. God has given me a do-over, and I'm not going to mess it up this time."

She nodded and settled back against the seat. She, too, was getting a do-over. There was a chance that she could finally have the relationship she'd thought she was building with Norman.

If she just didn't screw it up, she might get her happily ever after, after all.

CHAPTER 26

KYLIE

*W*ITH HER SMALL shopping basket slung over her arm, Kylie wandered the aisles of Second Time Around, pulling whisks and wooden spoons and a beat-up set of measuring cups out of the tangled piles on the shelves. She'd come down to the thrift store after work with the intention of buying a couple of things for the living room – maybe a lamp or end table – but had somehow found herself in the kitchen area instead.

Ahem. Yeah. Somehow…

She rolled her eyes at herself. She was incorrigible, truly.

Even though she really shouldn't be buying another large mixing bowl, she told herself that it'd make the Keep Adam Fed project a lot easier if she had two, and snatched the rose-patterned bowl off the shelf. It was gorgeous – a pale pink with hand-painted roses on the side, it would absolutely look at home in

Ruby's kitchen. Even better, it'd look at home in Kylie's kitchen, what with the shabby-chic vibe she had going on.

Shabby chic was a decorating trend that Kylie was almost positive originated with women who hadn't been blessed with deep pockets, but had been blessed with a sense of style. It was one of the few trends that was actually friendly on ye olde budget, something Kylie appreciated to the depths of her very empty bank account.

As she continued to browse, looking through the plates for some decent ones that could be vaguely thought of as matching, she spotted a small sign at the end of the aisle and wandered over to take a closer look.

Shopping at Second Time Around helps support the residents of the Long Valley Senior Citizen's Center. All profits are used to run activities and to provide creature comforts to the elderly in our community. Thank you for your support!

Huh. Kylie hadn't exactly shopped in Second Time Around as a high school student, and so somehow, she'd missed this piece of information.

She carted her overflowing basket up to the front counter and set it down with a thump. The older woman behind the counter, a cloud of white hair bobbing around her face with every movement, laughed a little as she began sorting out Kylie's haul so she could ring it up.

"You found some nice items in here," the woman

said admiringly. "I do love shopping at a thrift store. It's like a treasure hunt!"

"It really is," Kylie said with a satisfied grin. It was a treasure hunt, and she'd struck gold. "So, I noticed the signage back there about the profits going to the senior citizen's center. Somehow, I'd missed that before. How long's that been going on?"

"Well now," the woman said, ruminating as she separated the items into piles, "a long time, I s'pose. Second Time Around used to be run by the Methodist Church, but they had a hard time finding volunteers who were reliable enough to keep a store like this open."

She shrugged. "It's damn hard to find people who want to work for free all the time. Funny that." She let out a boisterous laugh. "But the gal who runs the senior citizen's center came up with the idea of taking it over; she said that one thing that seniors miss the most is a purpose in life. Although it sounds like fun to do nothin' but sit around on your hindquarters all day and play pinochle, you start to get bored after a while. Grandkids and kids...they have their own lives. They can't spend their days entertaining their grandparents. So, the Methodist Church signed the store over to the center with a real strict contract that it can't ever be converted to for-profit, and all revenue has to go back to the center. We've been keeping it running ever since."

She'd been steadily beeping the items through the scanner as they'd talked, and once she'd worked her way through the pile, she looked up at Kylie. "That'll be $39.42, please."

Kylie gulped, but handed over two twenties. She obviously couldn't indulge in a shopping spree every day after work, buying up gorgeous mixing bowls, but just this load would be a huge help in making her rental into a home.

As the volunteer was counting back her change, Kylie's mind jumped back to Ruby, sitting at home, gnarled hands keeping her from doing much, but a real desire to still contribute to the world. "How long are the shifts when you work here?" she asked, dropping the coins into her purse and slinging it over her shoulder.

The older woman shrugged. "As long as you can work," she said simply. "You tell the director what you're physically capable of, and she puts a schedule together. They have a bus that runs back and forth from the center to here pretty much all day long. Some people like to sort donations in the back, some people like to stock the shelves, and some like to run the cash register. Up here is my favorite because then I get to talk to people all day long, and not a soul who shops here wants to discuss how many times a day they drink Metamucil to keep themselves regular, either!"

Kylie snort-laughed, her eyes huge as she stared in disbelief at the elderly woman. "Metamucil?" she choked out.

"Some of the topics they talk about over breakfast

at the center…" The woman shook her head in disgust. "I try to tell 'em it isn't good for digestion, but they still keep talkin' about it anyway. Working here… I can't stand too long—" she gestured to a cane in the corner, "but it's amazing how having something to do each day changes your mindset."

"Thank you," Kylie said with a grateful smile. "I appreciate the information, and your hard work as a volunteer here."

"Sure, sure!" the woman said cheerfully. "Be sure to come on back real soon; we get donations all the time."

With a wave to the friendly woman, Kylie carted her treasures out to her new-to-her car and loaded it up. After Adam had taken her out on their first real date the day before, he'd cancelled all of his appointments this morning and had spent the day tuning up her car instead. He'd proudly handed over the keys to the Grand Marquis at closing time.

Despite the fact that it was so oversized, calling it a boat didn't quite do it justice, Kylie still couldn't believe it was hers. Or that she had a whole house to herself. All the way home, she just kept shaking her head in wonderment. It was like she was a real adult or something, with a car *and* a home of her own.

Home. What a lovely word. As she began putting her thrift store finds away, she looked around her with a huge grin. The old farmhouse was slowly becoming hers, a reflection of her values and what made her happy.

She ran her hand over her rounded belly and said softly, "You hear that, baby? We've got ourselves a home, you and me. I can't wait to show it to you."

She grabbed her laptop from the corner and settled down into the worn couch, the springs creaking beneath her weight as she began browsing the internet, doing another round of research on ways to use goat and cow's milk. She didn't want to be in charge of pasteurizing the milk or getting a health and safety certificate in order to sell milk or cream to others. But lotion, soap, and other body products didn't require any certification at all, and as long as she only mixed in healthy ingredients to provide a rich scent, she certainly couldn't make someone sick from the products.

She pulled up a how-to article and got to work with a piece of paper and pen, taking notes. She'd crack this yet.

CHAPTER 27

ADAM

*A*DAM PULLED the front door open, the doorbell jangling overhead, and breathed in deep. *Ahhh…coffee.* Even if Kylie did nothing but make coffee for him every morning, he'd still think she was amazing.

The fact that she did so much more than that…he really felt like God had been smiling down on him when she'd shown up at the clinic all those weeks ago.

Kylie came hurrying up from the back. "Good morning!" she said cheerfully when she spotted him. "I have the coffee started."

"I could smell it as soon as I came in." He pulled her into his arms and nibbled on her neck. She squirmed at the contact, moaning sexily with pleasure, and he felt his dick rising to the occasion, happy for the contact. *Down, boy. Not now.*

He pulled back, if only to give himself some breathing room from her. "I used to think that one of my favorite smells in the world was the scent of animal and coffee together."

"Animal?" she repeated, looking at him askance.

"Yeah, but I've changed my mind." He bent back and began nuzzling her neck again, and his dick sprang right back up. "I like wildflowers more."

"Oh, really," she said faintly, tilting her head to the side to give him better access to her neck. "You're a flowers kind of a guy, huh?"

"Your perfume has been driving me wild since day one," he admitted as he breathed in her unique scent. "I even thought about telling you that I was allergic to it, because my self-control was struggling with the idea that I had to keep my hands to myself."

She looped her hands around his neck and sent him a saucy grin. "Hmmm…good to know…I may just have to use this information at a future date."

He rubbed his stubble against her neck, and she collapsed with laughter against him. "Be kind to me," he murmured in her ear. "It's been…a long dry spell. A man can only take so much."

She pulled back and bit her lower lip as she looked up at him through her eyelashes. "Something else I will keep in mind…"

The neanderthal in him wanted to throw her over his shoulder and cart her back to her place and make love to her all day and if he was lucky, all night, but he barely restrained himself.

Barely.

He had a full load of patients today, all here in the

clinic, which meant that he got to spend the day around Kylie. He wasn't sure if this was the best thing that had ever happened to him, or pure torture. Keeping his hands to himself in front of the clients was gonna be a *real* test of self-restraint.

Speaking of, he needed to get to work. He reluctantly moved away from Kylie and headed to the back where he grabbed a mug off the shelf. "Today's the last day of therapy camp using the school schedule," he said over his shoulder as he poured himself a cup of coffee. "Then I have a two-week break, then we start summer camp. I was thinking you might have fun coming over today and helping out with it. You'll love these kids – they're a real handful but boy, are they sweet."

"Oh, that sounds like so much fun!" Kylie said excitedly, shooting him one of her 100-watt grins. "I'd love to. Are you thinking we'll close the clinic again so I can come with you?"

"Yeah, one afternoon won't kill anyone," he said as he went to work checking on the patients, barking and meowing their hellos to him. "The kids are gonna think you're the best thing since sliced bread."

"Well, I can't wait," Kylie said happily, and then headed back up front to get to work.

Adam found himself whistling a tuneless song as he checked the animals over. When was the last time he'd been this happy? He couldn't remember. Forever, it seemed like.

Life couldn't get much better than this.

CHAPTER 28

KYLIE

THERE WERE ABOUT a million of them milling around, talking and laughing as they waited for class to begin. Most of the students had some sort of physical impairment that Kylie could spot – coke-bottle glasses or a limp or a protruding tongue. A few showed no scars on the outside, and Kylie knew that for these students, the hidden scars were probably even worse.

The scars you couldn't see were the hardest ones to get over, something she knew all too well.

"Okay, everyone, listen up!" Adam was standing up at the front of the barn, and almost instantly, every pair of eyes were trained on him, and the constant hum of noise disappeared. Kylie was impressed – Adam had obviously been working with these kids for a while now to garner that sort of attention so quickly. "I have a helper here today who I want to introduce you to. Kylie, can you come up here?"

"Oh, sure," she said, embarrassed as every eye in the place swung towards her. She hadn't expected this and gave Adam a playful glare as she walked up to the front. He winked at her in return.

He'd *obviously* been intimidated. She sighed to herself. She really needed to work on that steely-eyed glare…

"This is Kylie VanLueven," he said to the group. "She's my secretary back at the clinic, and will also be coming out here to help with the camp sometimes. Can everyone say hi to Kylie?"

"Hi, Kylie," came a chorus of voices.

She looked at the group of eager faces and couldn't help but grin back. "Hi! I'm so excited to be here. I can't wait to get to know you all."

"Are you Dr. Whitaker's girlfriend?" shouted one of the boys in the back. Tittering and laughter spread through the kids at the question.

Kylie did a fine impersonation of a goldfish for a moment, mouth agape, not sure what to say, when Adam countered back smoothly, "Wouldn't you like to know! Quick reminder everyone, today is the last day of school hours. After this, we do summer camp hours. Did you guys all enjoy your last day of school?"

"Yeah!" a couple of the boys shouted, and then pandemonium descended as every student tried to tell Adam and Kylie what had happened that day. From what Kylie could gather, not much had changed since she was in elementary school – they'd had a water day, had eaten ice cream sandwiches, and had cleaned out their lockers. The city fire department had even driven a firetruck over to the school. The firefighters had turned on the siren while shooting a stream of water into the air for the kids to run under, which according to everyone there, was the highlight of the day, even above and beyond the ice cream sandwiches.

Hmmm…ice cream. I could eat some ice cream right now.

She felt her stomach rumble at the thought, but forced herself to concentrate. She could eat ice cream later. *Oh yeah…I could eat french vanilla ice cream with blueberries and chocolate syrup and gummy bears and coconut shreds and…*

Focus, Kylie! She was supposed to be supervising children, not daydreaming about cookie dough ice cream, with raspberry syrup and—

She forced herself to start walking around, and soon found herself working with a girl, brunette hair in pigtails and braces on her teeth, who quickly began giving Kylie lessons on how to brush a horse. "You have to go from the head to the tail," the little girl said seriously, flashing a mouth full of metal up at Kylie. "Horses don't like it if you go the other way. Sonny loves everyone but he loves me the mostest. Can you get the oats out of the barrel? I need to feed him."

Kylie's head spun, trying to keep up with the little girl's stream of thoughts, but hurried over to the barrels that she'd pointed out. Kylie grabbed a small bucket off the top of the stack and a scoop, and filled up the bucket.

"Thank you," the girl said politely, before turning to the horse, bucket in hand. Sonny began snuffling up the oats in record time, using his lips to suck up every last one in the bucket before plaintively nudging the little girl's shoulder for more. "Can we give him more?" she pleaded, her big eyes begging Kylie adorably.

Kylie looked down at her and panicked a little. "Uhhh…let me ask Dr. Whitaker. I'll be right back."

She hurried across the dusty barn to Adam, who was busy refereeing a dispute between two boys. When he finished and sent them off in opposite directions to get back to work, he looked up with a harried smile.

"Ummm…that little girl over there——" she pointed towards the pigtailed girl who was brushing Sonny carefully from head to tail, "—wants to know if she can give her horse a second bucket of oats."

"No," Adam said with a laugh. "Jenny knows better. She's just hoping that with you being the new person and all, you won't. Don't let her talk you into giving Sonny more than one bucket per day. She knows the rules."

"Okay, thanks," she said, flashing Adam a quick smile before turning to head back across the barn.

"Kylie!" he called out, and grabbed her hand.

She turned back, surprised, even as bolts of excitement shot up her arm. Would she ever tire of being around Adam? It was hard to imagine that happening, although intellectually, she understood that it was possible.

Just like it was possible for the moon to fall from the sky.

"Thanks for the help," he said softly. "And thanks for asking. Jenny would do almost anything for that horse, and that includes trying to bend the rules."

"Of course," she said, and reluctantly pulled away. Leaving Adam's side was painful, to say the least, but she wasn't here to make googly eyes at her boss/boyfriend. She was here to work with the kids. She hurried back across the barn.

"Okay, girlfriend," she told Jenny, "Dr. Whitaker said only one bucket per day."

Realizing that her attempt to play the new person had failed, Jenny instantly decided to change the topic. "My name isn't 'Girlfriend,'" she told Kylie seriously. "It's Genny with a G."

"Oh. Right. Of course." Kylie hid her grin behind her hand. "Well, Genny with a G, are you ready to saddle Sonny up?"

"Yes, please!" Thrilled that the topic was back to what she loved most of all – riding horses – Genny grabbed Kylie's hand and began dragging her across the barn to where the tack was stored.

Kylie was a bit rusty on how to saddle up a horse, but with Genny's guidance, they got it done. Genny led Sonny over to the mounting block and swung up onto his back, grinning like she'd just won the Kentucky

Derby. With a click of the tongue and a light tap on the sides of the horse, Sonny began ambling towards the open door of the barn and out onto the worn, dirt oval to join the stream of other horses and riders.

Kylie followed her out into the sunshine and over to the fence to lean against it, watching the horses plod by, grins and shouts from the kids over the sheer joy of it all. A few were working on cantering, which Kylie thought looked like a good way to bounce all of your teeth out of your head if you didn't know what you were doing, but hell, the kids looked like they were loving it, so who was she to question their choices?

Her eyes were drawn to a slender, Hispanic boy with large brown eyes and a look of total concentration on his face. He was young, of course, maybe ten or twelve years old, but Kylie could already tell he was going to be a heartbreaker when he grew up. Amidst the yelling and laughter of the other students, he seemed overly serious, as if every move he made was a life-or-death decision.

"Kylie, Kylie, look!" Genny hollered, pulling her attention away and back towards the girl bouncing along on Sonny. "I'm gantering!"

Kylie just smiled and waved, hiding her laughter at the mispronunciation. Genny was a force to be reckoned with, even if she didn't know how to pronounce every word properly.

Way too quickly, it was time to wrap up and the children began leading the horses inside to unsaddle them and brush them down. Parents began arriving, and heroics were shared as the kids began regaling them with all of their derring do.

Kylie watched as Genny began telling her tired-looking mother all about the excitement of the day, waving goodbye to Kylie as she left, never missing a beat in her story.

Kylie then saw the county deputy – April? Abigail? Annie? Something with an A – arrive, holding hands with the oldest Miller boy. They were both way older than Kylie – she'd probably been a babe in arms when they were graduating from high school – but their love for each other appeared to still be just as strong as ever. She wondered when they'd gotten married. Had they been married since high school? Probably. They had that aurora of stable love about them, as if they knew what the other person was going to do or say even before it happened.

The quiet Hispanic boy Kylie had been watching earlier went hurrying over to the couple and began chattering up a storm about riding Ladybug and he'd saddled her all by himself and he rode faster than the other kids and…

She was completely fascinated by the abrupt personality change. Before the Millers had shown up, she hadn't seen him say a word to anyone, but now, he was lit up like a Christmas tree.

Once he'd finally wound down, Mr. Miller looped his arm around the boy's shoulders and said with a big grin, "C'mon, Juan, let's head home. Mom's got dinner in the oven already, and you know she won't put up with us being late for dinner."

"Hey, I heard that," Mrs. Miller said, laughing. "You make me sound like an ogre!" They continued their playful banter out the door and into the sunlight. Kylie watched them go, her curiosity piqued. Had the Millers adopted Juan? It sure sounded like it.

Once again, she was regretting not being plugged into the Long Valley Gossip Network. There was a real difference between knowing all of the gossip, and being the center of all of the gossip. One was significantly more pleasurable than the other, that was for damn sure.

Finally, all of the kids were gone and it was just her and Adam left in the barn. "So, what did you think?" he asked as he came striding over to pull her into his arms. Before she could say anything, he leaned down and gave her a thorough kiss. "I've been waiting for hours to do that," he told her with a lazy grin when he pulled away.

She couldn't help the silly answering smile that spread across her face. "Me too," she said, and then blushed. She still wasn't used to the idea that Adam Whitaker was her boyfriend. "Anyway," she said, hurrying on before her face could turn a brilliant tomato red, "I can see why you do this, but also why you're exhausted from it! These kids…they're amazing. A real handful, but amazing. Speaking of the kids, what's the story with Juan? Was he adopted by the Millers?"

Adam nodded slowly. "His parents weren't stand-up citizens, to put it mildly, and when Juan first started coming to camp, he had a chip on his shoulder the size of Texas. He was in the foster care system at that point, and boy, was he pissed at everyone. Defensive, snarky, always having to one-up everyone around him...he wasn't the most popular kid in the class, let's put it that way." They began wandering around the barn and cleaning up, putting stray pieces of tack and brushes away as they talked.

"So in January of last year," Adam continued, "Wyatt started helping me with these classes, and he and Juan hit it off. Wyatt said that Juan was his mini-me; he understood the attitude for what it was − a front to hide pain and fear behind. Anyway, so after Wyatt and Abby got married last September, they started the paperwork to adopt him." *Oh. So they definitely* haven't *been together since high school. Whoops...* "He's living with them full-time but the legal system moves slowly, and the adoption isn't official yet. They're hoping it will be this fall. It sure is funny to see a guy that you graduated with grow and change as much as Wyatt Miller has." Adam shook his head in disbelief. "Actually, Juan and Wyatt have both done a shit-ton of changing, and all for the better. I think we have Abby to thank for that."

"Hold on, you graduated with Wyatt Miller?" Kylie said, her stomach dropping to around her toes. Sometimes, it was easy to forget that there was an age gap between them, but when Adam said something like that so casually... "But, but Wyatt is *old!*" she protested.

Adam threw his head back and laughed. "I'll be sure not to share that assessment with him, or with Abby. She's only three years younger than Wyatt and me."

"Sorry," Kylie mumbled, her cheeks red with embarrassment. "I know that you're older than me, but sometimes...I guess I just forget how much older."

Adam pulled her back into his arms, wrapping them around her and snuggling her up against his chest. "An adult is an adult," he said seriously to the top of her head, his warm breath blowing over the part in her hair, like air kisses. "It's not like you're 12 and I'm 28. We're both adults, and we are legally and morally a-okay to love each other. Just...uh...leave all mention of how old you think someone is when you're hanging out with my friends."

Kylie nodded, rubbing her face up against his chest as she did so. "Deal," she mumbled, suddenly feeling exhausted beyond all reason. "Why am I so tired?" she asked rhetorically around a huge yawn.

"It takes a lot out of a person to grow another human being inside of them," Adam said seriously, pulling back and looking down at her with concern. "Are you okay to drive home? Or do you want to go inside my mom's house and take a nap before you drive back?"

"I'm all right," she insisted, rubbing her eyes. "I'll go home and sleep this off. It's not that far of a drive."

Adam led her out into the brilliant summer sunshine and slid the barn doors closed behind them. "Well, I'm going to be a hovering pain in the ass and follow you back to your place, just in case. If you need to talk to me while you drive, you can always put your phone on speakerphone and we can chat as I follow you."

"No, no, I'm good," Kylie insisted. She gave him one last kiss goodbye and climbed into the Marquis. True to his word, he followed her all the way back. She waved goodbye to him as she unlocked the front door and stumbled inside, heading for the couch and dropping like a rock onto it. Her eyes closed and she fell asleep almost instantly, out like a light.

She awoke, disoriented in the darkness. The sun must've set long ago, which meant...*Oh shit!* She sat straight up on the couch, fumbling for her phone where she'd dropped it on the hardwood floor when she'd done her swan dive onto the couch. Yup, 10:22 at night. *Dammit.* She was late feeding and milking the animals. They were going to be unhappy with her, that was for sure. She hadn't even managed to get her shoes off when she'd gotten home, so at least she was able to save that step and just hurry out the backdoor towards the barn.

Except, Dumbass and Skunk weren't lowing their displeasure into the summer night, and the barn door between the pasture and the barn appeared to already be closed. Kylie squinted through the darkness, trying to figure out if it was closed, or if the shadows were just playing tricks on her. She opened up the main door to the barn and stepped inside to find all of the animals bedded down for the night, and pails of milk in the fridge, along with a fresh carton of eggs.

Kylie looked at it all, shaking her head in wonder. If there was one thing Adam was good at, it was showing her that he loved her through his actions, not just his words.

She flipped off the light and closed the door behind her, heading back towards the house, a smile of joy and love spreading across her lips. After six months of listening to Norman declare his love for her, only to find out that he was actually married… protestations of love didn't mean much to her. Words were easy to say, and completely meaningless if the person saying them was a jackass.

But actions…Adam was thoughtful and kind in a way that Norman could never even dream of being. More than Adam's inadvertent declaration of love earlier that week, his actions yelled his love for her from the rooftops.

Kylie climbed the stairs to her bedroom, shucked off her shoes, and crawled into bed, still in her clothes. She didn't care; right now, she could sleep anywhere, anytime.

She drifted right back to sleep and dreamt sexy dreams of a cowboy with whiskey brown eyes, cradling a baby in his arms.

"*H*EY, ADAM," Wyatt's voice came through the phone loud and clear, "I just realized that it's coming up on a year since the last check-up of Maggie Mae. Are you gonna be anywhere in the vicinity of my farm in the next day or two?"

Adam cradled his phone between his ear and shoulder as he cleaned out Hero's hoof. "Yup. I'm out at your brother's place right now, actually, so I can be over right after this."

"Great, see you then."

Adam hung up and slipped his phone back into his shirt pocket before getting back to work on Hero's hoof. When Wyatt had been locked up in the Long Valley County Jail for months by the local judge who had a vendetta against him, his loyal and faithful dog, Maggie Mae, had just about starved herself to death, refusing to eat without Wyatt there beside her. Ever since then, Wyatt had insisted on yearly wellness checks of his dog, certainly not something most farmers and ranchers in the area did. It was good to see a person love his dog as much as the dog loved that person.

Some people took a dog's love for granted, but not Wyatt.

Adam stood up and patted Hero's hindquarters. "All done, handsome," he told the gelding. "Ready for some sweet grass?" He led the horse out of the barn and out into the adjoining pasture, waiting for a moment to be sure that he was settling in happily, and then looked around for Declan.

There was no sight of him, though; hell, Declan was probably off kissing his new wife, Iris. They were two lovebirds who could hardly keep their hands off each other. Just a couple of months earlier, it'd been hard for Adam to see the lovestruck gazes they were sending each other, but now...well, it reminded him a bit of him and Kylie.

Just a little bit.

Obviously, Adam and Kylie's lovestruck gazes to each other weren't nearly as painfully clear for everyone to see, though, or as vomit-inducing.

Obviously.

Oh well, Adam could catch up with Declan later. He really should be heading out to the Cowell's place again to check on their mare's progress instead of going over to Wyatt's, but hell, Wyatt's farm was just a hop, skip, and a jump away. It wouldn't take him long to look Maggie Mae over, and then he could hurry over to the Cowell's with no one the wiser about his detour.

He pulled up in front of Wyatt's new place – a giant of a house that Wyatt had built specifically so he and Abby could adopt a "whole passel" of foster children and give them a true home. Like Adam had told Kylie a couple of weeks ago, watching Wyatt change and grow over the last 18 months had been a sight to behold, and in some ways, Adam was still in disbelief. A *good* disbelief, but one nonetheless. He'd always known Wyatt had a heart of gold, but he'd buried it so far down, it had required some heavy-duty mining equipment to get to it, and a whole lot of patience.

Luckily for the world, Abby was just stubborn enough for the job. Adam figured Wyatt ought to be down on his knees daily, thanking God for sending him Abby. Getting that lucky just didn't happen every day.

Maggie Mae came darting out of the shop, circling Adam's truck, her tail wagging enthusiastically. She sure seemed healthy, but of course, looks could always be deceiving. Adam grabbed his vet bag and swung out of the truck, giving the loving cattle dog a brisk pat on the head before heading into the shop. Wyatt looked up from the workbench, and shot Adam a huge smile.

"Thanks for coming over today," Wyatt said, striding over and shaking hands with Adam. "She looks like the picture of health, of course," he gestured down at Maggie Mae that'd made her way back inside and was sitting loyally next to him, "but you never know. I—" He cocked his head. "Hold on," he said, moving towards the shop door and poking his head out. This time, Adam could hear it, too – Abby was asking him something, her voice floating on the breeze. "The wife calls!" Wyatt said to Adam over his shoulder with an easy grin. "I'll be right back."

Maggie Mae began to follow Wyatt, but he stopped her. "Stay," he told her, and she sat down with a whine as she watched him go. Adam laughed a little to himself. It was hard to know who loved Wyatt more – his dog, his wife, or his soon-to-be adopted son. It was quite the contest at this point.

When Wyatt had left, Adam knelt in front of the sweet mutt and began doing a quick inspection, checking her teeth and tongue, then moving to check her pupils and their responsiveness—

"Hi, Dr. Whitaker," a softly accented voice said behind him shyly. Adam swung his head around, astounded that Juan had snuck up on him like that.

"Hey, Juan!" he said with a laugh, turning back to Maggie Mae to continue his examination. "You're sure good at sneaking up on a person. What's happenin'?"

"Ummm…I wanted to ask you a question," Juan said seriously. Adam began feeling up and down Maggie's legs to make sure there weren't any lumps or tender spots to be found.

"Yeah?" he said distractedly. "What's going on?"

"I have...I have a friend at school, and he's Mexican but his adopted parents are white and all of the kids at school are teasing him and asking him if he's Mexican or white now and...well, he doesn't know what to say to them."

Adam's hands stilled over Maggie Mae's glossy coat as Juan's story fully registered in his mind. His heart hurt as he turned towards the overly serious boy, who was busy digging the toe of his shoe into the dirt covering the concrete floor.

He absentmindedly began petting Maggie Mae as his mind raced, trying to find the right words to say. "Has your friend talked to his parents about this yet?"

Juan shook his head frantically. "He really likes his parents and he doesn't want them to be angry or sad or somethin', you know? That's why I—*he* thought I should ask you what to do. And then I can tell him."

Adam's stomach twisted with dread and anger. If this was already starting, what was it going to be like when Juan hit junior high?

"What grade are you and your friend in?" he asked softly, studying the worried boy in front of him.

"Fourth grade. Well, school just finished. I'll be in fifth grade next year. And my friend, too," he added hastily.

Adam fought to hide his smile. Juan could be many things when he grew up, but a professional liar wasn't one of them.

Instead, he just nodded slowly. "I have a good

friend who teaches fifth grade – Miss Lambert. Do you know her?"

Juan nodded enthusiastically. "She's cool! When she does recess duty, she actually talks to the kids instead of just yelling all the time."

"She is a real nice lady – she even owns horses of her own. I helped her mare Wildflower give birth to a little foal not too long ago. Anyway, is most of this happening at school?"

Juan nodded again, back to kicking the dirt. "Yeah, during recess and stuff."

"Well, I think it's real important that your friend gets Miss Lambert as a teacher this next school year, and if other kids start in on that shi–crap," he quickly corrected himself, "your friend can tell Miss Lambert and get help."

"But…is he white? Or is he Mexican?" Juan whispered, his eyes huge as he stared at Adam pleadingly.

Oh God, oh God, oh God, I don't even know how to approach this topic…

"Did you know that I went to school for eight years to be a vet?" he asked Juan rhetorically. Juan shook his head anyway. "In all of that time in school, not once did a teacher say that a black dog needed to have different treatment than a white or spotted dog. You know why?" Juan shook his head again. "Because there is no difference at all underneath the skin. If you look at the muscle or the bones or the heart or the liver, they're exactly the same, no matter what color the skin is on top. It's true for animals, and it's true for humans.

"Now, you might start to notice over time that your Mexican friends celebrate holidays that your white friends do not, like Cinco de Mayo, and the same is true the other way. The really awesome part is, because you're part of both cultures, you get to celebrate *all* of the holidays. You get to eat yummy tamales *and* steak and potatoes. You don't have to choose one or the other, you can pick the best out of both worlds. It's like language – you speak Spanish, right?"

"Of course," Juan said with a little *duh* in his voice.

"But you speak English, too."

"Yeah…" he said, his eyebrows creasing, obviously trying to figure out where Adam was going with this.

"Just because you speak Spanish doesn't mean you can't speak English, right? And the other way around. As soon as you speak English, your Spanish doesn't just magically disappear. You have them both in your brain. Well, it's the same with your culture – you can be white *and* Mexican. You can choose the parts you like, and ignore the rest. Anyone who says you have to choose one or the other just isn't lucky like you are. Just because they've chosen one or the other doesn't mean you have to."

"Thanks, Dr. Whitaker!" Juan said, his face lighting up with understanding. "I'll…I'll tell my friend that."

"Of course." Adam stood, brushing the dirt off his knees studiously, struggling to hide his smile.

"What are you going to tell your friend?" Wyatt asked, walking up.

Dammit. Adam hadn't heard him come in. Juan's eyes shot to Adam, pleading for him to keep his secret.

"I was just asking Juan here if he'd be willing to be my assistant at the therapy camp," Adam said smoothly. "He's been with me almost from the beginning and he knows every horse I've got and how to take care of them. I'd love to have another set of hands on deck. I was thinking…five dollars per class?"

"Five dollars!" Juan repeated, his eyes round as saucers. He spun on his heel. "Can I, Dad? *Please?*"

"We'll have to ask your mom, but I don't see why not," Wyatt said, patting his son on the back with pride. "I'm sure glad to hear that you're doing so well at camp."

Juan shot his father a huge grin. "It's easy," he told him. "I don't know why people are scared of horses. Just move slowly, don't stand in their blind spots, and don't scream in their ear."

Adam let out a roar of laughter. "Someone's been listening to my lessons," he said approvingly. He turned back towards Wyatt. "Maggie Mae is looking great. I think she's good to go."

Wyatt shook Adam's hand, gripping his shoulder for a moment. "Thanks," he said softly, just loud enough for Adam to hear. "For everything."

Adam paused, searching his friend's eyes. Had

Wyatt heard what he and Juan were talking about? He couldn't break Juan's confidences, but he hoped Juan would choose to talk to his parents about this soon. Things were only going to get worse the older Juan got.

Finally, Adam nodded slowly and said, "Anytime," just as softly. He turned to Juan. "Therapy camp starts up again on Monday. Come ready to work, okay?"

"Okay!" he exclaimed excitedly. "Thanks, Dr. Whitaker."

"You bet." He did a fist bump with Juan, and then headed out for the Cowell's. The unexpected stop may've put him off his schedule, but it'd been worth it anyway. What Abby and Wyatt were trying to do for the foster children of the world was downright admirable, but that didn't mean that it was easy.

As he drove to the Cowell's, his mind skipped back to his childhood. His mom had loved *South Pacific* and Adam had been forced to watch it dozens of times growing up. The lyrics echoed in his mind...

You've got to be taught before it's too late
Before you are six or seven or eight
To hate all the people your relatives hate
You've got to be carefully taught

How was it that a movie made so long ago, before color TV was even invented, was still so applicable today? Depressing, that's what that was. Would humanity ever learn? He wasn't sure, and wasn't *that* just an awful thought.

That evening, he arrived at his mom's house even

later than normal. He dragged himself out of his truck and up to the front door, trying to stifle a yawn behind his hand as he went. Chasing cows, horses stepping on him, arguing with sheep…his discussion with Juan had ended up being the highlight of his day, and that was really saying something, considering that he still didn't know if he'd said the right thing or not.

Hell, *was* there a "right thing" in that situation? Who knew.

"Hi, Adam," his mom said, cutting into his thoughts. "Rough day at work?" she asked just as he let out another yawn.

He laughed a little. "That obvious, huh?" He pressed a kiss to his mom's cheek and then headed into the kitchen for a glass of water. "How was your day?"

"Fine," she said, in that tone of voice that meant anything but.

Adam went back into the dining room, glass of water in hand, and leaned up against the cool wall, not letting himself sit down at the table with his mom. He was afraid if he sat, he'd never get back up again.

Thanks to Kylie's Keep Adam Fed project, he'd had a healthy breakfast and lunch that day, and for once, it didn't feel like his stomach was eating his backbone. Actually, his stomach was just about the only part of him that didn't ache at the moment.

"What's going on?" he asked, trying to focus on his mom's face through bleary eyes.

"I was wondering if you've called on that CNA

yet," his mom said, staring at the far wall, refusing to meet his eye, embarrassment from even mildly broaching a sensitive topic staining her cheeks red.

"No," he said, the guilt washing over him. "I'm sorry, Mom. It totally slipped my mind. I'll call tomorrow, I promise."

She nodded, unhappy but not arguing the point. Adam felt the guilt pound through him as he kissed his mom goodnight on the cheek and headed to his bedroom. Even with Ollie and Kylie's help, he was still behind on everything and disappointing everyone.

If he didn't find a way to clone himself, and soon, the guilt would be the thing eating through his backbone. He *had* to make his mom more of a priority, starting right now.

He was damned if he knew how, though.

CHAPTER 30

KYLIE

K YLIE SLICED THE BOX OPEN and pulled out every piece of soap-making equipment and ingredient for this project that a body could want, and then some. After her last paycheck from the clinic, she'd set aside what she'd absolutely need for gas, food, and utilities over the next two weeks, and then went online in a wild shopping spree, blowing the rest of the check on soap supplies.

She'd told herself that she had to spend money to make money, but honestly, it'd also been fun to just let loose a little. She'd always been frugal with her money – her roommate had once said that she was tighter than a clam with lockjaw, a phrase that'd caused her to shoot milk out of her nose with laughter when she'd heard it – but even for her, the last two months had been squeezing it pretty tight.

She wrinkled her nose, though, at some of the

ingredients that she pulled out of the box. "Lye? Castor oil? Really?!" she muttered underneath her breath. "I know I live in Idaho, but dayum, this *is* the 21st century. I didn't even know people used castor oil anymore." She huffed out a breath of indignation. "I seriously thought there'd be more rose petals and less lye involved in this project."

It was at this point, looking around her empty house, shadows creeping into the corners from the evening sun, that she regretted not adopting a pet. Adam had taken her to the county animal shelter a couple of times as he went to do check-ups on animals, and the last time, there'd been an adorable dog – a playful ball of white fur and pink tongue – that had been just begging for Kylie to take him home.

Now, she rather wished she had. If she had a pet as a companion, at least then talking out loud wouldn't be *quite* so strange.

She put her hand over her belly. "Soon, I'll have you to talk to," she said down at the rapidly growing bump. "Even better, next week at my doctor's appointment, I get to find out if you're a girl or a boy, and really get to start in on picking out baby names and decorating your room. You already know what you are, but you're not telling, are you?"

She felt a slight flutter underneath her hand in response and she grinned so hard, her cheeks hurt. She'd just started being able to feel the baby kick a couple of days earlier, and honestly, it was an insanely strange and magical feeling that she wasn't sure she'd ever really get used to.

Concentrating on the project again, she made herself get back to work. Once she had everything laid out and inspected for damage, she pulled her laptop over to her side.

"Let's start working through the steps..." she muttered to herself. "Hmmm...frozen goat's milk, coming right up." She pushed herself up off the floor and headed for the freezer. Once she'd found out that to make handmade soap, she should start with frozen goat's milk, she'd given a little cheer. It was perfect, really. Being able to stockpile the milk away without worrying about it going bad before she could get to it had been a load off her mind.

She pulled one of the many quart-sized Ziploc baggies out of the freezer and put it on the counter. She started to cut the bag open – reusing the plastic bag wasn't going to be an option, she could already tell – when she heard Adam's voice calling out. "You here?" he asked, his voice muffled, his boots echoing on the hardwood floors as he wandered through the house, looking for her.

She dropped the frozen block of milk on the counter and wiped her hands on a kitchen towel. "Adam?" she called, hurrying into the living room. "Hey darlin', what are you doing here?" she asked, her heart skipping into overtime at just the sight of him.

Shhiiittttt. This was a gift she hadn't expected to receive. She'd woken up that morning, depressed that it was Saturday and thus she probably wouldn't get to see Adam. She had to be one of the few employees in the world who didn't look forward to weekends. He was always so busy with projects, she felt bad for wanting a piece of his time outside of work.

Having him here in her living room? Best thing that'd happened all day.

He pushed his baseball cap up a little on his forehead, scratching at it, looking insanely tired and bemused at the same time. "I honestly don't know," he said as she threw herself at him, wrapping her arms around him. He pulled her tight up against his chest and she felt just as much as she heard him say, "I just finished with a pig birthing out at Declan Miller's place, and I should've gone home to take a shower and hit the sack since I didn't get much sleep last night, but somehow, I found myself here."

She pulled back just slightly and looked up at him. Close up, she could see the bone-deep tiredness etched across his face, a weariness that just a few hours of sleep wouldn't remedy.

He needed a vacation or a clone, or both. "I'm really sorry to hear it, babe," she said, pressing the palm of her hand to his cheek. "You look tired enough to fall over at any moment."

"I feel tired enough to fall over at any moment," he admitted wryly.

"You should go take a shower. My landlord is

awesome, and he installed a tankless water heater," she winked at him, "so your shower can be as long as you want it to be."

"Hmmm...good idea." He looked down at his filthy clothes and said thoughtfully, "I keep a spare set of clothing in the truck just in case a cow kicks me into a watering trough or something, so I could even put clean clothes on when I'm done. But, are you sure you don't mind? I didn't mean to barge in here just to use your shower."

She laughed. "I'm pretty sure my shower doesn't have a limited number of uses on it," she told him. "Now, go grab your stuff from the truck and head upstairs. When you're done, I *just* might have a meal on the table for you."

His eyes lit up. "Now we're talkin'," he said with a huge grin, but the grin quickly fell away and he looked depressed for a moment. "Dammit, I really want to kiss you right now, but I have so much grit and dirt in my teeth, you could probably start row-croppin' in there." Kylie shuddered as she laughed, and he grinned again. Yup, she could see some dark spots between his teeth. "Let me clean up and then I'll give you a proper kiss. I give you my word." He winked at her, and then headed back out the front door to his truck.

With a happy grin of her own, Kylie headed into the kitchen and straight to the freezer to put the goat's milk back in. She'd tackle that project another time.

Actually having Adam all to herself, without animals or clients or friends around?

Priceless.

She hummed happily as she dug through the fridge, deciding to make a shepherd's pie. It was hearty and filling and not too complicated. As her hands flew over the ingredients, she began to get a quiver of anticipation in her gut...and lower. Adam hadn't said that he'd come over to make love to her, but that didn't mean that it couldn't happen, right?

They'd been taking it plenty slow, what with Adam's past history with Wendy, Kylie's sorry disaster of a relationship with Norm, and then of course, the pregnancy. They'd been restricting themselves to just kisses...okay, and one major make-out fest at his mom's house that'd ended with them scrambling off the couch in record time when they'd heard Ruby stirring around in her bedroom.

Although Kylie applauded the reasons for Adam living with his mom, it did tend to make things...interesting.

Okay, fine, awkward as hell.

But if tonight was the night...

Kylie tried to remember the last time she'd shaved her legs and armpits. *Shit.* She'd gotten out of practice after moving back home to Idaho, because honestly, who was going to complain about hairy legs? The dogs as she helped wrap their legs up in a cast? Not bloody likely.

Maybe she could try slipping upstairs while Adam was otherwise occupied, and run a razor over her legs dry. Yeah, it'd hurt like a son of a bitch, but she could survive. Probably.

Oh, what a girl does for love...

CHAPTER 31

ADAM

*A*DAM CAME DOWNSTAIRS, smelling a little bit like roses but feeling about a million times better. Hell, if rose soap was what it took to feel good again, he'd take a bath in it every day.

Just taking a shower, knowing that Kylie was downstairs, making him dinner, no stress of places to go or other people to take care of...it was heaven on earth.

After his mom's frustrated reminder to kick his ass in gear and make some phone calls a couple of weeks ago, he'd actually carved some time out (okay, okay, he made the calls while driving between appointments) to get his mom taken care of. The CNA had started showing up last week – it was the younger sister to Moose Garrett, actually. Zara was just a kid and originally, the idea of hiring a 16 year old to take care of his mom had seemed like a shitastic idea. What could a teenage girl possibly know about how to take care of an elderly woman?

But Zara and his mom hit it off almost instantly, which had been a huge load off his mind. He'd been able to breathe a huge sigh of relief – his mom was now taken care of.

…Except, if he was going to be honest with himself, she really wasn't. She was still by herself pretty much 75% of the time, and cooking most of her own meals, and doing light household chores and even some heavy duty ones when she thought she could get away with it.

A CNA was only part of the solution, as much as he hated to admit it, no matter how much Zara and Mom liked each other.

"What's wrong?" Kylie asked softly, jerking him out of his thoughts. He looked around the living room, dazed. When had he sat down on the couch?

"Wrong?" he echoed.

"Yeah. You just let out a huge sigh, like the weight of the world is on your shoulders."

"That's because it is," he sniped back instantly. It had slipped out of him – cutting and mean and snarly – and he let out another groan. "I'm sorry. I don't mean to be so…negative. I'm just tired today." *And every day…* But he managed to keep that one to himself by sheer willpower.

She was standing in front of him, his head about even with her chest, and with a mumble about too much stress for one soul to bear, she pulled him forward, cuddling his head against her tits as she rubbed his back and shoulders.

Well, today just got a whole lot more interesting.

She was talking about taking time off work and not booking so many clients and…something something something, but his hearing shut off as he turned his head to nuzzle against her chest. "I know what I want for dinner," he growled, cutting off some piece of advice that he was just sure was accurate, but he really didn't care at the moment.

She let out a delicious giggle. "I worked really hard on this dinner," she protested, even as she let out a happy sigh as he began working her shirt upwards, revealing her rounded belly to his mouth and hands. "We can't let it…let it get cold." She was breathless by the time she finished her sentence.

"I'm sure it'll taste really amazing…later." He pulled her down on top of his lap so he could get better access to all of her fun parts, her crotch rubbing against his fast-awakening dick as she settled down into place.

"Oh, hello," she growled, her eyes lighting up as she began wiggling her ass back and forth intentionally. "What do we have here…"

He let out a shout of laughter as he yanked her shirt out of the way. "Some fun things to play with," he told her, reaching behind her and unsnapping her bra, flipping it across the room. "My oh my," he said softly, taking in her breasts. He reached up and cupped one and then the other, the heavy weight of them sending a shiver of desire through him. "You have no idea how horny I am right now," he growled, and then leaned forward, wrapping his lips around a large pink nipple, just as oversized as the rest of her tits were. There were some definite perks to pregnancy...

"Oh, I think I do," she said with a breathy laugh. "It's been months for me, too."

He looked up at her through his eyelashes, desire shooting through him like sparklers on the 4th of July. "Darlin', it's been *years* for me. I don't want to hear any whining out of you."

She threw her head back and laughed. "But, but, but," she protested, "I have pregnancy hormones running through my veins, and those make you even hornier than usual. I'm pretty sure I've out-hornied you."

It was Adam's turn to let out a belly laugh. "'Hornied'? Dare I say that your creativity is quite impressive? I know that for me, it's hard to think when..." He stuttered to a stop when Kylie deliberately turned and rubbed her generous boobs across his face.

"Ah...ah...ah..." But he couldn't manage to get anything else out because he'd completely forgotten what they'd been talking about anyway. There was nothing but gorgeous, full tits to suckle on and a rounded belly to run his hands over. Nothing else existed in the world.

All of the humor drained out of Kylie, too, and

she began pulling at his shirt, fumbling at the small buttons marching up the front, letting out a curse that a sailor would be proud of as she lost the battle and simply ripped at it instead, buttons popping everywhere like popcorn in a microwave. Adam wanted to laugh but he also wanted her so badly, he wasn't sure if he was still breathing.

Yeah, laughing was totally out of the question.

She shoved the sleeves down his arms and he fought to get it off him like a wild octopus flailing around, arms going everywhere. With a final pop of the remaining buttons, the shirt slid off his arms and was instantly forgotten. Kylie leaned down and began hungrily nipping at his chest and abs. "Do you know…" she panted, "do you have any idea how sexy you are?"

He flung his head back with a body-shaking groan. "Nooo…" he sighed. "I…"

What were they talking about? He couldn't remember. She was frantically unbuttoning his jeans and he realized that he'd be much faster at this project than she was, so he plucked her up and sat her off to the side, shucking his jeans and boxer-briefs in one quick, economical movement, and then he pulled Kylie across his lap, the desire so strong at this point, he thought he might pass out.

Through the film of desire that'd descended over his eyes, he could see that Kylie had taken her yoga pants and underwear off at some point, leaving her naked under his hungry gaze.

"Yes," he growled, and with one swift movement, he picked her up and set her down on his dick, the warmth and liquid and pressure around him almost his undoing. He panted, trying to push down the heat licking through his veins long enough to give Kylie some sort of pleasure out of the experience, but she was moaning and bouncing up and down on his lap, shouts of lust spilling out of her, and then his seed was spilling out of him as he went rigid and the whole world went dark and he couldn't see or think or breathe or hear but could only feel.

His orgasm lasted so long, a small part of his brain began to worry that it might never stop and he would literally die of pleasure, but finally, ever so slowly, his body began to relax back into the couch and he managed to pull his eyelids apart to look down at Kylie. She'd collapsed against him, nuzzled up against his chest and neck, groaning.

"Are you…" He coughed, trying to clear his throat and make it work. "Are you okay?" he finally got out.

She sat back with a dreamy smile. "Ohhh yeaaahhh…" she said, and laughed. "That was…is sex always like that with you?"

He let out a pained groan. "To be honest with you, it's been so long since I've had sex, I can't remember." He gave her a lopsided grin as he sank further down into the couch. "I tried one time after my wife died – some chick I picked up in a bar in Franklin. It was so awkward and just flat-out weird that I never tried again."

"Weird? Like the girl had a tongue piercing and it felt weird when she was sucking you off?"

Adam let out a little laugh at that. He wasn't used to bluntly discussing sex with another person. It was refreshing. Definitely out of his comfort zone, but refreshing. "No, no tongue piercing. It was just weird because it wasn't my wife, you know? She liked different things, and I didn't know what they were and I felt like I was auditioning for a part, and if I pleased her enough, she'd acquiesce to letting me have sex with her again. It was just...weird."

"It sounds like the chemistry was all wrong," Kylie said seriously, her green eyes trained on him. "'Cause, well, I'm not your wife either. I hope you didn't feel that way just now."

His eyes grew wide with surprise. "Oh *hell* no!" he exclaimed. "This was..." He gestured between them. "This was like nothing I've ever felt before. I don't mean to compare you to Wendy because it isn't fair to either of you, but I will say that from what I remember of sex with my wife, what you and I just did was incredibly different."

He couldn't believe it, but he felt a blush steal up his cheeks like a little boy confessing his sins as he said, "I...uhh...I usually last longer than that. Just so you know. I think it'll take a while to get my friend here back into shape. When you've been starved for attention for as long as I have, it's easy to go off a little on the early side." He stumbled to a stop. He felt like a randy 14-year-old boy, trying to explain away premature ejaculation to a disappointed girlfriend.

Kylie threw her head back and laughed. "You'll notice that I wasn't complaining," she said when she finally got her laughter under control. "It's been way too long for me, too, and…I was raring to go, I think it's fair to say." She flashed him a naughty grin. "And, just so we're all on the same page, I'll be ready to go again soon. *Real* soon."

She climbed off his lap and looked down at her body with another naughty grin. "That's the most fun I've had getting sweaty in a very long time. Let me go clean up. I'll be right back."

She headed up the stairs, muttering something about hair as she went, and Adam headed to the kitchen sink to wash up there. Afterwards, he slipped his jeans back on but when he attempted to put on his shirt, he quickly realized that he was missing more than a few buttons. He held the shirt up with a chuckle.

He had exactly one button left on the whole thing – the top one, which hadn't been fastened when Kylie went apeshit on it.

"What are you laughing about?" Kylie asked, coming back down the stairs.

"Remind me not to get between you and sex. Ever," Adam said dryly, pulling his shirt on to model the problem for her. She looked at the open front and sent him another naughty grin.

"Huh. I have to say I rather like this," she said,

coming to a stop in front of him and sliding her hands up his abs. "Easy access, easy on the eyes...can't say I'm complaining." Her light green eyes flashed desire and sex up at him and he sucked in another breath at the sight.

"You...you weren't kidding about being ready to go again, were you?" he asked, running his hands through her thick blonde hair, straightening out the tangles.

"Not at all." She bit her lower lip as she looked up at him through her fan of eyelashes. "Anytime, anywhere," she breathed, and leaned forward to nip at his nipples. She sent him a saucy wink and then headed into the kitchen. "Let's dish this up, huh?" she called out, normal and boring and totally non-sexy.

"Bu...uh...urgh..." Adam wavered a bit on his feet. What had just happened here? Going one direction, and then another...How could she put her hands all over him like that and then act like everything was normal?

He shook his head as he headed into the kitchen after her. Women. It's a damn good thing they were so amazing and sexy, because they also happened to be confusing as shit.

Living through a relationship with Kylie would be hell on earth...and worth every minute of it.

CHAPTER 32

KYLIE

*Y*UP, the shepherd's pie was cold. She knew it would be. She wished she'd been able to afford a microwave during her last shopping trip so she could easily heat the meal back up, but that particular appliance was on the "Buy soon" list, not the "Already bought" list, dammit.

As she watched Adam shovel the food into his mouth, obviously starving, she decided that if he didn't care, she didn't either, and dug in too.

"So how's your mom doing these days?" she asked as she took a sip of creamy, thick cow's milk. One thing that was never in short supply: Milk and eggs. If nothing else, her baby would have strong bones, that was for damn sure.

Adam looked down at his empty plate with a deep sigh.

"Hold on, before you explain that sigh, do you want another helping?" Kylie asked.

"Oh, sure!" he said eagerly. "This is the best thing I've eaten all day."

She slipped into the kitchen to dish up another helping, even as she rolled her eyes at his praise. If she knew her Adam – and she was pretty sure she did at this point – this would be the *only* thing he'd eaten all day. She rather wondered if she ought to start following him around, shoving food into his mouth between vaccinations.

"I love my mom, and…I just feel like I'm failing her," he said in a quiet voice as she came walking back into the room with a heaping serving in her hand. "Zara Garrett – do you know her? Younger sister to Moose and Rhys?"

She slid the plate in front of Adam and then topped off his milk. "Yeah. She's quite a bit younger than me – I was closer in age to Rhys – but I know *of* her, of course. Doesn't she work at the hospital as a CNA or something?"

Adam dug into the shepherd's pie with a hearty groan. "Thank you," he said in a heartfelt whisper. "It's so nice to have someone else take care of me for a minute. Anyway," he said, waving his fork in the air dismissively, obviously trying to hurry past that admission he absolutely hadn't meant to say out loud, she was just sure of it, "I stole her away from the hospital and have hired her to come over to help take care of Mom. She'd been asking for me to hire someone to help her – a *female* person – but wouldn't tell me anything more than that. I was happy because even though Zara is just a kid, she and Mom hit it right off."

He let out a deep sigh. "Which sounds like yay, problem solved, but honestly, it isn't. I can't afford to have Zara move in, and anyway, she's still in high school. She needs to be living at home. But I think my mom needs more help than she's letting on. For her to even ask for Zara's help is…" He shrugged. "Nothing short of a miracle, honestly. I just don't know what else to do. There's only so much of me to go around."

He lapsed into silence, digging back into his meal with gusto as Kylie sat and thought for a while. "I don't know your mom well," she finally said slowly, "and I don't want to intrude where I'm not wanted. But, have you ever thought about having her move into the Long Valley Senior Citizen's Center? They have staff there all day, every day. They can help take care of her better than a teenage girl coming over a couple of times a week."

But he was already shaking his head, even as she was talking. "My mom was born in that house," he said, the frustration and bewilderment about what to do stamped across his face. "She's said it a million times – she was born in that house, and she wants to die in that house. If I take her out of it, she'll die from heartbreak."

Kylie nodded. "It's…it's hard," she said weakly. *Ugh. Such a worthless comment to make.* She hated the words even as they came out. It was like the empty phrase, "Thoughts and prayers." It was such a generic platitude, it had virtually no meaning except, "I'm saying something because I know I'm supposed to."

She pushed that away and thought over the conundrum, rubbing her earlobe as she did. Finally, she said thoughtfully, "I kinda wonder if your mom's attachment to the house isn't actually just an attachment to independence. I mean, I'm sure she loves that house, absolutely, but it's gotta be hard to be by herself so much. She's a really gregarious woman, sharp as a tack, not slipping mentally at all that I can tell, and yet, right now, she's basically in solitary confinement. A teen comes over a few times a week, and she sees her son for a few minutes every morning and night. I can't imagine that a woman as outgoing and friendly as your mom is happy about that."

Adam pushed back from the table, drumming his fingers, thinking. His shirt lay open, giving her easy visual access to his chest, and just the sight of his abs...she had a hard time keeping her mind out of the gutter and focused on the conversation, that was for sure.

"I...uhh..." She tore her eyes away from the visual feast in front of her, forcing herself to meet his gaze. "Have you been into Second Time Around?"

"No," he said slowly, confused about the apparent change in topic. "I mean, I know what it is, but they don't tend to have a lot of veterinarian tools or horse tack in a thrift store, so I've never had much reason to go in there."

Kylie laughed a little. "I have to admit, I didn't see

a single horse saddle in the place when I went in. Anyway, I had to get some items for the house, and thought I'd check out their offerings. Did you know that it's actually run by the senior center? Everyone who works there, they all live in the retirement home. The home sends a bus back and forth between the store and the home all day long, shuttling workers to and fro. All money from the store is used for activities and other items for the home. I personally think that your mom wants to still be busy. Important. Needed. She doesn't want to be shunted off to some old folks' home to die, and really, who would? But if they could find some task for her to do down at the store to keep her busy and wanted, I think that'd mean more to her than anything else. And you wouldn't have the strain of taking care of her on top of everything else you have on your plate."

Adam's mouth twisted. "I'll be honest, that sounds lovely. I just don't know if my mom will actually go for it. Ruby Whitaker can be sweet and kind to almost everyone she meets, but when she digs her heels in… watch out. It's a side to her that most people don't see, but as her only living relative, I can attest that it's there."

Kylie reached out and took his work-hardened hand into hers. "Give it a try," she said softly, rubbing her thumb over his calloused knuckles. "The worst she can do is say no."

CHAPTER 33

ADAM

"*I* AM *NOT* going to be dragged off and stuffed into some old folks' home to die!" his mom shouted, her normally pale face red from anger.

Kylie had been wrong. Oh so very wrong. His mother wasn't just telling him no, she'd told him what a terrible idea it was using phrases from other languages that he didn't even recognize. Or maybe his mom was just hurling made-up swear words at his head. He wasn't quite sure at this point.

He held up his hands in front of him defensively. "I'm sorry!" he blurted out. "Kylie thought that you might enjoy working down at the store, and—"

"So now you're listening to Kylie, huh?" his mom yelled, cutting him off. "Is she trying to get rid of her future mother-in-law so she can have you all to herself?"

"Now, hold on a minute," he growled back, glowering at his mother, his worry about upsetting her morphing into anger. "Kylie was just trying to help. She is one of the nicest people to ever grace this planet, and I won't have you saying shit like that about her!"

"Don't you swear in front of me!"

"Don't you give me cause to swear in front of you!" he retorted.

They were breathing heavily, just staring at each other, neither one willing to move an inch, when his mom snarled, "So. Is this why you wanted to sell my car to her? Just wanting to start the process of selling off everything I have and leaving me with nothing at all?"

"What?" he yelped, jerking his head back in surprise. "Mom, what are you talking about? You begged me for years to sell it for you but I was always too busy. You were thrilled with having Kylie take it over. Why are you acting like this?"

"Why are you trying to get rid of your mother?" she shot back. She struggled to her feet. Instinctively, Adam hurried to her side to help her but she waved him away. "I'm going to my room," she announced. "Maybe by tomorrow, you'll have realized what a terrible mistake you've made."

Head held high, she pushed the walker down the hallway, not looking back.

Adam collapsed into the wing-back chair and stared off into space.

Well, that went well.

It'd seemed so simple, so straightforward, when

Kylie had talked about it last night. And it would be…
if his mother wasn't so damn stubborn.

He pushed himself out of the chair and headed
outside. He needed to go do something. Just sitting in
the house, staring at the walls, his mother busy giving
him the silent treatment…that wasn't going to help.

Somehow, he found himself in front of the Long
Valley Senior Citizen's Center, without making the
decision to actually drive there. *Ugh.* He really needed
to stop driving on autopilot. He was going to get into
a wreck at some point if he kept it up.

He swung out of the truck and stared up at the
building in front of him. It was a sprawling building;
obviously, someone had made the wise decision to
build out rather than up. When the majority of the
residents have mobility issues, adding stairs into the
mix was never a good idea.

Despite its size, though, it still had that welcoming
feel, from the wisteria climbing up the side of the
building to the rose bushes in full bloom. There was a
large grassy area off to the left with some huge red
maple trees to provide shade, where families could sit
outside together and just hang out.

It was Sunday afternoon, so the place was bustling
with family members down to visit relatives for the
week. There was laughter and the Monkees belting
out *I'm a Believer* and small kids running around…

It sure didn't seem like the ass end of the earth
to him.

Ms. Blackburn came walking up. "Hi, Adam!" she

said, obviously surprised to see him. "Down here to visit someone?" She was the center's director and from the little that he'd heard over the years, she seemed to be doing a stand-up job. Not that he'd made much of a point to pay attention previous to now, but thinking back through his memories, it sure seemed like he'd heard good stuff.

"No," he said slowly. "My mom – Ruby Whitaker – her hands are getting worse. The arthritis…" He shook his head. "I broached the topic today about moving over here and you'd think I'd suggested she move to outer Siberia or somethin'."

Ms. Blackburn laughed dryly. "I know this doesn't help, but that's actually a really common response, at least at first. I'm sure your mom has been here, visiting friends, but still, another visit might be in order. It's one thing to go somewhere just to chit-chat with your friends; it's different to take an official tour and look at it as a potential future resident. It might help her realize that quite a few of her friends are here already, and there are some fun things to do, I promise."

"Actually, my girlfriend, Kylie, said that y'all are associated with Second Time Around. I think my mom would love to work there, once she got past her pride."

"Not everyone can work there," Ms. Blackburn said, "and even if someone wants to and is able, their shifts aren't usually for very long. And that's okay. I try really hard to match physical and mental abilities with tasks so that everyone can play a part, *if* they want to.

"It's all voluntary, but I'll be honest, I think that store is part of the magic of this place. At so many retirement homes, people move there right at the end, when the family can't take care of them any longer because their physical and emotional needs are too much. Being in a strange place – it's hard any time, but it's especially hard if you're not mentally capable of understanding what's going on. We do have some end-of-life cases like that here, but the people who do the best were moved here when they were still active and loving life. When that happens, residents find that they have friends around them again. They have a purpose. They have a job to do, a job that they've chosen and want to do. *And*, they get to hang out with their buddies while they do it."

She laughed a little. "Honestly, people don't change just because they get older – they still want friends to hang out with. Sundays are a pretty popular day for families to visit so you see lots of them here right now, but even on a Tuesday evening, you'll find residents out here, listening to music and chatting with their friends. Not everyone is happy 100% of the time, but that's because they're human beings, so…" She shrugged and laughed. "But for the most part, once people settle in, they love it here. They tell me that every day."

Adam nodded, looking closer at the elderly women scattered in chairs throughout the grounds.

Keeping track of who his mother's friends were had never been a specialty of Adam's, but a few of the women looked damn familiar to him. If nothing else, she surely had acquaintances here. "I'll see if I can talk her into a tour," he said finally. "I believe that she'd love it here, if she'd give it a try. I'm afraid she won't, though, just to spite me." He gave the center's director a wry smile.

"Some people are more stubborn than others," she said mildly, and he wondered for a moment how many residents had fought her tooth and nail when they'd first been moved into the place. She didn't have an easy job, that was for sure. In that moment, wrestling steers to the ground almost seemed relaxing by comparison. He sure couldn't do what she did.

"Well, thanks anyway for your time," he said, and headed back to his truck. More than ever, this seemed like exactly what his mom needed. He'd give her a few days to calm down, and then try the conversation again. By the end of this, his mother was either going to love the retirement home, or hate his guts, and he wasn't too sure which outcome he should place a wager on.

Oh, Mom…

*A*HHH…*Monday morning.*

Usually the most dreaded day of the week, Kylie found that hers was going delightfully. Since Adam hadn't been able to come over at all yesterday, their kiss upon him arriving to work that morning had been… **ahem** more than a little lusty.

By the end of it, she'd been pretty sure that Adam was going to throw her over the desk and pound into her right then and there, but then the phone had rung, interrupting them.

Damn phone.

Hours later, Kylie found herself squeezing her thighs together, practically vibrating with need. Now that Kylie knew what sex with Adam was like, it was hard to think, to breathe, to move, without sending desire sizzling to every nerve ending. Saturday evening had been an explosion of need and desire between them that they'd both been holding back for way too long, and she'd spent most of their dinner afterwards (when she wasn't worrying about Ruby, of course), waiting eagerly for round two.

And then, just as dinner was done and things were about to get interesting again, his phone had rung and he'd had to leave to go check on a mare who was in breech with her first foal.

She really was starting to think that the apocryphal story her history teacher had told about President Ulysses S. Grant dismissing the telephone as "not being something anyone would want to use" had been more spot on than she'd realized at the time. In fact, if she had her way, she'd unplug every phone in town for at least the next week, if not two.

Yum...two weeks of nothing but sex with Adam...

Kylie bounded up from her chair. Just sitting there, thinking about nothing but sex, sex, sex was gonna kill her off if she didn't quit it. She could...

She cast her eyes around the office, thinking. What was left to do? She'd cleaned and filed and organized the place to within an inch of its life. She'd already scrubbed the nose prints off the glass front door from yesterday, and there hadn't been any dogs in yet today.

Oh! She could check the batteries in the smoke detectors. She hadn't done that yet.

Before she could discover where Adam had the ladder stored, though, a gold Lexus sports coupe pulled up in front of the clinic and an older woman, about the age of her mom or so, swung out of the car, a small Yorkie in her arms. The little ball of brown fluff was completely adorable, especially with the red ribbon tied on top, and Kylie mentally added Yorkies to the list of potential dogs to look into adopting.

The heavier-set woman, salt and pepper curls around her head bouncing with every step, came striding into the clinic. She put the dog down on the ground to sniff around before walking over to the counter. "I'd like to set up an appointment for Yorkie Poo," she said imperiously, not a hint of laughter at the ridiculous name anywhere on her face. "She's been acting weird lately, and I want Dr. Whitaker to take a look at her."

Kylie swallowed hard, trying to keep the bubble of laughter from actually escaping her lips. *Yorkie Poo?* She couldn't be serious. Was she being serious?

Another look at the woman's face...*Alrighty then. Yorkie Poo it is.*

"Do you have a date you prefer?" Kylie asked, scooting into place in front of the computer and clicking over to the calendar. "It looks like Dr. Whitaker will be spending the day in the clinic on Friday, so if that works for you, he could put you in at 2:00 p.m."

"Sure," the woman said dismissively, almost as if she were completely uninterested in this appointment she'd supposedly come all the way in here to set up. Kylie shrugged to herself. Weird but whatevs.

"And your name?" she asked, clicking to create a new appointment.

"Mrs. Richard Plossy," she announced imperiously, rather like she was introducing the Queen of England. Or thought that she *was* the Queen of England.

Well, at least now she knew why the woman looked vaguely familiar. Her youngest had graduated with Kylie, something Kylie'd tried her best to forget over the course of the last four years.

Mrs. Plossy's son was an asshole of the first water, to put it mildly.

Kylie ignored her instinctive dislike of the woman in front of her, putting on her best customer service demeanor like a knight arming himself for battle. She had to treat all of Adam's clients politely, even the ones who'd mistakenly left their crowns at home that morning.

"Well, Mrs. Plossy, here's your appointment card," Kylie said, sliding the business card across the counter to the woman. "Friday at—"

"Are you and Dr. Whitaker dating?" the woman interrupted.

"Wha—what?" Kylie sputtered. *She did* not *just ask that. I'm having some sort of alternate out-of-body experience right now. I have to be.*

"I heard around town that you two were dating, but since you're knocked up with a bastard's child, I was just sure that was wrong," the woman said, her voice dripping with saccharine sweetness as her gaze dropped down to Kylie's rounded belly and then back up to her face. "There's no way that Dr. Whitaker would saddle himself with a home wrecker like you, right? So I told all of my friends that I'd come down here and find out for myself so we could set the record straight, once and for all."

Kylie had never understood the phrase *seeing red*... until that moment. It wasn't a metaphorical thing after all. It was literal. The world went red with black around the edges and a roar echoed in her ears but even through it all, she didn't punch the woman or call her a bitch, something she was rather proud of, actually.

"Mrs. Plossy, taking a second look at the calendar," she said evenly, keeping her eyes pinned on the woman in front of her, "it turns out Dr. Whitaker will be busy on Friday after all." She picked up the appointment card from the counter and tore it into little pieces, letting them flutter into the trashcan, and then marched around her desk and over to the door to hold it open. "I'm sure you can see yourself out."

"How...how dare you!" the woman gasped. "Do you know who my husband is? The Plossy Ranch is one of the largest in the area. When he hears about what you just did, he's never going to use Dr. Whitaker as a vet again."

"It seems like if more people were willing to tell you the truth, maybe you wouldn't be so inclined to think it was okay to be a bitch," Kylie said mildly. "Have a good day."

Hmmm...so, she'd failed on the "not calling the woman a bitch" front, but in her defense, the woman had deserved it, and a whole lot more, so ehhh. She just couldn't find it in herself to feel bad about that particular slip-up.

The woman marched over, snatched Yorkie Poo off the immaculate floor, and cuddled him close. "There's probably diseases on this floor that I don't want him to get anyway," she huffed and brushed past Kylie, head held high. "Some people!" she harrumphed, right before slamming her way into her car.

Some people was right. Kylie let the front door swing closed behind her as she marched back to her desk, righteous indignation in every step. How *dare* she say that to her. How *dare* she think that it's okay to talk to another human being like that.

She felt her eyes stinging with hot tears but she absolutely refused to let them slide down her cheeks. No way, no how was she going to let that woman make her cry. It was something the Plossy boy had taken great pleasure in for years, and Kylie wasn't about to let that damn family win now.

She sat down and then sprang right back up, too much anger and rage boiling through her veins to sit in a chair. She wanted to beat something, she wanted to throw something, she wanted to…

She wanted to clean.

She marched into the employee bathroom and attacked the toilet, scrubbing it furiously. "You… you…*asshole!*" she yelled into the toilet bowl. "You entitled piece of shit! I am not your subject or your servant, and I don't care if your husband is the freaking King of England, you still don't get to treat me that way!"

"So, you wanna tell me what happened with Mrs. Plossy?" Adam asked quietly, standing right behind her.

Startled, she swung in a circle, toilet water flying everywhere. She looked down at the brush, horrified, and then dropped it back in the toilet. She leaned over and washed her hands – the bathroom was so tiny, she didn't have to move an inch to do it – and then planted her clean hands on her hips.

"Mrs. Plossy," she snarled at Adam, "is a first-rate asshole, and so is her son."

"Hold on, her son was here?" Adam asked, confused.

"No, he wasn't. That was just a general statement on the assholishness of the Plossys in general. *Any*way, she had the balls to call me a home wrecker to my face and she demanded to know if we were dating and she called my baby a bastard's child and…and…I called her a bitch," she announced. "You can fire me if you want to. She deserved it and I won't take it back. I don't care if I have to be homeless. I won't do it. I—"

Adam pulled her against his broad chest. "It's okay," he said soothingly, trying to cuddle her rigid body against his. "I'm not upset with you, I promise. I just wanted to know what your half of the story was when I called her back. I was pretty sure she'd left out more than a few details."

"But...but..." Kylie sputtered, all of her righteous indignation leaking out of her at his understanding words, leaving only worry and mortification in its wake, "she said that she was going to tell Mr. Plossy what happened and that you'd lose all of his business!" The tears that she'd been so heroically holding back finally came spilling out. "He's one of the biggest ranchers in the area. I *can't* keep costing you money like this!"

Adam continued to stroke his hands down Kylie's back, never wavering, never pausing, just long, even strokes down her spine. "Kylie, darlin', we've already talked about this," he said softly once she'd stopped blubbering. "I have enough work to keep me *more* than busy. You know that. If Mr. Plossy decides to drop me because you actually had the balls to tell his wife the truth, I'll be just fine financially, I promise. But," he said, cutting off her protests before she could even sputter them out, "the truth is, the man will probably buy me a beer."

"What?" Kylie gasped, pulling back and staring at Adam in amazement. Maybe he'd had one too many kicks to the head by ornery calves, and the brain damage was just starting to show.

Adam gave her a naughty grin as he snuggled her back against his chest, restarting his strokes down her back. "He'd call me a liar to my face if that statement ever got around town, but truthfully? He can't stand his wife. They've been on the outs for years. He can't afford to divorce her, though, so they keep up this façade in public…Honestly, I can't blame the man. Have you ever met him?"

Adam's hands were making Kylie melt into a puddle in front of him, and his words just barely registered in time for her to answer. "Uh-uh," she said, pressed against his chest, not moving a millimeter.

"Okay, imagine Mrs. Plossy. Now, imagine the exact opposite of Mrs. Plossy. Mr. Plossy couldn't be a nicer guy. Down to earth, hardworking, humble…he doesn't throw his weight around, which is part of his wife's problem. She wants him to act like the lord up on the hill, and he won't. It drives her crazy. So, with that in mind, are you ready for me to call her back?"

"Oh, yes please!" Kylie exclaimed, pulling back *just* her head and flashing Adam a huge smile. She didn't want to lose contact with the rest of his body. Not until she absolutely had to. "I'll just stay right here so I can hear every word of it."

Adam was already pulling up his call history on his phone, using his other hand to continue to snuggle Kylie against his chest.

"Hello?" came the tinny greeting from his phone.

"Hi, Mrs. Plossy, it's Dr. Whitaker. I've had a chance to talk to Kylie about the situation—"

"Oh, good!" the woman said. "So I take it she's fired now?" The smugness in her voice made Kylie roll her eyes in disbelief.

"It's more like you're fired," Adam said bluntly. "As a client. Although I enjoy my time with Yorkie Poo, I can't say the same about you. You're not welcome back here."

"What?!" the woman shrieked, even through the speaker on the phone. "How dare you! Just wait until I tell—"

Adam hit the red icon and the sound blessedly went silent.

Kylie looked up at Adam, her eyes huge. She began to giggle from the insanity of it all. "You...I... Oh my God, Adam, I can't believe you actually did that!"

He grinned back. "A part of me can't either. Honestly, I've been wanting to do that for a very long time. So! To celebrate, I say we play hooky," he said, pulling her out the front door and flipping off the open sign as they went, "and go on down to the Muffin Man. I never did buy you that donut I promised you, and Gage has finally finished with the remodel, so they're back to serving them again. That alone is cause for celebration. I mean, muffins are fine, but they aren't *donuts*."

Kylie's stomach rumbled even as she tried to protest. "I really shouldn't..." she mumbled without an ounce of conviction as he began striding down the street towards the Muffin Man, pulling her along behind him. "Processed sugar isn't at all good for you," she felt obligated to point out.

"Yolo," he said, shrugging his shoulders, still pulling her along.

"Yolo?!" she said, laughing until her sides ached. "I can't believe you know that phrase."

"Ollie has been trying to teach me teenage slang so I can be cool. I keep telling him that he's more likely to get pigs to fly, but at least a few phrases have stuck. You Only Live Once seems like a pretty good motto to live by, *especially* when it comes to donuts."

"Somehow, I am not surprised by this," Kylie muttered under her breath. She was pretty sure Adam lived for donuts. How he survived this long with the Muffin Man operating at only partial capacity was inexplicable, honestly. She'd been trying her best to feed him carrot and celery sticks as part of her Keep Adam Fed project, and although he'd eaten them, she'd heard more than a few mumbles about rabbit food while doing it.

Mumbles she'd chosen to ignore, of course.

As they walked, her hand brushed against her belly and like a flash flood, the roundness of it brought all of her panic and worry back, but ten times worse. "Adam, are you *sure* you want to claim me in public?" she exclaimed, seemingly apropos of absolutely nothing, but she knew that she was right to ask, to doubt what Adam was doing for her. "We don't have to hold hands while walking down the street. We can just be employer and employee in public, I promise. I won't be offended." *Oh, but I'll be heartbroken...*

She pushed that thought away. She couldn't guilt Adam into a relationship with her, especially one that hurt him financially.

He pulled her into the shade of the awning over the hardware store. "Darlin', I'm not going to pretend that this," he ran his hands lightly over her baby bump, "doesn't make me want to panic a little inside. I still haven't told you about helping Chloe give birth to Tommy in the middle of a blizzard. Human births are *scary*. But if you'll have me, I want to be there for you every step of the way. You are not just my employee, you are my girlfriend, and I love you very much. I don't care what the Plossys or the Tiffanys of the world have to say on the topic. They don't matter to me. *You* do."

She rubbed her hands over the curve of her belly unconsciously as she listened. A part of her wanted to protest − *but, but, but* − but she swallowed that down. She couldn't turn into a needy girlfriend who spent her days asking her boyfriend to reassure her over and over again that he loved her. That also wasn't fair to Adam.

"All right, let's go get fat," she said finally, grabbing his hand and tugging him back down the street with her.

He let out a roar of approval. "Now that's a plan I can get behind."

CHAPTER 35

ADAM

$\mathcal{A}$DAM DRAPED HIS ARM around Kylie as they walked down the street. It was hot today, even in the shade, but he didn't want to be any further away from her than absolutely necessary.

It was funny, Kylie's concerns. It wasn't that they weren't legit – having a baby changed a person's life forever, and being in love with someone who was having a baby meant that his life changed almost as much – but he was surprised no one seemed to care about the age difference between them. He never would've guessed that someone who was 16 years younger than him would make him so damn happy. He would've dismissed the idea out of hand...*if* it'd been anyone else but Kylie.

She completed him in a way that he hadn't felt in a long time.

Looking back on Chloe, he wondered if a bit of his infatuation with her wasn't actually based on the fact that they never went anywhere. It was easy to be in love with someone if you never got into an argument with them or walked into a bathroom after they'd really let one loose or had never spent an entire dinner arguing about which was better – *Star Trek* or *Star Wars*. (*Star Trek*, of course. Not even worthy of a discussion, as anyone in their right mind would know).

But when he put Chloe up on a pedestal and never saw the negative side to her – never saw her with her hair unbrushed or with sleep lines running across her face – well, it was easy for him to think of her as perfect.

Theirs was a friendship, which meant that he didn't see the hidden sides to her.

Was love based on superficiality still love? Or had it just been a really long infatuation – a nine-year infatuation?

Before he could properly debate that out in his mind, they got to the bakery, Adam pulling the door open for Kylie and jangling the bell overhead.

Walking into the cool of the air-conditioned bakery was paradise. They both sucked in deep breaths of cold air, trying to bring down their internal body temperatures. *And this is up in the mountains. I can't imagine trying to live in Death Valley or something...*

He'd never been meant to live in a desert, that was for damn sure. Give him snow over heat waves any day of the week.

Sugar Stonemyer, soon to be Anderson, looked up from the counter and shot them both a big smile. "It's nice in here, isn't it?" she called out. "After the heat of outside, it's lovely to breathe in air that isn't trying to bake you alive."

"Bake? Really? In a bakery?" Adam teased Sugar. "That's a pretty bad pun right there."

Sugar laughed, her dark brown eyes lighting up. "I hadn't even thought about it, honestly," she protested. "Although now that I have…"

Gage came walking up from the back. "Are you flipping our best customers shit?"

"Yes!" Adam said just as Sugar protested, "No!"

Gage looked back and forth between them, and then turned to Kylie. "Okay, you're the tie-breaker."

"I'm just here for the donuts!" Kylie said, holding her hands up in mock surrender. Even as she spoke, she didn't tear her eyes away from the display case in front of her. For all of her protestations about how processed sugar wasn't good for a body, she sure was excited about picking out a donut.

Adam turned back to Gage. "So, how's the remodel coming along? If you're serving up your whole menu again, does that mean that everything is wrapped up?"

Gage nodded, pushing his glasses up the bridge of his nose. "Pretty much. We still have painting left to do, but that's just about it. I can't wait to have everything back to normal. All of that chaos – the saws and hammers and yelling back and forth…Much more of that and I was gonna go insane." He pushed his glasses back up his nose again.

Which was when Adam finally realized why Gage looked so different. "Hold on, did you used to wear glasses?" he asked.

"Observant," Sugar said dryly.

"Hey, I at least picked up on your puns," Adam tossed back.

"I began wearing them when the construction started," Gage put in, ignoring them both. "All of the sawdust in the air was irritating my eyes and I was constantly having to rinse off my contact lenses. And then…" He shrugged. "I just got lazy. No flour dust underneath my contacts anymore, no more sticking myself in the eye with my finger; it's pretty nice, really. I've been trying to remember why I ever started wearing contacts to begin with, and I'm coming up with a big fat 'Hell if I know.' Hey, do you guys want to tour the back and see the new kitchen?"

"Sure!" Adam said, grabbing Kylie's hand and tugging her away from the cheesecake display case. She muttered something about how he should never get between a pregnant woman and her sugar, but he pretended a sudden case of deafness, just like he'd ignored her comment earlier about his love for donuts.

Sometimes, it was convenient to be deaf.

Gage pushed through the swinging doors and into the kitchen, with Adam and Kylie following on his heels. Adam had only been in the back once or twice before the fire, but from what he remembered, it was a lot brighter and whiter now than it had been previously. He listened with half an ear as Gage showed off every pot, pan, and appliance in the joint. Kylie was practically bouncing off the walls with excitement as they compared baking secrets and shortcuts.

As Adam enjoyed watching Kylie's tits bounce around under her flowing pregnancy top, the actual words they were saying flowed around him like the meaningless babble of a creek rushing by. He was in the middle of trying to decide what color her bra was when he heard Kylie say, "Right, Adam?"

He jerked his head up from her delectable chest, his cheeks flushing. "Yeah, of course," he stammered.

Kylie and Gage went back to discussing the intricacies of baking flour versus…Adam zoned out, not even keeping up with the discussion long enough to know what they were comparing. He realized as he was enjoying Kylie's dramatic gestures, especially the ones that stretched her top across her delicious breasts, that his smug laughter the other day when Kylie told him that she didn't want to learn how a car ran…well, it wasn't warranted.

Thinking about it now, he ought to apologize to her for it, even though it had been internal smug laughter and she hadn't realized he was doing it.

Did he love donuts? Yes.

Did he actually want to learn how to make donuts? Not even a little bit.

It was totally possible to love an end result without

having the slightest desire to learn how to follow the process yourself.

Huh.

"Are you ready?" Kylie asked, jerking out him out of his ruminations.

"Sure, sure," Adam said, and grabbed her hand as they headed towards the front. If he wasn't going to be able to ogle her breasts, he could at least hold her hand.

When they got back up to the main area, Adam spotted Mike from the mechanic's shop, busy buying some donuts up at the cash register. He reluctantly let go of Kylie, knowing that it was only polite to go shoot the breeze with the mechanic for a minute or two.

"Hi, Mike," he said, walking over and putting his hand out to shake.

Mike's leathery face broke out into a big grin as he gave him a hearty handshake. "Hey, Adam! How's life treatin' you?"

"Fine, fine. How's Kimber and Rex's little one doing?"

"Oh, she's just beautiful," Mike gushed. It was a little funny to see a man who could be his father get all mushy over a baby, but Adam could already tell that this little girl had him wrapped around her pinky. "She's two months today, so I said I'd grab a box of sweets to celebrate. She's not quite big enough to eat one of these yet, but the way she's growin'…" He shook his head in bemusement. "I can't believe she's two months old already. She's got a mop of hair on her like you wouldn't believe."

He turned back to Sugar, grabbing the box of donuts from the counter. "Thanks, Sugar," he said. Turning back to Adam, he said, "I better get to it. Rex's parents are up from California visiting, here to celebrate her birthday so I best be on my way." He headed out the door, his limp a little more pronounced than normal as he hurried for his truck.

Sugar turned back to him. "You two know what you want?" she asked. As Kylie picked out two for herself, Sugar sliding them into paper sleeves, Adam couldn't help but feel a little nostalgic for a dad he never knew. Would his father have been that excited over Kylie's pregnancy? He liked to think he would have.

"And what for you, Adam?" Sugar asked, breaking into his thoughts.

"Chocolate icing with sprinkles and a jelly donut," he said without hesitation.

"I don't even know why I asked," Sugar teased him with a wink.

"Chocolate? Sprinkles? Were you deprived of sugar as a child and now you're trying to make up for it?" Kylie asked, laughing.

"Hey, I don't think bear claws and maple bars are all that much better," he pointed out.

Before Kylie could come up with an adequate response – he could almost *see* the wheels turning in her head – Sugar began ringing up their donuts. "So, are you two coming to the wedding this weekend?" she asked as her hands flew over the cash register.

Kylie and Adam both asked in unison, "Which wedding?"

"Mine, of course." She laughed, tossing her braid over her shoulder. "It's nothing big or fancy, but Jaxson and I thought it'd be fun to just throw a huge party. We're skimping on things like wedding invitations and just putting everything up on Facebook. We're using these cut corners to be able to afford a real throwdown."

"We'd love to come!" he told Sugar, and then turned towards Kylie. "You don't have anything going on on Saturday, do you?"

Kylie shook her head. "No, nothing in particular." Something passed across her face and then it was gone. Adam cocked an eyebrow at her questioningly, but Kylie just smiled back and then turned towards Sugar. "It'll be fun! Where are you getting married?"

"The Methodist Church – the ceremony starts at 11 a.m., but the party starts here that evening at 5."

"Here at the bakery?" Adam asked.

"Yeah. We thought it'd be a fun grand reopening for the bakery *and* a great wedding celebration for Jaxson and me. At first, I was just going to have Gage cater the wedding, but then I decided oh hell, why not just have it here? People can wander up and down Main Street, we'll have a street dance, and I've even talked a couple of local bands into coming and playing."

"Wow," Kylie said. "If I ever get married, I think I want to do exactly that. It sounds like a blast and a half." She took a bite of her bear claw and moaned with enjoyment, a little flake of sugar stuck to the corner of her mouth. Adam's gaze fixated on the tempting morsel, and he began having fantasies of licking it off. Sugar wouldn't mind, right? She and Jaxson probably did that sort of thing all the time.

Kylie's tongue darted out, pink and cute, and snagged the sugary goodness. *Dammit!* "We better get going," she told Sugar. "We closed up the clinic to come down here, so we should probably head back. Good luck with the wedding!"

They headed back outside, the oppressive July heat beating down on them as they began meandering back towards the clinic.

"So," he said mildly, taking a small bite of his jelly donut, trying to extend the sugar rush for as long as possible, "what's wrong with going to Jaxson and Sugar's wedding?"

CHAPTER 36

KYLIE

*a*DAM'S QUESTION caught her off-guard, her maple-glazed bundle of goodness halfway to her mouth. Her eyes shot up to his. "What?" she sputtered. "Who says that there's anything wrong with going to their wedding?"

He cocked an eyebrow at her as they walked. "I'm not gonna pretend that I've known you forever and thus can read you like a book," he said bluntly, "only because I've only really known you for about two months now. I don't count that time you listened to my 'You can be a vet!' presentation in the fifth grade. But, I will say that I can read you like a book because every thought you've ever had flashes across your face like you're telegraphing it to the world. If you want to become sneakier about your thoughts, you're gonna have to learn how to play poker 'cause right now, you suck ass."

Kylie laughed at that one. "Has anyone ever told

you that you should start being more blunt?" she asked dryly. "I'd hate for you to be holding back on *my* account."

He waved his donut around in the air dismissively, sugary crumbs flying everywhere. "When I asked you about going, you got a funny look on your face, like you'd just bit into a lemon but were trying to pretend that it was a lemon drop instead. What's going on in that head of yours?"

"Well…I mean…well, it's one thing to walk down the street holding hands or whatever," Kylie burst out. "This is Gossip Central and yeah, some tongues might wag over it. But actually showing up to a wedding together? That's like…Seriousville. That's what couples do who've been together for three years, and have adopted a dog from the pound, and have picked out curtains for their living room that match their couch. If you take me to this wedding, then people will know it's *real* and you won't be able to back down from it."

"Huh. Strange that," Adam said dryly. "Turns out, I don't want to back down from it."

Kylie rolled her eyes. "That's because you haven't seen all of the backlash from this yet. Tiffany and then Mrs. Plossy…who's next? You could lose half of your business from this. I'm just not worth it."

She clapped her non-donuted hand over her mouth. *Shit.* She hadn't meant to say that. Not out loud.

"Not worth it? Maybe you've met a different Kylie

than I have. To me, you're worth all of this, and more."

She just shook her head. He was wrong. Sweet and nice, but oh so very wrong. He was going to figure that out, sooner or later, and it just wasn't fair for him to destroy his business in the meanwhile. She needed to be strong enough to save him from himself.

The thing was, she just wasn't sure if she was that strong. To voluntarily give him up…it felt like someone was asking her to rip her right arm off.

Lost in her thoughts, Kylie was jerked back to the present when Adam announced, "Holiday today! We're going to go home now." They'd apparently reached the clinic somewhere in there because there went Adam, dragging her over to his pickup, practically pushing her inside.

"We can't just close up for the rest of the day!" Kylie protested when he'd walked around and climbed in on the driver's side. "You're supposed to check up on Mr. Miller's piglets, you've got that castration to do out at the Cowell's place, and then—"

One hand on the steering wheel, he clapped the other hand over her mouth. She squealed in surprise. "Sometimes, you're too good at your job," he said over her squeals. "If the boss says that it's vacation day, then it's vacation day. That's how this whole self-employed thing works. If the boss is any good, he won't say it very often, but when he does, you don't ask questions."

Tired of waiting for him to pull his hand away, she licked him right across the palm, causing him to jerk his hand away instinctively. "Hey!" he protested.

"You're the one who put it there," she said mildly. "I figured that just meant you wanted me to lick it."

He rubbed his palm on his jeans. "I guess I deserved that," he grumbled.

"Yeah, pretty much," she said sweetly. "So anyway, when I get to work tomorrow, do you want me to call and reschedule all of your appointments from this afternoon?"

"Yes, please. Tell them..." He paused for a moment. "Tell them that something came up."

She couldn't help herself. Her eyes dropped down to his crotch and then back up to his face. "'Something'? Usually guys have more creative names than that for their dicks."

Adam almost drove off the road in surprise, and then the laughter started. "Oh Lordy!" he said around gasps of laughter. "Remind me to never think of you as some delicate flower who can't handle vulgar language."

"It's because I'm so short," she said, shrugging.

Wait for it...wait for it...wait for it...

"Because you're so short *what?*" Adam finally said, obviously not making the connection himself and thus was forced to ask for clarification. She could tell it drove him crazy to do that, which she figured was only fair, considering his hand-over-her-mouth trick.

Next time he pulled that stunt, she'd be tempted to add a little teeth into the mix.

"People think I'm this delicate flower who is all innocent and naïve," she explained, "because I'm short and thus I look young."

"But, you *are* young."

"Hmmm…" she said, tapping her chin as if thinking hard, "and all this time, I thought it was that you were old!"

He leaned over and tickled her, keeping one eye on the road. "We'll see who's old!" he yelled over her screams of laughter. "Let's see who begs for mercy first."

She was finally able to wrestle his hand away from her stomach. Putting his pinky into her mouth, she began sucking on each calloused finger, one by one, looking at him through her eyelashes as she did it. He grabbed the steering wheel harder with his left hand. "Holy shit, Kylie, are you trying to drive me insane?" he said through gasps for air.

"Why, yes I am," she said, overly sweetly as she flipped his hand over and began nibbling her way up his wrist. "Is it working?"

His knuckles were white as he clung to the steering wheel with all of his might. "May-be," his voice cracking halfway through the panted word.

Kylie sent him a naughty grin. "Good."

Adam pressed on the gas pedal. "Lord, please don't let there be any cops out here today," he groaned. "I don't wanna have to explain why I thought it was okay to go 90 on a country back road."

She let his arm drop to the armrest between them and instead reached over with her left hand, lightly stroking his crotch through his jeans.

"Kyyylliieeeeee…" he moaned, trying to warn her off. "If you keep that up…"

"Oh look, we're here," she said pleasantly as they pulled up in front of her house, as if remarking on nothing more than the weather. "I'm ready to go inside now." She pulled back, unbuckled her seatbelt, and slid out of the passenger side of the truck as if she were perfectly fine. As if her legs weren't shaking from need and desire, and as if her breath wasn't short and choppy.

Torturing Adam just a little bit…yeah, she was okay with that.

He hurried around the truck and swung her up into his arms, carrying her up the dirt pathway to her front door. "Adam!" she hollered, throwing her arms around his neck and clinging to him for dear life. "You can't just pick a girl up and carry her around wherever you want."

He grinned down at her mischievously. "Well now, that's where you're wrong," he said as he juggled her and the door knob, finally getting the old door to creak open. "I figure God made you fun-sized for a reason. I wrestle steers and stallions and Great Danes around all day. A little thing like you? I hardly even notice I've got you in my arms." He carried her into the living room and up the stairs towards her bedroom.

Hardly even notices I'm here, huh? That just seemed like a challenge to her. She nosed apart the collar of his shirt and began sucking on the triangle of skin she found there, swirling her tongue over the dips and valleys, and then pulled back and blew softly on the wet skin.

"Kyyyllliiieeee," he panted, finally getting to her bedroom and laying her down on the antique brass bed.

"You keep saying my name like you think I've forgotten what it is," she said, straight-faced as she looked up at him. "I promise you, I know what my name is."

"Oh, I know that," he said, his eyes dark with promise. "But what I'm aiming to do is to make you scream mine."

She sucked in a breath at that, staring up at him. "Oh," she said weakly, all of her teasing and bravado gone. *When you put it like that…*

He pulled off her ballet flats and thin socks, and then reached up and began tugging down her maternity pants, the wide elastic band easily puddling once it got past her belly. "Have I ever told you how sexy I think maternity pants are?" he said as he pulled them off her feet and tossed them in the corner.

That jerked her out of the world she'd been blissfully drifting in and back to the present.

"Maternity pants?" she asked incredulously. "You're kidding me, right?"

He shrugged as he began nibbling his way up her legs. Her shaved, lotioned legs, thankyouverymuch. After this past weekend, she wasn't taking any more chances. She'd never been the best about keeping her legs shaved, but she had a three-day streak going now. "Just that they say to the world that you're pregnant," he explained, doing delicious, probably illegal things with his tongue. "After trying for years with Wendy and never having her get to the point where she needed them, they just mean a lot to me." He kissed and sucked and blew on her legs, working his way up to the juncture of her thighs.

Groaning with lust, she lay back on the bed. She could argue with him over his strange fetishes later. Right now, that required too much… "Oohhhhh…" she breathed as he moved over the curls and began blowing lightly on them, sending waves of heat through her. "That's…oh my…I can't…" He nosed between her curls and ran his tongue over her clit, sending her hips straight up into the air. "Oh my God," she hollered. "Oh God!"

"Now see, that's where you're wrong," he said mildly, sitting back on his heels. Her eyes fluttered opened and she stared up at him, completely confused. English. He was speaking English, but the words weren't making any sense at all.

"Whatswrong?" she mumbled, trying to concentrate even as waves of desire washed over her.

If he didn't get back to her clit and pronto, she was gonna go insane.

"My name. It isn't God, it's Adam. I told you that I'd make you scream *my* name with desire."

Her mouth opened and closed wordlessly – *again* with the goldfish impersonation! – and then she bust out laughing. "I don't know if you've ever heard of a thing called humility, but it might be something to look into."

"Just telling you what I'm aiming for," he said with a nonchalant shrug, and then went back to work with his tongue and fingers and—

"Ooohhhhh!!!!" she yelled, her back arching. "Yes, yes, yes…" It was that red haze again, but this time, it was a wonderful red haze and she couldn't stop thrashing as shocks of electricity coursed through her.

He was pulling off her top and bra and then running his hands all over her body. "Beautiful Kylie," he murmured. "So gorgeous." She heard him, distant, like someone shouting from the end of a tunnel, every nerve ending centered on his fingers and mouth. Then Baby moved around, kicking her, and she let out a muffled "Oof!"

"Are you okay?" he asked, worried, immediately pulling back, staring down at her with concern in his eyes. "If you don't want to—"

"No, no, I promise you I do. Baby was just making their presence known, is all. Gonna grow up to be a world-class soccer player at this rate." She decided to use their small break to roll him over onto his back.

"Well now, this is better," she murmured, running her hands up and down the valleys and peaks of his body appreciatively. His long, lean muscles – not built in a gym but out in the field, working with his hands every day under the Idaho sun – they were oh so delicious. And tempting.

She followed his happy trail down his flat abs to his *very* attentive dick. She wrapped her fingers around it and began sucking and pumping, licking up the precum that'd teetered on top.

"Oh Kylie!" he hollered, his head tossing back and forth on the pillow. "Yes, please, feels, yes, need—"

"Turns out I'm not the only one who knows how to shout names around here," she said with a naughty grin, and then bent over to begin sucking again. She had to spread her knees just a bit to allow for room for her belly – she could already tell that sex was going to become more gymnastic the farther she got in her pregnancy – and sucked happily.

"I, you, can't—" He pushed her shoulders away. "You have to stop," he said in one breath, "before all of the fun comes to a stop for us. Buddy here is still relearning, you know." He closed his eyes and took a couple of shuddering breaths. "God almighty," he finally said, opening up his eyes to look up at her, "where on earth did you learn to do that?"

"You mean suck cock?" she asked, confused.

"Yeah. Wow. I remember it felt good, but that…" He screwed his eyes closed for a minute and then they popped back open. "I've never felt anything so good in my life."

She sent him a pleased smile. "I think it's best not to discuss my previous sex life with you," she said awkwardly, "but I'm gonna take the compliment and roll with it."

He pulled her up so she was straddling his stomach, his dick pressing up against the crack of her ass. "Good," he grunted. "I really didn't want to talk about Norm right now anyway." She let out a snort of laughter and then a groan of desire as he pulled her forward, her dangling breasts sliding — one and then the other — into his mouth.

She'd always been on the smaller side up top, but she was quickly discovering one side benefit of being pregnant – along with her belly rapidly expanding, so were her breasts. After years of wearing padded bras and moaning about her complete lack of cleavage, she was really starting to appreciate this.

And then Adam was picking her up and sliding her into place over his dick, his eyes closing in ecstasy. "Yes," he moaned, guiding her hips up and down as she bounced in rhythm to the desire pounding through her. "Yes, yes, yes—"

"Adaaaammmmmmm!" she hollered, throwing her head back and arching her back and the world was going dark and then light and she couldn't breathe and every muscle was tensed—

Just as she was starting to come back to earth, Adam let out a shout and she felt him tensing inside of her, his dick pulsating as he came. Finally, he relaxed and his eyelids fluttered open. He grinned up at her and said with a wink, "I told you I'd get you to scream my name."

And she laughed and he tugged her down beside him on the bed, tucking her next to him, drifting off to sleep together.

*A*DAM AWOKE SLOWLY, his eyes fluttering open, his brain trying to figure out where he was. The light was all wrong…

Kylie turned over, mumbling about carrots as she moved, and it all came back to him. He was in his rental. In Kylie's bedroom, to be specific. In Kylie's bed, to be even more specific. He lay back with a happy groan. Waking up with Kylie by his side, after the most mind-blowing sex he'd ever had…well, other than the first time he and Kylie had made love, that was.

Yeah, life was going pretty damn awesome. He stacked his hands behind his head, staring up at the ceiling, a feeling of déjà vu washing over him as he lay there. How many times had he done exactly this with Wendy? It was weird to be in the same house, the same bedroom, the same bed even, but a different woman. He waited for the guilt to come – the self-recriminating thoughts about how he shouldn't be so happy since the love of his life had died in his arms and he hadn't been able to do a damn thing to save her, but...it didn't appear.

Instead, he felt a sense of peace wash over him and for the first time, he wondered how Wendy would've felt about him basically becoming a monk since she passed. Would she have wanted it?

Maybe it was just him wishing for this answer, but he couldn't help but think that she wouldn't. She'd loved him with everything she had, and he'd loved her just as much. In the year after she'd died, all he could think was that he wished he'd died that day in the stream, too.

Anything to escape the pain.

But she wouldn't have wanted that. He knew that – he'd always known that – but for the first time since his wife's passing, he *believed* that.

Kylie turned back towards Adam, stretching out her fingertips and grazing his side lightly. "I can smell the burning rubber all the way over here," she whispered, her eyes still shut, her fingers dancing over him. "Whatcha thinking about?"

He chuckled and snuggled her closer to him. "That it's damn nice to wake up next to you," he whispered into her hair. Which was close enough to the truth. She didn't need to know how messed up he'd become over the years, trying to deal with the pain of Wendy dying in his arms.

No one needed to know that.

"Liar," she said softly, burrowing deeper into his side.

Speaking of liars…

"I know you think that I took you here to make wild, passionate love to you—" she snorted with laughter at that and he grinned for a moment before continuing, "—but I'd actually wanted some privacy to talk to you."

"Talk? About what?" she murmured, her hand drifting across his chest and over to his suddenly very erect and very interested nipples.

He captured her wandering hand in his and held it tight. If she kept that up, they'd never get anything important discussed. His dick could wait for a minute.

It wouldn't be happy, but it could do it.

"About what happened when you told Norm that you were pregnant," he said seriously, and she instantly went rigid in his arms.

Bingo.

She probably had no idea that her body language was so revealing, but based on just that response, he was now *damn* sure that there was something that'd happened that night that she wasn't telling.

And if he was right, it'd relate to that comment she'd made earlier about not being worth it. He was about 98.2% sure that this Norman guy (who really deserved to have his teeth rearranged and as Adam figured it, he was just the guy to do it), had screwed with her head big time.

"I already told you about that night," she said,

sitting up and pushing her hair out of her face. She crossed her arms across her chest. "There's really not much more to say."

"During our walk by that damn river," Adam said mildly, "you told me that you told Norm about the pregnancy, and that's when he revealed that he was already married."

"Yeah? So?" she asked defensively. "What else is there to say?"

He rolled over onto his side, propping his head up with his hand, intentionally keeping his body language loose and welcoming. He reached out and stroked her knee. "Well, I'm going to guess that the conversation continued after that," he said, keeping his voice even and calm. She was on the verge of hysterics, he could tell. It was building up inside of her, like a volcano just preparing to explode. "When he told you that he was married, what did you say?"

"I was in shock. I sputtered and yelled and cried a bit."

"And what did he say in defense of it?"

"Just that he was gone from home a lot and it was hard for a man with his needs to go that long between each session of…you know…sex." She waved her hand in the air dismissively.

"All right, so he said it was okay to cheat on his wife because he was incapable of keeping his dick in his pants. And then what?"

"And then what *what*?" Kylie repeated, her whole

body so rigid, he was pretty sure he could use her as a ruler in that moment.

"Well, he didn't divorce his wife and move to Sawyer, Idaho with you," Adam pointed out. "You're not engaged, you're not married, and unless you're hiding it pretty well, you're not in contact with him. Are you?"

She shook her head, lips pressed tightly together.

"So after you two established that he's a scumball and asshole extraordinaire, what did you guys discuss about the future? About the baby?"

Her gaze dropped to the bedspread between them and she began plucking at a loose thread. She didn't say anything for a long time, and as Adam studied her face, waiting patiently for her to keep talking, he knew she was debating whether or not to tell him the truth. Whether or not their relationship was worth the pain of reliving that night.

Then, finally…

"He walked over to his jeans piled on the floor," she said in a dead voice, "pulled out his wallet, and threw five one hundred dollar bills at me. Told me to take care of the problem. Told me I wasn't worth marrying; wasn't worth screwing up his life over. Told me that he'd been thinking he would stop coming to Bend for a while now, but that I'd been so needy, so desperate for him, that he'd continued to come just to placate me, but that we were over now. He put his clothes back on, and as he was leaving, he told me one last time that I better 'take care of it.' Then he walked out."

Her voice was robotic, like she was reciting an entry from the encyclopedia, but the tears...

There were tears streaming down her cheeks that gave it away. No matter how hard she tried to shut herself down, the tears betrayed her. She didn't make a move to wipe them away, almost as if she believed that if she didn't acknowledge them, then they didn't exist.

Adam continued to stroke up and down her thigh, trying to convey a sense of calm and peace and love. He felt like a world-class asshole himself even as he quietly asked, "That's it? He just walked out?" He didn't want to pry, he didn't want to break her, but he could also feel something else there, something under the skin that she wasn't letting out.

"He threw me around a bit, okay?!" she snarled, head jerking up, pale green eyes glowing with pain and hatred and anger and hurt. "Are you happy? He made sure not to touch my face but the rest of me was fair game. I'm lucky I didn't lose the baby that night. He whaled on me, told me I was a dumb bitch, he couldn't believe I'd gotten pregnant, couldn't believe he had to clean up this mess. Told me I wasn't worth his time. I wasn't worth...I wasn't worth anything at all."

And then she broke.

The thing he hadn't wanted to see but somehow

knew needed to happen, happened right before his eyes.

She curled up in a ball on the bed, crying hysterically, screaming into the mattress, nothing making sense, shoulders shaking, deep shuddering breaths. Adam curled himself around her, his body shielding her from the world, from Norman, from everything. She shook and sobbed and cried for what seemed like hours. As he held her, he thought about the words she'd said, how this monster had beat her.

Adam had thought before that he knew what hate was. He hated getting stepped on by a cow. He hated lima beans. He hated not getting everything done in a day that he needed to.

But this…this was hatred that went bone deep. Beyond reasoning, beyond thought, beyond explanation, he hated Norman. Adam had never thought of himself as being a particularly violent man but in that moment, all he could think about was if he ever met this Norman, he'd kill him.

He'd kill him, and it'd be worth it. Because anyone who did this to a sweet person like Kylie…they didn't deserve to live anymore.

"After he left," she said dully, her words breaking into his anger and hatred, drawing him back into the moment, "I picked myself up off the floor. Everything moved okay, and I realized that he didn't break anything. So I started packing. He knew where I lived and where I worked; I couldn't stay there. I wasn't about to have an abortion of my baby. My roommate came home in the middle of it and totally freaked out because I looked like a mess, but I just kept packing. I took everything I could fit into my suitcase, left everything else behind, and bought a ticket home on the Greyhound bus. I used his money to escape him. I think the irony is rather well deserved, to be honest."

She stopped talking and just lay there, bones loose, face pale and streaked with tears, staring off into the distance. She had nothing left in her. He continued to stroke down her body, pushing her hair away from her face, holding her, loving her.

"I haven't told anyone what happened," she whispered, breaking into the silence surrounding them. "Well, my roommate guessed, of course, but she promised not to say anything. When I got here to Sawyer, I just told my mom about the baby and him being married, but nothing else. You know how Mom is." She waved her hand in the air dismissively. "She would've wanted to file a police report and drag his ass into court and get him behind bars, but I know him. I know how charismatic and charming he can be, and it'd just be my word against his. So what if I had a few bruises on my body? I could be a clumsy person. I could've been robbed by a maniac on the street. How can I prove that it was him who did it to me? Plus..." She drew in a deep, shuddering breath. "I was a wimp when he first showed up that night. I didn't want to tell him and ruin the beautiful relationship that we had."

She rolled her eyes at herself. "I had myself

convinced that he was going to propose to me when he heard the news, but there was some deeper part of me that knew that this revelation would be destructive. So instead of just telling him the truth right away, we had sex first. I was the one who initiated it. I wanted to just forget everything for a minute. So yeah, we had consensual sex and then he beat on me. A defense lawyer could say that maybe I just liked things rough and it was part of our sexual relationship." She shrugged. "So, he gets away with it."

Adam knew that it was his job to listen and to console, not to try to solve the problem, *if* there even was a solution for it. Short of tracking the guy down and doing some dental work on him, it was too late to file a police report against him or press charges. Sure, it wasn't too late under the law, but without pictures to prove injuries, it would be a horribly difficult case to prove at this point.

Despite knowing that, it was still unreasonably difficult to keep his anger in check. What if Norm was doing this to other women? Defenseless women who were smaller and weaker than him? He was a stereotypical bully – he'd never pick on someone who could actually put up a fair fight. That wouldn't be any fun at all. But fun-sized Kylie...she made an easy target.

How many other Kylies were there out there?

Adam was sick at the thought.

"I'll be leaving now," she said dully. "I can pack

up my stuff and be out by morning." She swung her legs off the bed, trying to push herself upright. "My mom will help me move out, so you don't need to let me use your truck again."

Adam's hand snaked out and grabbed Kylie's arm. "What?" he asked, totally bewildered. "What are you talking about?"

"You've been sitting there, trying to think of how to tell me to get out of your life," she said, her eyes dead, her voice wooden. "I'm trying to make it easy on you. Isn't that what all men want? For the women in their lives to just shut up and go away and stop being so needy all the time?" She let out a short, humorless laugh. "Please take your clothes and get dressed elsewhere, though. I'd like to get dressed now, and I don't want to do it in front of you."

"Kylie, darlin', we need to take a step back for just a moment," Adam said, trying to maintain the calm demeanor he'd been using all along. It began to slip on him, though, when he faced the thought of losing her. "I haven't been sitting here, trying to think of how to get rid of you. I've been sitting here, trying to understand how monsters like Norman still exist. There's a large part of me that wants to track him down and do some dental work on him, but I know that—"

"Dental work?" she interrupted him, eyebrows creased, looking puzzled. It was the first time she looked anything but robotic since he forced this topic out into the open, and Adam clung to that small improvement like a lifeline tossed from the Titanic.

"Yeah. You know, rearrange his teeth a little. Punch him in the face. Show him what it feels like to be on the receiving end for once."

She looked genuinely puzzled, as if Adam had begun speaking Swahili on her, and he reached out his hand to stroke her cheek, laughing a little as he did so. "Honey, falling in love with a charming, narcissistic asshole doesn't mean that you deserve to be treated like shit. It just means that he was convincing and manipulative, and you, being the sweet person that you are, believed him. It's a commentary on him, not on you."

"Don't call me 'honey,'" she said quietly.

He cocked an eyebrow, waiting patiently for her to explain her request, because there was *absolutely* a story behind that one.

"It was his nickname for me. It's common, of course, but I don't think he called me Kylie but once or twice. It was *always* 'honey.' Now that I know the truth, I think he did it because it was easier for him to just call everyone 'honey.' What if he'd accidentally screwed up and called me by his wife's name or something?"

"I imagine for a serial philanderer, it's a difficult problem to manage," Adam said with a small laugh. "I'd pretend to have sympathy for him, but I'm afraid I don't have much at this point."

"Yeah. Me either." Kylie shot him a grimace that

he guessed was supposed to be a smile, and then they sat in silence for a minute. Adam wanted to make sure she'd said all that she wanted to say. This was her time to get this shit off her chest, and he wasn't going to interrupt her if she had anything left to spill.

When she didn't say anything else, though, he reached out his hand and stroked it over her cheek, staring up into her red-rimmed eyes. "Darlin', God only knows that this is easier said than done, but I'm telling you right now: Whatever bullshit that man told you, he was wrong. You need to not only *know* that, but *believe* that. With me, right here, right now, I want to start over."

He drew in a deep breath for courage, and then plunged on.

"When I tell you that I love you, when I tell you that you're the world to me, when I tell you that I'd give up almost anything to make you smile, I damn well mean it. I don't play games. It isn't in my DNA. My mother loved one man her whole life. She'll be the first to say that she's a 'one man woman!' and she shakes her finger in the air when she says it. I'm up to two, but yeah. I'm definitely my mother's son."

"Two?" Kylie asked, confused. "I thought you loved Wendy and Chloe before me."

"Wendy – absolutely. Wholeheartedly. I loved her since I knew what love was. But Chloe...I've been thinking about it for a while now. I helped her give birth on the side of the road, in the middle of a blizzard, and then was a big part of her life for nine years. She friend-zoned me out of the gate, though, and I never really had a chance with her.

"To be honest, I think she was more attractive to me *because* of that. She was safe. We would never go anywhere as a couple, and after Wendy's death, that's actually what I wanted, even if I didn't know it myself. I wasn't ready to move on yet, so I put her up on this pedestal, a pedestal that no woman could actually live up to. If you never really get to know someone, then they can appear perfect. It was easy to retain that illusion from afar. But no one is truly perfect."

"What?!" Kylie gasped in mock outrage, a bit of a laugh sneaking into her voice that had been missing since this whole awful discussion began. "Are you trying to imply, sir, that I am not perfect? Tell me, in which way do I fall short of perfection?"

"Well, speaking of being short, you obviously didn't eat your Wheaties growing up, a terrible failure on your part." He ignored her protests that being compared to a giant just wasn't fair, and continued on. "Then there's your insane predilection towards carrots instead of donuts, which is *obviously* a sign of some sort of mental defect—"

"Mental defect?!" she half yelled, half laughed. "Just because I think that eating healthy is—"

"And then, of course," he continued on, bowling right over her, "you have this unhealthy obsession with mops and brooms and Windex. I mean, have you *seen* the floor of the clinic lately? I swear to God, you could eat off it. It just isn't right." He shook his head mournfully. "Oh, for the days of cobwebs and gray walls and dirt-encrusted everything. Don't hate me too much, spiders − *I* wasn't the one who took your home away."

Kylie was laughing so hard, she couldn't even protest anymore, but rather collapsed onto the bed, holding her sides as she roared with laughter.

"I don't even know how it is," he said softly, hovering over her with a gentle smile, "that I can put up with you." He kissed her and she looked up at him, laughter and a bittersweet happiness in her pale green eyes. "Not with such a terrible list of flaws like you have," he whispered.

"It is awfully kind of you," she said solemnly. He could see that she was drifting in that in-between world, between laughter and crying, and just the slightest push could send her spinning back the other direction. She was fragile in that moment; far beyond the fragility of her small frame, but rather it was a deep fragility, a hairline crack running through her emotions that could be broken with just the slightest pressure. "Speaking of being kind," she whispered, "would you be so kind as to just hold me for a minute?"

"Anytime," he whispered, and pulled her against him, wrapping his arm tight around her waist, drifting through the summer evening with her in his arms.

CHAPTER 38

ADAM

*A*DAM OPENED the front door of his mom's house quietly, hoping she was still asleep by some miracle. He'd ended up falling asleep at Kylie's on accident and didn't wake up until her alarm went off this morning. Unfortunately, Kylie got up later than he did, so he was running behind even more than usual, which was saying something.

His mom looked up from the dining room table and without a word, folded up the *Franklin Gazette* and set it off to the side.

Shit. He'd been caught by his mother, trying to sneak into the house without her noticing, and of course, she'd noticed. He swallowed his groan. He was *way* too old to put up with this sort of thing from his mother, for hell's sakes.

But when she opened her mouth, she surprised him. "Adam, I want to apologize," she said solemnly.

He felt his jaw hit the deck. His mother?

Apologize? This wasn't exactly something that she did regularly. Or, ever, to be more precise.

"You can wipe that look of shock off your face," she said mildly. "I've apologized to you before."

About what? And when? But he decided that if he was ever going to actually hear this apology of hers, he should keep his sarcastic thoughts to himself.

Instead, he slid into his chair kitty corner from his mom's and took her soft, spotted hand in his. "What's going on?" he asked.

"The other day, when you talked to me about the retirement home, I didn't take it well."

The corners of Adam's mouth threatened to curl up at that one, but he fought hard to keep a straight face. To be fair to his mother, she didn't exactly have a lot of experience apologizing to other people. He needed to cut her some slack. But still... "Not well"? Sure, and he'd heard that the Titanic's maiden voyage didn't "go well," either.

"This whole arthritis thing has really been difficult, but I kept telling myself at least I was staying in my home. It was my consolation prize – maybe I can't crochet anymore, but darn it all, I can sleep in my own bed under my own roof."

She shook her head, her faded blue eyes downcast as she pulled her hand away from Adam's and began fiddling with the head of her cane. "Asking you to move in with me...I should've known from that, that I wasn't going to last much longer here. Well, I guess in the end, it did give me quite a few more years, but still, I shouldn't have even asked you to move in here. That was me being selfish and wanting to extend my independence for as long as possible.

"Zara…she's wonderful. And I really appreciate her coming over, and I appreciate you arranging for that." She leaned over and squeezed his hand. "But she's a girl and she needs to live in her own house with her parents, not here with me, and…I need more help than some afternoons a couple of times a week." She swallowed hard, looking rather like she'd just bit into a wormy apple. "Margaret and Susan both live up at the retirement home, and they love it. They volunteer down at the second-hand store and say it's the best part of their week. I'd like to go outside and do something for other people. I feel so worthless, just sitting around and reading all the time. I want to help other people. I want to be wanted."

This was exactly what Kylie had told me. She knew my mother better than I did.

She let out a big, shuddering sigh, and then said softly, "I'm not going to tell you that I want to do something just yet, but will you take me over to the center? I want to look around, and then think about it. Would you be kind enough to take me there, even after I behaved so badly to you?"

Adam pulled in a deep breath. "I would love to, Mom, but we need to talk about what you said about Kylie. If I'm lucky, I'll marry her someday, and I won't have my mother talking about my wife like that. Did you mean what you said, or were you just angry?"

"To tell you the truth, I don't even remember what I said." She grimaced. "I was mad and wanted to make you mad. Which is a sad state of affairs for someone as old as me to find herself in, 'cause I should be old enough to know better. My momma raised me better than that. I...I was scared." She shrugged her thin shoulders.

Adam wasn't about to let her off the hook so easily, though. "You said she was trying to get rid of you so she could have me all to herself. You were also angry about the car being sold to her."

His mother's pale cheeks turned a bright red. "Oh my, oh my," she whispered, distressed. "I didn't mean it, I promise. You didn't tell her any of that, did you?"

"I generally don't start World War III before breakfast if I can help it," he said dryly. "No, I knew you weren't yourself in that moment, and I wasn't about to report any of that to Kylie. She is just trying to help. She likes you a lot, and I want to keep it that way."

His mom reached out her liver-spotted hands to pat his. "Thank you," she said softly. "I really like Kylie, too – she makes you happy, and for that, I'd love her even if she were a three-headed monster who ate cats for breakfast, although I have to say that her being sweet and hardworking certainly doesn't hurt her case."

"Sassy, did you hear that?" Adam called out. She lifted her calico head and stared at him, yawning as he talked. "Your momma says it's okay if a three-headed monster eats you for breakfast."

Deciding that nothing of interest was happening, Sassy snuggled back down into the couch and went right back to sleep.

"She's terrified," Adam said, turning back to his mom.

"I can see that," his mom said dryly, and laughed. "I don't know what your schedule looks like this week," she said, returning to the topic at hand, "but if you can take me over to the home at some point, I'd like to tour it with you. Then I can decide."

Adam's mind skipped back to his "Let's play hooky" attitude yesterday afternoon. Had it really only been 18 hours ago? It felt like a lifetime ago. But because he'd skipped his appointments yesterday, that meant he was even more behind today.

And yet…

"Let's go right now," he said impulsively. "I'll have Kylie move my appointments from this morning. I don't have anything pressing going on – no one is giving birth or dying on me – so what I'm doing can be moved by a day or two."

"Today?" Mom said, her eyes lighting up with excitement. "Well then, I best get ready! I can't go there looking like *this*." At Adam's blank look – she looked like she always did – she shook her head in disgust. "Men," she muttered, and then pushed herself to her feet. "I'll be back in a jiffy," she promised him, pushing her walker down the hallway as she hurried as fast as her old bones would allow her.

She came back wearing a string of pearls, a matching pantsuit he hadn't seen in ages, and bright red lipstick. "C'mon," she said, winding her arm through his, "if we hurry, we might be able to catch breakfast. I want to see what they consider to be a meal. Bad food will kill me off faster than you can say 'Kentucky.'"

As Adam escorted his mother to his truck, helping to get her into the passenger seat safely, he couldn't wipe the grin off his face. Really, life couldn't be much better than this.

CHAPTER 39

KYLIE

KYLIE LEANED OVER, trying to snag the paper off the ground that she'd just dropped. "Oof," she gasped, as her belly squished up against her knees. She really wasn't used to having to maneuver around a volleyball, sticking out of the front of her everywhere she went. "Sorry, girlfriend," she said, patting her stomach reassuringly. "I remember that you're there. I just forgot for a moment that I can't bend over anymore." She carefully slid off her chair and knelt down, finally giving her access to the damn piece of paper. She heaved herself back up into the chair.

"Everything all right up here?" Adam asked, popping his head around the corner from the back room.

"Oh yeah. Me and the baby, we're just gonna have to decide who's gonna be where so we can start making reservations a week before we need to get there." She was trying to make a joke about how her belly was arriving places a week before the rest of her did, but based on the blank look Adam was giving her, she could tell she'd lost him. "So," she said, hurrying on – explained jokes were just never very funny, "I was thinking about going for a little walk, just to stretch my legs, and I thought I'd go down to the Muffin Man to pick up coffee or something. Do you want me to get anything for you?"

He gave her a hang-dog look and she bust out laughing. "Chocolate donut with sprinkles and a jelly donut it is," she said with a teasing sigh. "But only if you eat those carrot sticks I cut up and put in the fridge first."

"Deal," he said, giving her a long, thorough kiss.

"And feeding them to Mr. Mopsy doesn't count," she whispered against his lips.

"What? Who me?" he asked innocently, pulling back a bit and batting his brown eyes at her. "I'd never dream of such a thing."

"I'm gonna tell Ollie to keep an eye on you. He won't let you cheat."

"I don't know where you get this idea of me," he said, flabbergasted. "Why, I am the very picture of good health and good eating."

"You tried to argue last week that Snickers was good for you because it has nuts in it," she reminded him dryly. "You keep this up, and you're gonna be 900 pounds. Ollie!" she hollered.

Adam snuck one last kiss from her, muttered

something about being henpecked, and disappeared into the back again. Kylie rolled her eyes, trying and failing to keep a grin from spreading across her face.

Hmmm…well, it's okay to smile since he can't see me, she decided. *Encouraging him, though…that would* not *be a good idea.*

"Yes, Ms. Kylie?" Ollie asked, appearing in the doorway to the back.

"First off, there's carrots and celery sticks back in the fridge. I want you and Dr. Whitaker to have them all eaten by the time I get back from the bakery. Second, I want them eaten by you two, not by Mr. Mopsy. He's here to get testing done, not to eat his weight in carrot sticks. Third, what donut do you want me to get for you from the bakery?"

"Oh, Bavarian creme!" he said, his face lighting up at the talk of donuts. He looked…decidedly more excited about that than the carrots and celery she was insisting he eat.

Why was she not surprised…

"I'll be back in a minute," she told him. "If the phone rings, just let it go to voicemail. I'll call 'em when I get back." She'd done her best to teach him not to lecture clients on whether it was okay to have a business card, but still, it seemed best to leave client relations up to her.

She walked out into the heat of the late July sun, letting the warmth pound down on her for a moment, and then began meandering towards the Muffin Man. She was excited by the chance to get out and stretch her legs, sure, but she was more excited to go chat with Sugar.

After attending Sugar and Jaxson's wedding three weeks ago, Kylie felt like she finally had a friend in the area. She'd never been real close to anyone in Sawyer growing up – definitely one of the reasons why it'd been so easy to move to Oregon for college and leave Long Valley behind – and the few people she would've reached out to since she moved back home had also moved away, so other than her botched attempt to make friends at Knit Wits, she hadn't had much of a chance to expand her social circle.

Sugar had been four years older than her in school, which had seemed *so important* back then, but didn't mean diddly squat now. Post high school was a pretty nice world to live in, after all.

She walked into the cool of the bakery and sucked in a deep breath. "Oh, that's nice," she murmured to herself.

"Hi, Kylie!" Sugar said, coming out of the back and wiping her hands on her apron. "How are things going?" Her eyes dropped down to Kylie's belly and back up to her face. "Wow! For some reason, I thought you were only like five months along or something."

Kylie sent her a pained smile. "It'll be six months in another five days and before you ask, no, I'm not having twins. I'm apparently just like my momma – I carry my babies up front and proud. I just made a joke to Adam about arriving somewhere a week after my belly did, and he just looked confused. I'm afraid pregnancy humor is rather lost on him." She sighed. "He's started seeing a lot more patients in the clinic, making clients take their animals down to the clinic whenever possible, rather than driving out to see them at their house, because he doesn't want to leave me alone. He's got the helicoptering part down flat, and I'm not even due for another three months."

"You should've seen Jaxson after the bakery fire," Sugar said, laughing. "Every time I sneezed, he wanted to take me to the emergency room. I finally had to tell him, 'I love you, baby, but if you don't go back to work and stop hovering over me, I'm going to leave you.' Apparently, I finally convinced him that I meant it, because he went back to work the next day. That didn't stop him from hovering over me before and after work, and sometimes during work, but I at least got breathers in between."

They laughed together for a moment, and then Kylie said, "So, I'm on a donut run. I'm making Adam and Ollie eat carrots and celery before I give them their donuts, but I figure that if I promise them sugar in return for veggies, at least they get veggies into their system at some point."

"Bavarian creme, jelly donut, and a chocolate one with sprinkles?" Sugar asked, already starting to pull the sleeves out to ready them.

"I'm not sure what that says about the eating habits of the employees of Whitaker's Veterinarian

Clinic that you have that memorized," Kylie said wryly.

"The only one I don't have memorized is you, and that's because you actually pick a different one every time."

"*Moi?*" Kylie said, placing a hand over her chest innocently. "Why, I hardly ever eat sugar. But since I'm here..." She began wandering along the display case. "Oh, the coconut one," she said decidedly, pointing to the delicious-looking donut with shredded coconut heaped on top. Sugar scooped it up and slid it into its own bag.

"I've been meaning to tell you that we got pictures up on Facebook from the wedding," Sugar said, ringing up the total on the cash register. "Apparently, the photographer forgot to get one of just you and Adam, even though I specifically asked her to, but there were a few with you two in the background. Between customers, I've been doing nothing but tagging people in pics. I can't believe how much your stomach has grown just since the wedding! I mean, in the wedding pictures, I could see the baby bump, of course, but it's definitely gotten bigger since then. You're just about the cutest pregnant woman I've ever laid eyes on. It isn't fair how adorable you make it look, honestly. Have you found out if it's a girl or a boy, or do you want to be surprised?"

Kylie had heard the words, off in the distance, registering somewhere in the back of her mind, even as the rest of her mind was busy screaming in panic and terror. *Not on Facebook. I can't be on Facebook. Not Facebook. He could find me. Oh God, I should've taken my Facebook profile down…*

"A girl," she murmured, answering Sugar's question even as she tried not to retch in fear. She smiled broadly at Sugar, panic thrumming through her veins. "A girl. I couldn't be happier." She shoved a ten-dollar bill across the counter and snagged the bag of donuts, practically running for the door.

"Are you oka—" and then Kylie was outside, heading down the street. Towards the clinic and her phone and Facebook.

Stupid. So stupid. She'd been careful since she got home, making sure to only take pictures of her face when posting on Facebook. No mention of the pregnancy at all. She'd ducked Sugar's photographer all night, making sure to head the other direction whenever she seemed intent on her and Adam. She'd even turned off all of the geographical tagging that Facebook liked to include, and had stuck to generic posts about, "Having a good day today!" She hadn't wanted to go completely silent because people might worry over that, but she'd hoped…

She'd hoped for the impossible, honestly. Why would Sugar make sure not to tag her in photos on Facebook if Kylie didn't tell her the truth about Norman? Why would anyone think to be careful about that?

And if it hadn't been Sugar's wedding, it would've been something else. She should've just gone silent and deleted her account. Let a few people worry. Better than letting that dickwad track her down. She didn't want to lose all of the pics and posts and videos she'd been making on Facebook ever since her mom *finally* let her get an account when she was 13 – way past the age most of her friends got their own account – but was that truly worth it in the end?

Stupid, stupid, stupid Kylie...

She hurried into the cool of the clinic and directly over to the front desk, leaning over the counter and grabbing her phone to log into Facebook without even bothering to walk around the counter so she could sit down. Every second counted. Hands trembling, she brought up her Facebook app, a big bell of notifications sitting there. She quickly untagged herself from every picture at the wedding, grimacing at the roundness of her stomach so blatantly noticeable. Sugar'd seemed to think that Kylie'd grown a lot since the wedding, but honestly? She really hadn't been that small back then.

"Hi–oh, hey Ms. Kylie," Ollie said, coming to a stop when he saw her. He'd obviously heard the ringing of the bell over the doorway and had thought a customer had come in. "Everything okay?" he asked, taking in her sweaty clothes from her jog through the summer heat, the panic that was no doubt registering on every cell in her face, and the fact that she was standing on the wrong damn side of the counter.

Yeah, probably not hard to figure out that something was wrong.

She flashed him a casual smile. *Everything is fine...* "Oh yeah, just forgot to send a text message before I left. Did you guys eat your veggies?"

"Yup, all of them. We split them in half. Dr. Whitaker said it was fairer that way." Even as Kylie was sliding her phone back onto her desk – the tags deleted – and grabbing the donuts nonchalantly, like absolutely nothing was wrong, a small part of her brain celebrated the fact that Ollie was actually talking to her. Real sentences and everything. Although she was a human, and even worse, a *girl*, he must've decided that since she was also a regular purveyor of donuts, she was okay to like anyway.

"Well, in that case, I say we celebrate by enjoying some donuts." She flashed him another smile, promising herself that she'd go ahead and completely delete her Facebook account that night. As tough as that was to lose all of that information she'd posted over the years, not giving Norm the breadcrumbs to find her? Priceless.

*a*DAM DROVE DOWN the street towards the clinic, singing along lustily to the song on the radio.

I had a barbeque stain on my white t-shirt
She was killin' me in that mini skirt
Skipping rocks on the river by the railroad tracks
She had a suntan line and red lipsti—

"What the hell?" he exclaimed, his eyes focusing on a bright red antique convertible parked in front of the clinic. He turned down the radio and then squinted into the bright August sunshine. It wasn't a car that he recognized and as many miles as he put on his truck, driving around the area, checking on animals…

That was really saying something.

As he pulled in next to it, he noticed the Utah

license plates. Definitely not from around here, then. Why were they stopping at his clinic? A hurt pet while on the road? The Long Valley area was a tourist destination, sure, but the Whitaker Veterinarian Clinic was definitely not on the list of the Top 10 Things You Must Do While in Idaho.

He swung out of his truck and headed for the door, taking one last look at the older car over his shoulder as he went. There was something wrong here. There was something about this car that was setting off alarm bells in his head, and it wasn't worry about an animal potentially hurt and waiting inside for him. No, there was something else—

A Karmann Ghia. It was a Ghia.

Holy shit, it was a cherry red antique Karmann Ghia.

He grabbed the door handle of the clinic and yanked it open just as he heard Kylie cry out, "Don't!" His eyes swept the room, taking it all in, everything in slow motion, bile rising up in his throat. There was his precious Kylie, being held by a short, muscular guy, shaved head, a long, thin knife held to her throat.

A knife. Oh God, a knife.

His eyes popped up to Norman's – because it could only be Norman standing in front of him – and saw that he was watching Adam closely in return.

"You must be the new boyfriend," Norman said, snarling as he pressed the knife further into Kylie's throat, cutting off her mumbled pleadings for him to stop. "Did you know that this dumb bitch here doesn't even know how to follow directions? I told her to get rid of this thing, but look at her. She's huge. No doctor is going to take it out now. Because of her incompetence, I have to clean up her mess. Again."

Just stay calm. Don't agitate the man further. Maybe Ollie will get to work unseen and can call 911. His eyes swept the room fruitlessly as his mind spun. Was Ollie already there? He might be in the bac—

"Your sniveling teenage boy is tied up in the back," Norman said, reading Adam's searching eyes correctly. "I didn't want to have to deal with two people, in case one of them decided to act like a hero. And then *you* had to come along. Well, it can't be helped." He snorted with disgust. "I mean, I doubt you'd agree to turn around and walk away."

Adam's eyes went wide at that, and the first sounds he'd made since he arrived came out – a low, nasty chuckle. "*Hell* no, I'm not walking away," he growled, his eyes jumping between Norman and Kylie. Was the man psychotic? Adam couldn't see something like this and walk away, even if he didn't know Kylie from Eve. What kind of human being could? *Oh, so sorry to interrupt your abortion in process with a giant fillet knife. Let me just get out of your way and let you two get to it.*

As his eyes flicked between Kylie's – pale green and terrified and begging for help – to Norman's – pale blue and icy and lifeless – he debated his choices. He could charge the man, but Norman would be able to hurt/maim/kill Kylie long before Adam got there, and considering the soulless look in the man's eyes, he was pretty sure Norman was more than happy to do that.

Could he talk the man down?

Maybe?

He held up his hands in the air pleadingly. "Look, I think that this has just been a misunderstanding," Adam started out. "If you put the knife down, maybe we can all talk and decide together on what to do." *Right after I punch your teeth down your throat and then turn you over to the cops.*

Yeah, right after that.

Norm let out a snort of laughter. "Do I look that stupid?" he asked condescendingly. "I didn't think that I appeared to be the village idiot, but maybe I was wrong. Was I wrong, Kylie?" He jerked on her hair, causing tears of pain to spring to her eyes. Adam's heart twisted inside of him. Dammit, he was a country vet who dealt with badass bulls, not psychotic wannabe murderers. And if he screwed this up…

"No," Kylie whispered carefully. Adam could read the terror in her eyes from across the room.

"Look, no reason to think I meant that," Adam said calmly, shuffling forward just a bit, hands still held up in a surrender position. If he could just get within arm's reach…

"Back up or I slit her throat," Norman said, pressing the blade to Kylie's throat. A small red line appeared across it. Kylie didn't even dare whimper.

Adam stumbled backwards. "No need to do that," he said, still holding up his hands placatingly, terror ripping through his stomach. He thought he might be sick.

He had to keep calm. Figure out a way to force Norman to make a mistake. "Look, let's not move too hastily here. We can slow down and think through our choices. You don't want to hurt Kylie, right? You have your business, your wife, your family…you can't go back to all of that if you kill someone. So let's try taking a step back to see if we can find a solution—"

"I told this dumb bitch to get rid of this thing!" Norm growled, cutting Adam off. "She didn't do it, so I have to do it for her. *That's* the solution."

I can't reason with him, I can't call the police, I don't carry a gun with me, I can't get to his side fast enough to get Kylie away from him before he just slits her throat. The only other person who knows what's going on is tied up in the back and is absolutely no help to me. What other choices do I have?

And then the thought he'd had over a month ago, when Kylie had first shared the truth of what had happened the night she'd told Norm about the baby, rang in his mind.

This guy is a stereotypical bully – he'd never pick on someone who could actually put up a fair fight.

Bully…

Bully…

Bully…

Adam had been lucky growing up – he hadn't been picked on much. A little here and there, but he'd tended to be on the tall side and none of the bullies had wanted to pick on someone bigger and taller than them. Just like right now – Norm didn't want to take on Adam in a fair fight; he wanted to hurt and abuse a woman who was smaller and weaker than him in every way.

But what was one thing that was true about almost every bully out there? They were thin-skinned megalomaniacs. They couldn't stand having someone think that they were dumb or less than in any way, because secretly, *they* think they're dumb and less than.

Adam opened up his mouth, praying that his new plan wouldn't end up with Kylie on the floor in a heap. *Please God please God please God…*

Adam forced out a taunting laugh. "You think that you're not the village idiot, huh? That's not what I see in front of me. A smart man would've planned this out so much better. A smart man would've made sure to pick a time or a place where no one else would walk in on him. But you…you picked right here, in the middle of town on a Thursday. And you honestly thought you'd be able to pull this off without a hitch? They must grow 'em stupid in Utah."

Norman's body tensed up, his icy blue eyes narrowed and angry and pissed as hell. "How dare you, you stupid country bumpkin!" he roared. "What do you know – you drive a pickup truck old enough to date and work in this tiny cinder block hellhole. Obviously, I am a lot more successful than you, and—"

Adam laughed sarcastically, cutting his tirade off, while Kylie sent him pleading looks to just stop pushing this guy's buttons. Adam didn't dare look at her. He knew he wasn't a good enough actor to pull that off.

"Shiiitttt..." Adam drawled, adding in a thick country twang that hurt his ears to even use. "I might just be a country bumpkin, but I at least know not to be such a dumbass like you." The color began to climb in Norm's cheeks, and Adam could tell he was starting to get to him. *Just keep going...* "I mean, Lordy, could you even have been more retarded? Only an idiot would walk into a business like this and attack a *girl*. How low can you go?"

With a roar that seemed to come from deep inside of him, Norm threw Kylie to the side and charged at Adam, his knife in a death grip in his hand. Adam waited until it was *almost* too late and then reared up, a cowboy boot straight to the shorter man's face. The momentum of the charge put so much force into the boot kick, Norm dropped to the ground, his hands cradling his face, blood pouring out of them, screaming in pain.

Adam sprinted past the man, intent on getting to Kylie's side to console and protect her, when she instead did a sharp about-face, snatched the phone off the cradle, and dialed 911. "Yes, this is an emergency," she snapped. "An insane man just tried to kill me."

Adam stumbled to a stop. He'd thought that...

well, that Kylie would be crying. And would need him to hold her and tell her that everything was okay. Instead, she was doing her part to take Norman down.

He couldn't be more proud of her than if she'd just won an Olympic gold medal. Anyone who underestimated Kylie was in for a hell of a surprise.

He turned around and instead snatched the fillet knife off the ground where Norm had dropped it and hurried into the back, slicing through the duct tape holding Ollie's wrists and ankles to an old wooden chair, and then turned on his heel to head back towards the front. Norman may be thrashing around on the floor now, begging for his mom, but that didn't mean he'd stay there.

"Holy shit!" Ollie yelled, as soon as he got the duct tape off and the cotton out of his mouth. "I can't believe that jackass! He taped me to a *chair*!"

"C'mon, Ollie," Adam said, laughing a little inside at the teen's disbelief. He was heady with emotion and relief and his legs were rubbery but he had to keep going. He couldn't sit down until this psychopath was behind bars. "The police should be here soon."

They hurried back upfront to find Kylie still on the phone, telling the dispatcher everything that had happened while Norman...Norman was busy crawling towards the door.

"Oh no you don't," Adam said, grabbing the man's collar and yanking him backwards. He was a little too pleased to see that Norm, in fact, had broken teeth as he gasped and begged for mercy. "It's not so fun when you're on the receiving end of an ass-whooping, is it, shithead. I do hope your job comes with a nice dental plan." Norm got up on his hands and knees, making a drunken attempt for the door, but Adam grabbed his collar and flung him back down on the ground again. Sprawled out in front of him on the floor, Adam put his shit-and-straw-covered boot on the guy's chest, pinning him to the ground.

"Huh. Well now, Ollie," he drawled to the teen who was standing on the sidelines of the action, looking terrified and excited by turns. "I think it's rather fun to keep him pinned here like the insignificant insect that he is. Kylie, how you doin'?"

"Good," she called back calmly. "The dispatcher says the police are almost—oh, that's them now." There were sirens in the distance, tearing up the street towards them. "Thanks, Mr. Behrend. You be sure to bring your cat by next week when you have a chance." She hung up the phone as Adam turned to shoot her a look, his boot still firmly planted in Norman's chest. Norman let out a pained groan and Adam smiled to himself.

Maybe more than a little firmly planted.

Kylie shrugged at Adam's surprised look. "Mr. Behrend started telling me about his cat while we were waiting for the police to show up. I mean, you have to talk about something. Apparently, she's been dry-heaving lately and he doesn't know why."

"Sounds like a major case of hairballs…" Adam

said, tapping his finger on his chin, pretending to think. The piece of shit on the ground began whining and mumbling, and Adam knew that pretending to ignore him, as if he were literally not worth worrying about, was the worst thing someone could do to him. Worse than breaking his teeth, not paying attention meant they weren't giving Norman the Great the due respect and attention that he deserved.

Police were jumping out of their cars, doors slamming, sirens wailing, and still, Adam pretended to stay focused on the mystery hairball case. "Did you ask Mr. Behrend if she's been shedding more than usual lately? It could be—"

The front door burst open as Officers Knittle and Morland moved in, guns drawn, shouting. Adam turned back to them, grinding his heel into Norman's sternum one more time as he did so, and then waved. "Hi, you guys," he said pleasantly, ignoring the whimpered pleas for help from his footstool. "Everyone is fine, but I imagine you'll want to have the dentist meet you at the station along with a doctor. He's gonna need a full check-up."

He stepped back and let the men in blue do their job. Kylie came up and stood next to him, wrapping her arms around him. "I can't believe he came here," she said, her voice shaky and uneven now that the danger was over. "I can't believe I ever thought I loved him."

Adam hugged her tight. "The good news is, he's gone," he said softly against the crown of her head.

The smell of wildflowers wafted up and tickled his nose, reminding him of everything he almost lost. He pressed a kiss to the crown of her head. "Everything is gonna be all right now," he whispered.

And as Officer Abby Miller came in and began asking them questions, and as the police car pulled away with Norman in the back, Adam couldn't help comparing this to the last time the person he loved desperately needed him. That time, it'd ended in funeral flowers and caskets and people awkwardly hugging him and endless casseroles, brought by neighbors who wanted to do *something* to help, even though eating had been at the very bottom of his priorities list.

Yeah, everything was gonna be all right now.

CHAPTER 41

ADAM

*H*E SWUNG the saddle up onto Ladybug's back, centering it over the saddle blanket and starting in on tightening up the straps. Kylie would be here any minute, and he wanted to have the horse ready to go for her so she wouldn't be tempted to do the saddling herself. With all of the drama and anxiety surrounding last week's attempted kidnapping and abortion, Adam wasn't taking chances with the baby. Lots of stress wasn't good for anyone, but it was *especially* not good for an expectant mother.

After what seemed like ages but was probably just seconds, he heard his mom's car rumbling down the dirt road and he smiled to himself. There was something comforting about his mom's car being passed down to Kylie. You know, the whole circle of life thing, but with cars.

She pulled into view, peering over the steering

wheel of the giant boat of a car and, spotting him, gave a huge wave. He waved back, holding up the reins of Ladybug and Sonny who stood there placidly, not even twitching an ear as Kylie came to a stop and cut the engine.

There was definitely a reason why he was able to use these horses for the therapy camp. They were virtually unshakeable, an excellent trait in horses that worked with any children, let alone special needs ones.

Kylie pushed herself out of the car and then, reaching into the back, pulled out a backpack – her part of the picnic. He provided the horses; she provided the food.

Considering his cooking skills and her complete lack of horse ownership…well, it seemed like a damn good arrangement to him.

"Hi, baby," he growled when she came walking up, pulling her up against him and nuzzling her neck. "Damn, I've missed you."

"I just saw you this morning," she pointed out, laughing softly while also tilting her head to the side to give him better access.

"I know!" he murmured against her soft skin. "It's been like four whole hours." He began blowing on the kiss-moistened skin and she shivered in his arms.

"I…I can see the problem," she murmured, eyes closed. "It's surprising you lasted as long as you did."

"It really is," he said, sadly pulling away. As much fun as it was to kiss and suck and nibble on Kylie's neck, he had more important things to do that afternoon. "You've got our lunch in there?" he asked, nodding towards the backpack she had slung over her shoulders.

"I do! Hand-breaded, deep fried chicken, since that's a requirement for any self-respecting picnic, a salad," he let out a mock groan that she ignored, "sweet rolls that I baked up this morning, and an apple pie that I finished just last night."

"You got all of that into your backpack?" he asked, his respect for her rising to a new level.

"I did," she said, beaming a smile of excitement as she patted the straps of her backpack. "You've got the blanket, right?"

He pointed to a knapsack slumped up against a boulder. "Ready to go. Let's make this happen." Fissures of excitement sparked through him as he led Sonny over to the mounting block and helped Kylie up onto his wide back.

Please, please, please…

He snagged his bag from the boulder and swung up onto Ladybug's back, then led them down the well-worn path away from the barn and towards a small grouping of hills about a mile away. "So," he said, turning to Kylie as they meandered along in the warm August sun, "how are the soap sales doing? I keep meaning to ask. I've been seeing them pretty much everywhere, and I swear that half the women in town smell like lilacs now."

Kylie threw her head back and laughed. "Well,

I'm not sure my sales have been as good as that, but I'm damn happy with them anyway. There's only so much milk and cream that a body can consume, and even with you helping me out...I don't know how Chloe used it all up. Anyway, I just got the Shop 'N Go to agree to carry the soap in their bath and beauty aisle, so the sales oughta go up even further here in a bit. Now that I've pretty much covered all of Sawyer, I want to go over to Franklin next. They've got a lot of cute little shops, all there for tourists, and I figure that handmade soap oughta sell well with them, right?"

She patted her burgeoning belly – she was the cutest pregnant woman he'd ever seen in his life, for sure. Seeing her perched up on top of Sonny, swaying as they meandered along, her belly expanding even as he watched...yeah, life didn't get much better than this.

"The income from it has been coming in in spurts, but I've tried to sock away every bit of it that I could so I can use it to pay for expenses when the baby comes. The one thing my mom keeps telling me is that babies are expensive. She thinks I believe that babies poop gold bars or something." She let out a light laugh. "Mommas...what would you do without them?" she asked rhetorically. "I swear, it doesn't matter how old I get, there's a part of my mom who still sees me as a toddler in diapers." She shrugged. "Speaking of moms, how is your mom settling into the retirement home?"

"Oh, she's loving it," Adam said, happy to have

good news on that front. Considering her original reaction to it all, it was nothing short of a miracle, honestly. "When we first moved her in last month... well, you saw her. Nervous and excited as a kindergartener on the first day of school. She's found some friends to hang out with and seems to be settling in. They have her starting down at the thrift store, looking over donated items and deciding what to sell, what to fix, and what to throw away, and so she's in seventh heaven over that. Oh, and she says to tell you hello and that she's running low on soap, so she'd like to buy a bar the next time you stop by."

"Oh, great!" Kylie said, a huge smile on her face. Her hand went automatically to her pocket and then she grimaced. "I left my phone in the car. Remind me when I get back to put a date into my calendar to go out to see her. Otherwise, it'll never happen."

He nodded, trying to keep a straight face. With any luck, they'd be seeing her soon. As a couple. With things to announce. And stuff.

Please, please, please...

They finally reached the shade of the pine trees dotting the hills, and they both let out a sigh of relief at the same time, and then laughed. As Adam looked over at her, her golden hair glinting in the sun filtering through the canopy, he wondered anew at how it was that he'd managed to find such a wonderful woman, right here in Sawyer. First Wendy and now Kylie. He really couldn't get much luckier, honestly.

She looked over at him and then cocked an

eyebrow in confusion. "Why are you grinning?" she asked.

"I was just thinking how lucky I was to find you, and then I realized – I didn't really have to look too hard. After all, you showed up on my doorstep. I didn't so much find you as open my eyes to realize that you were standing right there under my nose."

She threw back her head and laughed. "Was that a short joke?" she demanded, wiping the tears away from her eyes. "Need I remind you – again – that I am not so much on the short side as you are on the Jolly Green Giant side."

He sent her a mock disgruntled look. "I'd tickle you into admitting that I am much more handsome than the Jolly Green Giant, but you are balanced precariously on top of a horse, so I *suppose* I shouldn't tickle you until you fall off." He said it magnanimously, as if granting her a kingly favor, and she bust out laughing again.

"So kind, so kind…" she said dryly. She pulled to a stop and looked around at the forest floor spreading out before them, a small stream rushing by, falling over the rocks in its hurry to get to the ocean. "How does this look?" she asked.

He took the idyllic scene in, a small stroke of fear brushing down his spine at the similarities between this picnic and the last one he'd gone on. "It looks good," he said cautiously, "but promise me you won't wade in the stream?"

"I promise," she said solemnly, and the fear faded

away. Maybe, someday, mountain streams wouldn't freak him out anymore.

That day was not today.

They swung down from their horses and went on the hunt for the perfect spot to set up for their picnic, finally finding a soft, relatively flat bed of pine needles underneath a group of trees. Adam laid out the blanket while Kylie got to work unpacking the food.

"Oh. Whoops," she said in an embarrassed voice, and looked up at Adam with a grimace on her face. "Sooo…that didn't work out so well." She held up a mangled mess of tinfoil and oozing brown glaze. "I don't know what I was thinking. The tinfoil…I thought it'd protect the apple pie, which, looking back on it, is a really stupid thing to think. Tinfoil isn't rigid enough to keep its shape. Duh." She looked on the verge of tears over it.

Shit! Ruining this moment over crushed apple pie simply couldn't be allowed. Adam stepped up next to her, wrapping one arm around her thickening waist while snatching away the messy tinfoil with the other hand.

"Hmmm…" he said, licking the juicy goodness spread all over the tinfoil. "Delicious. I have a new idea for lunch. I think I should spread this stuff all over your nipples and then lick it off."

Her eyes shot up to his in shock and surprise, and then she laughed. "You are *such* a guy sometimes," she said, snatching the tinfoil disaster out of his hands and licking the side of it. Watching her pink tongue go to town…Adam swallowed hard. Was breathing a thing? Hopefully not a necessary thing. "Yeah, I did pretty good with this one," she said around swipes of her tongue. "Maybe a little bit more cinnamon in my next one, though."

He couldn't stand it any longer. Between the tongue and the talk of more apple pies and the scent of wildflowers and the way her laughter made him feel like he could take on the world and just how damn happy she made him…It was time.

He dropped to his knees in front of her. Both knees, not just one, because she deserved both. "Kylie Carol VanLueven, will you be my wife?" he asked, before he could wimp out and do something ridiculous like claim he was down there just to tie his shoes.

Which, considering he was wearing cowboy boots…

She stopped, her tongue up against the tinfoil, her eyes big and growing bigger as she stared down at him.

Her arm lowered as she continued to stare.

Birds were singing to each other, squirrels were chattering with each other, insects were buzzing around…

Her pale green eyes were trained on him, unblinking, shock stamped across her face.

If she didn't say something right this very minute, he was going to throw up all over her shoes, which were *not* cowboy boots but were instead tennis shoes, which meant they were fabric, which meant that they would soak up his throw-up and—

Please, please, please…

Except this time, he realized that he was saying the words out loud. "Please…" he whispered again.

"YES!" she shouted, finally moving, throwing herself at him, knocking him over with the shock of it, apple pie and dirt flinging everywhere. "YES!" she shouted again, laughing and crying and then they kissed long and hard and all thoughts about discussing the wedding date – before the baby was born would make the logistics of claiming their little girl as his even easier – flew right out the window.

Turns out, that sort of thing can be discussed just fine *after* he showed her how much he loved her with his mouth and lips and fingers and soul.

EPILOGUE

KYLIE

OCTOBER, 2018

KYLIE PUT HER HAND on the small of her back and groaned. If this baby didn't come out soon, her back was going to give out from the pain of it. Carrying what the doctors estimated was a nine-pound baby upfront, sticking out of her like she swallowed a beach ball for breakfast…

It was rough on a person's spine, she could testify to that much. It really was too bad her mother had been spot on all those months ago, when she'd warned Kylie about this stage. Kylie had hoped that she'd somehow miraculously escape this fate, but nope.

She was her momma's daughter.

"Hurting?" Adam asked, rubbing the muscles at the base of her spine as she groaned in pleasure. Ollie looked up from the box he was picking up, worry etched across his face, and she waved him off.

"It's fine," she told the teen. "Keep going. I'd love to have everything inside by tonight if we can." He nodded and headed for the front door, box in hand.

"Watching Oliver hover over you," Adam said in her ear as his hands continued to work magic on her back, "well, it's a little surreal. I keep wondering where the awkward teen went that I hired over a year ago. You know, the one who refused to speak to girls."

Kylie let out a little laugh that segued into a sigh of pleasure when Adam hit a particularly sensitive spot. "Bavarian cream donuts," she murmured. "They're the key to Ollie's heart."

"Donuts…hmmmm…I knew there was a reason I liked that kid."

Kylie shook her head and laughed. Despite her best efforts, Adam still had a sweet tooth more appropriate for a four year old than an almost 40 year old. At least he was eating more veggies now, if only because she gave him the stink eye when he pushed them to the side of his plate.

A shiver ran through her at the cold wind beginning to whistle through the pine trees. It was almost Halloween, and the weather had already turned, the leaves long gone, the flowers killed with the first heavy frost.

Almost Halloween. Which meant that it was almost her due date. Halloween had never been a favorite holiday of hers – Thanksgiving and all of its baked goods was much more her style – so she'd spent the last five months of her life hoping and praying that her baby would either come early or be late. Anything but a Halloween baby. Everyone thought she was crazy ("But a baby all dressed up in a Halloween costume would be adorbs!" Sugar had protested) but Kylie was adamant. Even if she had to cross her legs for 24 hours straight, no baby was coming out of her womb on October 31st.

After their rushed (if amazeballs) wedding, Ruby signed her house over to Adam free and clear as her wedding present to them. Since she'd happily settled into the retirement home, she didn't need another house, and her one request had been that the house would stay in the Whitaker family. "I don't mind leaving it," she told Kylie a few weeks ago, "as long as Adam, you, and our grandchild lives there. That home is the legacy of the Whitaker bunch."

It was a request Kylie had been *happy* to comply with, considering it had a lot more room and was a bit more updated than Adam's rental. But, it meant that they were busy moving just days before her due date. They'd brought the animals over to the new barn yesterday, and Dumbass was already doing her best to chew through the fencing.

"Any day but today," she told her belly sternly. "Well, or Halloween. But I've got to put your nursery together before you can make your appearance."

Adam gave her a light hug from behind and a kiss on the top of her head. "I better get back to work," he said regretfully. "You stay here and continue to supervise the troops. Don't lift a thing!"

She waved and nodded, watching him as he walked over to chat with the Miller brothers – Wyatt, Declan, and Stetson – and Luke Nash, another friend of Adam's, all there to help them move. It seemed like everyone in the valley loved him, and for good reason. She'd never met a more solid, thoughtful, understanding man in all her life. Even when she insisted, in a fit of pregnancy cravings, that jalapeños and Fuji apples absolutely went together, he didn't call her insane.

Well, at least, not out loud.

Just then, a truck pulled up, its headlights cutting through the growing darkness, and Kylie shaded her eyes against the brightness.

Who is this…

The headlights cut off and it was only then that Kylie could see that it wasn't a truck but rather an SUV – a bright green one. *Ah.* Sugar's husband, Jaxson, the fire chief. He was just about the only guy in town that Kylie could name who drove an SUV instead of a truck, and he was *certainly* the only one to drive a bright green one.

But instead of just Jaxson hopping out, a bunch of guys started pouring out, like a cowboy version of a clown car. Sugar walked over, squinting in the fading light, trying to pick out faces. It looked like the local volunteer fire department had shown up to help – Moose, Jaxson, Levi, Troy, and Dylan were swarming towards Adam, asking him what it was they could do. A shaggy looking Dalmatian was trailing after them, tail wagging as it went.

Kylie came up behind the group, listening to Adam give orders, divvying up the workload between everyone. He caught her eye and after all of the men got to work, hauling in boxes from the moving truck, Adam came over and put his arm around her. "Still feeling okay?" he asked worriedly. "You've got that 'I'm in pain but I'm not going to admit to it' look on your face."

Kylie shook her head and laughed a little. "I'm fine, I promise. I can't believe everyone came over to help."

Adam squeezed her lightly. "I know. Me either. I sure am a lucky guy." With another squeeze to her shoulders, he headed to the group of guys to help them maneuver a dresser when…

"Oh. Ohhhh…Ohhhhh!" Kylie began moaning as she felt a rush of liquid run down her legs. "Adam!" she hollered. Everyone froze, and then as one, began yelling, all hell breaking loose.

"Get her into the truck – I'll drive her!"

"No, take the SUV! The backseat lays down."

"I've got leather seats – that's easier to clean up. Take her to the hospital in that!"

Adam swooped her up into his arms and, ignoring them all, headed straight for his truck. Kylie was shivering, her teeth chattering from the cold wind against her wet legs, and from the fear of what she was about to endure.

Suddenly, all of her wishing for the baby to just come already seemed premature. Giving birth was damn *terrifying*. Maybe the baby could just stay where she was for a while longer.

A lot longer.

Another year or two would be fine.

Adam slid her into the passenger seat carefully and shut the door behind her. He shouted something to the guys that she couldn't hear through the glass, and then hurried around to the driver's side.

"What did you tell them?" she asked, her hands clutching her stomach, rubbing at the skin, trying to ease the wave of pain building up inside of her.

"Tell what? Who?" Adam asked, tearing down the road just short of the speed of light.

"The guys. I couldn't hear you through the window." She honestly didn't give a damn about what he'd told them – she just wanted *something* to take her mind off the pain in her stomach.

"To just put everything into the living room and we'll sort it out later. Wyatt said that he'll return the rental truck tomorrow for us, so we don't have to worry about it. Oh my God, why am I talking about rental trucks? Shit! Where's your birthing bag? Is it in here or the car?"

The pain radiated from her head down her body, squeezing her like a tube of toothpaste. "Ummm....uhhhhh.......ummmm..." She couldn't breathe or think. *Why was I hell bent on doing this again? Is it too late to take it back? JUST KIDDING! I DON'T WANT A BABY AFTER ALL! HAHAHAHA!*

"Kylie!" Adam yelled, jerking her back to the present. She looked over at him, eyes woozy. The pain began to recede and she could breathe again.

"Yes?" she asked, panting. Drugs. She wanted all the drugs. She wanted drugs that hadn't been invented yet.

"Yes, it's too late to take this back," he said, turning the corner on two wheels. Kylie gripped the armrests, knuckles white from panic.

When all of the wheels were safely back on the ground, she un-gritted her teeth enough to ask, "Too late to take what back?" She was confused. What was he talking about? Hadn't he just been talking about their move? She didn't want to take that back.

"You were mumbl…never mind. How are you doing? How's the pain? Where's the birthing bag? You forgot to tell me."

"Oh. Right. Bag. Behind us. In the backseat. I put two together, just in case. One for each car. Exact duplicates of each other."

Adam let out an admiring laugh and shook his head. "I don't think I've ever met a more organized person in my life. Giving birth *before* your due date is probably the most spontaneous thing you've done in the past year."

"Are you kidding me? I've been praying for this for months. Before or after, I don't give a rat's ass. Just not on…aaahhhhhh!" she started yelling, the pain squeezing her again.

"We're almost there!" Adam shoved his foot down harder on the gas pedal, the diesel engine roaring through the darkness. "I am *not* going to help someone give birth in my truck again! Not, not, not."

"You never did tell me that story," Kylie said through pants. "What were you doing playing doctor on the side of the road?"

"Ummmm…" he stumbled, and Kylie could tell that panic was making it hard for him to concentrate. She just wanted something to take her mind off the pain, and finally, Adam started in on the story he'd been hinting about for months.

"Chloe was driving through Sawyer when her car broke down, a blizzard hit, and then Tommy decided to make an appearance. I was trying to make it home myself when I saw her on the side of the road, emergency flashers on, and so I pulled over to see if I could help. I was expecting a flat tire or the car to be out of gas, not a woman in labor." The Long Valley County Hospital came into view and Adam let out a whispered *thank you.* "So, I helped her into my truck, right back there," he jerked his thumb over his shoulder towards the backseat, "and that's where she gave birth. I always said I'd never be around a birth again. Animal births? Fine. Human births? Not so much. And then…you came along."

He pulled to a sudden stop in front of the ER doors, jumped out of his truck, and ran around to her side, not even giving her a chance to climb down from the truck but rather just scooping her up into his arms and running for the door. "I can walk," Kylie said weakly, wrapping her arms around his neck, trying to make it sound like she really meant it. It was only polite to insist, after all, even if walking sounded torturous just then. Actually, everything seemed torturous just then. Breathing, thinking, talking, blinking her eyelids...

"Nurse Knutsen!" he hollered as soon as the automatic doors opened, ignoring her mumbled protests. "Kylie's in labor!"

Things happened in a blur after that. There was a lot of screaming and crying and ranting and raving, and at one point, Kylie may've told Adam that she wanted Norman out of jail so she could kill him or at least yell at him, and apparently she was too far along for an epidural which made absolutely *no* sense to her, and between begging for death and threatening to kill the next man she laid eyes on, she continued to beg for *something, anything*, to take the edge off. A shot of whiskey. Cocaine. Whatever.

Okay, and so there might've been that part where she told Adam that if he ever knocked her up, she'd kill him with her bare hands. And that part where he passed out and Kylie demanded that the nurse pour water over his head because dammit all, if she was going to be awake through all of this, he should be too, and then a repeat fifteen minutes later when he passed out again...

But all of that sweat and tears and blood and puke and poop was a distant memory once she heard the cry of her baby, and the nurse saying, "It's a girl!" as if they hadn't already known that and planned for it for months. But still, it was good that it was for sure a girl, because Kylie really didn't want to repaint the nursery and buy all new clothes, and then they laid the squalling, red, slimy baby girl in her arms and she cried. Not tears of pain – no, she'd shed way too many of those over the past year.

These were tears of sheer joy and happiness. She looked up at Adam, whose hair was dripping from the second dousing of water over his head, and whispered, "Isn't she the most beautiful thing you've ever seen in your life?"

"She is," Adam said, but he was looking at her when he said it. He wiped a few strands of sweat-soaked hair from her face and then looked back down at their precious baby. "So are we sticking with the name we chose?"

"We are," Kylie murmured, running her fingertips lightly over the baby's skin. She couldn't believe how tiny her daughter was. She hadn't felt tiny just a half hour before, of course, but now that she was out, she looked ridiculously small for a human. "Hi, Ruby Carol Whitaker," she whispered to their baby girl. "Welcome to the world. You're gonna love it here."

AUTHOR'S NOTE

HI, AMAZEBALLS READER!

I sure hope you loved *Bundle of Love*. I know that for me, it was one of my all-time favorite books to write because I could finally give Adam the happily ever after that he deserved and has been waiting for since Book 1 of the Long Valley series.

Speaking of, if this is the first book you've read by me, you ought to start back at the beginning with Stetson and Jennifer's love story (*Accounting for Love*) and work your way forward. Although all of my books are standalones, it's a whole lot more fun to read them in order. Since everything takes place in Long Valley, people show up in each other's books all the time. Want to know how Sugar and Jaxson ended up together? That's *Flames of Love*. Want to know the backstory of Juan, the about-to-be adopted son of Abby and Wyatt Miller? That's *Arrested by Love*.

On the other hand, if you've read everything by

me that I've ever written, first off, *thank you*. I can't even tell you how much it means to me to have such dedicated, wonderful fans. I'm so damn lucky.

Second of all, do be sure to flip the page to check out "The Story Doesn't End" section, where I list out all of the upcoming books in the Long Valley world, and their release dates.

There, you'll find that Levi – Moose's best friend and a fellow volunteer firefighter – has his own story in *Fire and Love*. Troy, the quiet firefighter of the bunch and the one to adopt Sparky, gets the final firefighter story (for now!) in *Burned by Love*.

I say this at the risk of sounding a little OCD, but I actually have my writing schedule planned out until the spring of 2023. 😬 I like to know what I'm doing next, what can I say?

Hint: Be sure to preorder my books on your favorite storefront (I'm available everywhere – that will never change!) so you never miss an installment in the life and times of Sawyer's residents.

Speaking of, up next in the Long Valley world is *Lessons in Love*, the love story of Miss Lambert, 5th grade teacher extraordinaire. Although Adam never really gave her a second glance, it turns out that perhaps she'd been a little more interested in him than he'd ever imagined. Learn what she does in the wake of Kylie and Adam's relationship, and how she finally learns to open herself up to others...

Thanks again for all of your support and love,

~Erin

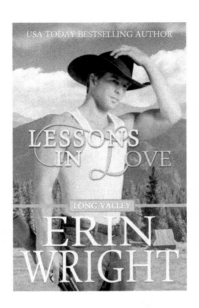

<u>Lessons in Love</u>

Forbidden love is never easy...

Elijah Morland only wants one thing.

Okay, so maybe there are two items on the list.

But more important than anything else is to spend more time with his daughter, Brooklyn, no matter how hard his ex-wife is fighting to keep them apart. Desperate, he takes a job at Brooklyn's elementary school to be closer to her, where she can be his entire focus.

Which was working just the way he'd planned... right up until he met her teacher, Miss Hannah

Lambert. He sees the way she cares for Brooklyn and despite his best efforts, he starts to fall for her.

He *can't* date his daughter's teacher, though – it's against the rules. Not to mention his ex-wife would have a field day in court if she found out.

But what if, for just one night, the rules didn't apply?

She's been hurt before...

It's simple, really. She cannot, under any circumstances, fall for Brooklyn Morland's father, even if Brooklyn is her not-so-secret favorite student.

But he's standing there in her classroom, looking at her like she's *not* invisible. Like she's *not* hidden beneath her coke-bottle glasses and oversized teacher cardigan.

With those gray-green eyes, he *sees* her.

The rules are clear: She cannot date a student's father. She'd be risking her reputation, her career, her everything.

But sometimes, love is worth risking it all...

∾

Read on for a taste of *Lessons*...

HANNAH LAMBERT LOOKED over the class roll for the year, double-checking that each child on the list had been assigned a desk on the seating chart. The names of Dayton and Tahlia caught her eye – they were both younger siblings to students she'd had in the past. It was always fascinating to see the differences between siblings. Was Dayton going to be a hellion like his older brother had been? It could be an...*interesting* school year if Dayton was even vaguely like his brother.

Speaking of hellions...

Her eyes stopped on the name of Brooklyn Morland. Just yesterday in the teacher's lounge, the teachers had been gossiping about who was getting which student, and Brooklyn's fourth grade teacher, Mr. Pettengill, had asked who'd been "stuck with that Morland girl" this year. Hannah's neck had flushed red with anger at his tone, and she'd been debating if she could get away with saying nothing at all when another teacher had ever-so-helpfully piped up and informed everyone that Hannah had her this year.

Thank you, Betsy. Really, you're awesome.

Every eye in the teacher's lounge had swung towards her, pinning her to her chair. Even now, a day later, she felt herself covered with goosebumps just remembering the ordeal. Despite having worked at the Cleveland Elementary School for the past twelve years, the idea of speaking in front of a group of adults...

Terrifying.

So, of course, she hadn't said a word; she'd just smiled a little at the group as she'd died inside.

No, worse – she *hadn't* died inside, which meant that she then had to listen as Mr. Pettengill began detailing Brooklyn's fall from grace. Oh, she'd been such a "sweet young thang" when she'd started the fourth grade but she'd quickly turned into a beast and he'd had to keep a firm hand with her.

Which was, of course, when Mr. Pettengill began lecturing Hannah on how to take care of an unruly child like Brooklyn; to make sure that she knew from Day One that Hannah was watching her and would punish her for the tiniest of infractions.

Which was when she died a little more inside.

There were days – like, 365 of them per year – where Mr. Pettengill resembled a boot camp instructor more than a fourth grade teacher.

Finally – *fin-a-lly* – the conversation turned to

gossip about other students, and the focus moved off Hannah, which meant she could breathe normally again. Honestly, if she'd had any idea how much she'd need to interact with adults as a teacher, she probably would've picked another profession. Maybe she could've been a deep sea diver where all she would have to interact with were sharks.

Sharks were honestly preferable to Mr. Pettengill, and didn't *that* just about say it all.

She heard a knock on the door of her classroom, yanking her back to the present. "Come in," she called out as she looked up to see who was there.

Mylanta!

As if thinking about the daughter had conjured up the father, there stood Mr. Morland in the doorway, his slim frame bulging with just enough muscles to make a girl drool.

'Just enough muscles to make a girl drool?' Where did that come from?

She shot to her feet, her chair skittering backwards and slamming into the painted cinderblock wall behind her. A deep red blush started at her toes and quickly worked its way up her body, staining her cheeks a flaming red she was just sure could be seen from outer space. Some satellite was probably being steered off course right now by the sheer luminescence of her cheeks.

"Hello, Mr. Morland," she said formally, trying to ignore the state of her cheeks and the fact that her darn chair was still sliding, ever so slowly, along the wall.

Stop rolling. Any day now. You can stop moving. Really, you can.

Mr. Morland walked in, his dark eyes tracking the progress of the errant chair, and then he turned them back towards her, and she was pinned into place yet again. They were this fascinating gray-green color that she'd never seen before; cool, aloof, but just a hint of something more beneath that.

"Hello, Miss Lambert," he replied just as formally as her, pulling on the brim of his cap. Her chair, thank the Lord above, had finally come to a stop. Hannah could just see it out of the corner of her eye, listing to the side drunkenly. She really needed to buy a new one, but that meant not buying any classroom supplies for the year and if she had to choose between a nice chair for her or pencils and markers for her students…

Drunken chair it was.

"Are you…" She cleared her throat, trying to get the croak out of it. Adults were just tall children, she reminded herself.

Very tall, very handsome children.

Hmmmm…actually, not *too* tall – the perfect height, really, especially for a person of short stature like her.

Okay, so that wasn't helping.

"Are you…are you here to talk about Brooklyn?" she finally got out. She scrambled inwardly as she talked to remember how old he was in relation to her, and made the vague guess that he was three years younger, maybe four.

A younger man…she didn't *do* younger men.

Ever.

Something her libido was apparently choosing in that very moment to forget.

"Oh!" he said, his brow wrinkled in surprise. "No, actually, I didn't realize she were gonna be in your class this year. My ex were the one who signed her up for school. I'm the new janitor here now that Mr. Longspee's retired, so I just wanted to say howdy to everyone and let y'all know that I'm gonna be the one cleanin' in here."

As he spoke, his rich voice with a thick hick drawl sent sparks up her arms. She scrubbed at them and then held them against her chest, hugging herself. Anxious to give herself something to do – anything that didn't involve looking Mr. Morland in the eye, that was – she hurried over and began tugging her errant chair back towards her desk. "Well, welcome," she said over her shoulder, concentrating fully on the listing chair. She didn't need to use every bit of concentration on the chair, but she wanted to, since the chair was a lot safer than Mr. Morland was.

Considering how her body felt on fire at that moment, nuclear explosions seemed safer than Mr. Morland.

Which was patently ridiculous. He'd graduated from Sawyer a handful of years after her, so she'd seen him occasionally at pep rallies, the grocery store, a football game…

But she'd never felt like this before. Not that she'd disliked him; it just hadn't occurred to her *to* like him.

Until today, that was. Suddenly, her body and libido were all sorts of awake and paying attention.

Now?! Right now you choose to sit up and pay attention?!

A couple of months ago, when Mr. Kiener had asked her out for coffee, all her libido had done was curl up in the corner and take a nap. It didn't help that he was 20 years her senior and missing some of his teeth. He was a nice enough guy; a widower looking for someone to cook for him now that his wife was gone.

Yeah, her libido had taken a real long snooze that day.

"Is there anythin' I need to work on or do for you here in your classroom?" Mr. Morland asked. He was busy looking around the room, apparently searching for a project to tackle, and she tried to control the panic flooding through her at the thought of him spending lots of time in her classroom, doing things.

Anything at all.

Like, breathing or something.

"No," she squeaked, and then cleared her throat. "No, we're ready for the new year. Thank you, though." She was so formal, her back so rigid, she would've been right at home in one of those atrocious whale-boned corsets women wore in the 1800s.

She knew she was being dumb.

She knew that this gut reaction to his presence was ridiculous.

a) She was an old maid;

b) She was never getting married – everyone knew that;

c) He was a younger man;

d) He was apparently now her coworker; and

e) He was the father of one of her students.

She couldn't have special ordered someone to be less suitable for her.

Too bad her twisting, turning, trembling stomach didn't agree.

Mr. Morland pulled on the bill of his ball cap, murmured, "Have a good one," and then was gone out the door. On his way to go torture another teacher with his muscles and his eyes and his tight butt.

Okay, so maybe Mr. Pettengill wasn't exactly panting over Mr. Morland's gray-green eyes and tight butt, which was not fair, honestly. Why did they have to affect *her* like this?

Hannah collapsed into her chair and stared at the empty doorway.

She was in trouble, all right.

Lessons in Love *is available on all storefronts – find it on your favorite store today!*

THE STORY DOESN'T END...

You've met a few people and have fallen in love...

You're probably wondering when and where you can meet everyone else. Here's the list of books, current and to-be-released, in the Long Valley world:

Accounting for Love – The bank's threatening to foreclose on Stetson's farm...and the auditor on the case is damn hot. Jennifer doesn't mind a tough job, but handsome Stetson is trouble. And then came the night she had to spend on the farm. Can she find a way for him to save his farm? And if she can't, will he ever forgive her?

Blizzard of Love – Luke never expects to end up

spending Christmas at the Miller farm. Everyone knows he hates Christmas. But Bonnie *adores* Christmas, so when her best friend invites her to the Miller farm, she jumps at the chance. When a blizzard hits, sparks fly. Can the magic of mistletoe tear down the barriers between them?

Arrested by Love – When Wyatt Miller ended up in the Long Valley County Jail over Christmas, he never expected to receive the greatest gift of all: Love and forgiveness...from his jailer.

Returning for Love – If Declan could turn back time, the rugged cowboy would do things differently. For one, he would've never let go of Iris Blue McLain. Fifteen long and lonely years, and the ache in his heart is as painful as ever. When he sees her again, he can't deny his feelings any longer, and vows to win the only woman he's ever loved.

Christmas of Love – This December, Ivy wishes she could just skip all the festivities. Parties? No thanks. Getting together with family? Not even. Mistletoe? Let's not go there. But everything changes when she meets a rugged cowboy with a slow, sexy smile. Austin's kiss melts her heart, but can two people with painful secrets have a chance at happily ever after?

Overdue for Love – When Dawson left Arizona nine years ago, he never expected to see Chloe again. Until he runs into her at a diner in Sawyer, Idaho, and finds that she has a memento of their last meeting in tow...

Bundle of Love – Dr. Adam Whitaker, vet extraordinaire, has spent the last nine years helplessly in love with Chloe, and deserves his own happily ever after. Except, what if the love of his life comes with one condition...a baby?

Lessons in Love – Elijah hasn't exactly made stellar choices in life, but the one thing he's never regretted? His daughter, even if his ex-wife is doing all she can to keep them apart. In the midst of their custody battle, something unexpected happens: He begins to fall in love. Everyone knows your daughter's elementary school teacher is off-limits, but someone forgot to tell Elijah's heart...

Baked with Love – When Gage took over his grandparent's bakery three years ago, love was the last thing on his mind. Despite the best efforts of his wanna-be-matchmaker sister, Emma, he was content to keep his nose to the grindstone, work his ass off, and make the bakery the success he knew it could be.

That all changed the day the neighbor from hell bought the shop next to his and began remodeling, destroying Gage's well-ordered life in the process. It really was too bad she was so damn gorgeous... [COMING APRIL 2019]

Bloom of Love – Carla has always been a romantic; after all, she couldn't run the flower shop in town, Happy Petals, if she didn't believe in true love, right? But she also happens to be single, and she'd just about given up on love for herself when Christian comes into her life. For one brief, shining moment, she thinks she might be able to have her own happily ever after. But nothing worth having comes easily… [COMING SEPTEMBER 2019]

Banking on Love – Tripp has a real talent for everything he touches: His job at the local credit union, the weights down at the gym, and the panties of women everywhere.

He's quite happy to continue honing these skills... right up until he meets his match: Amelia. She's the classroom aide for a 5th grade teacher; she hates treadmills on principle; and she hasn't had a guy catch a glimpse of her panties in years.

On paper, there's absolutely nothing about the two of them that should work.

It's a damn good thing Tripp's never paid attention to "shoulds"... [COMING MARCH 2020]

~ FIREFIGHTERS OF LONG VALLEY ~

Flames of Love – Jaxson's not interested in love, or the perils that come with it. His priority is caring for his two small boys, and being fire chief of Sawyer. Everything changes the day he catches sight of Sugar, the pretty girl with the fragile smile. He wants her all to himself, and preferably in his bed – a no-strings arrangement that won't break what's left of his heart. But love's as unpredictable as fire...

Inferno of Love – Georgia has spent a lot of years – roughly 26 of them – pretending Moose wasn't the finest man in town. For the record, she barely notices how his slow, sultry smile makes her knees weak, and always ignores the close fit of his faded jeans. But when she gets trapped in the flames of a wildfire out in the hills of Long Valley, Moose appears amidst the smoke, ready to walk through fire. For her...

Fire and Love – Levi has wanted Tenny for forever. Too bad the town's beauty queen is *waaay* out of his league.

While she grew up with money, he grew up dirt poor. While she's a daddy's girl, his father's a mean drunk with a vicious back-hand.

Levi should just forget about the high-class blonde, but she has a secret that changes everything. When the ghosts of the past return, he must choose between love...or betrayal.

Burned by Love – Nephew of the former fire chief of Sawyer, Troy was happy when no one looked his way to take over after his uncle retired. Troy appreciates his solitude, and just being a part of the background makes it easy to guard his secrets.

But secrets have a way of forcing themselves to the surface, no matter how hard one tries to hide them...

~ Music of Long Valley ~

Strummin' Up Love – Zane was on top of the world...

until a car wreck took his wife's life and left his son badly crippled. Late one night, he makes the rash decision that if he's going to hide out somewhere and lick his wounds, it might as well be in Idaho. But when Nurse Louise comes strolling into his life, there to help his son recuperate, Zane quickly realizes his son isn't the only one who needs her healing touch… [COMING JULY 2019]

Melody of Love – Georgette Nash's father hadn't exactly been an involved parent. In fact, just when the three Nash children needed him most – the night their mother walked out and never came back – was the night he disappeared into himself and never reemerged. So when Georgette met the father of one of her students and realized what a dedicated and devoted father actually looked like, it was hard for her to keep her distance. Who wouldn't love a handsome and caring man?

But sometimes, life isn't as simple as it seems, and secrets lurk just beneath the surface, ready to snatch any hint of happiness away… [COMING MAY 2020]

~ Servicemen of Long Valley ~

Thankful for Love – Gunner Nash left town the day after high school graduation, and hasn't looked back since.

He and his twin sister, Georgette, were happy living anywhere but Sawyer. But he's finished his stint in the Navy, and is now drifting, looking for a purpose in life, or at least a roof over his head. His older brother, Luke, offers him a place to stay until he can get back on his feet.

He never expects to find love in the process… [COMING NOVEMBER 2019]

Commanded to Love – Nicholas had grown up knowing that he wanted nothing more than to join the Marine Corps. It was his calling, his passion, and his duty. But after only one tour in the Marines, he came back to Sawyer, drifting and dispirited. It wasn't until he ran into his high school sweetheart that he realized maybe his life had a purpose after all; it just wasn't the one he'd dreamed of all those years ago… [COMING AUGUST 2020]

ALSO BY ERIN WRIGHT

~ LONG VALLEY ~

Accounting for Love

Blizzard of Love

Arrested by Love

Returning for Love

Christmas of Love

Overdue for Love

Bundle of Love

Lessons in Love

Baked with Love (April 2019)

Bloom of Love (September 2019)

Banking on Love (March 2020)

Sheltered by Love (October 2020)

Holly and Love (December 2020)

Forged by Love (August 2021)

Conflicted by Love (April 2022)

Dishing Up Love (September 2022)

Gift of Love (December 2022)

~ FIREFIGHTERS OF LONG VALLEY ~

Flames of Love

Inferno of Love

Fire and Love

Burned by Love

~ MUSIC OF LONG VALLEY ~

Strummin' Up Love (July 2019)

Melody of Love (May 2020)

Rock 'n Love (March 2021)

Rhapsody of Love (February 2022)

~ SERVICEMEN OF LONG VALLEY ~

Thankful for Love (November 2019)

Commanded to Love (August 2020)

Salute to Love (June 2021)

Harbored by Love (November 2021)

Target of Love (July 2022)

ABOUT ERIN WRIGHT

USA Today Bestselling author Erin Wright has worked every job under the sun, including library director, barista, teacher, website designer, and ranch hand helping brand cattle, before settling into the career she's always dreamed about: Author.

She still loves coffee, doesn't love the smell of cow flesh burning, and has embarked on the adventure of a lifetime, traveling the country full-time in an RV. (No one has died yet in the confined 250-square-foot space – which she considers a real win – but let's be real, next week isn't looking so good…)

Find her updates on ErinWright.net, where you can sign up for her newsletter along with the requisite pictures of Jasmine the Writing Cat, her kitty cat muse and snuggle buddy extraordinaire.

Wanna get in touch?
www.erinwright.net
erin@erinwright.net

Or reach out to Erin on your favorite social media platform:

facebook.com/AuthorErinWright

twitter.com/erinwrightlv

pinterest.com/erinwrightbooks

goodreads.com/erinwright

bookbub.com/profile/erin-wright

instagram.com/authorerinwright

CPSIA information can be obtained
at www.ICGtesting.com
Printed in the USA
LVHW021302270720
661634LV00015B/552